The First Advance  *on Tom Sharpe:*

"Tom Sharpe's comedy is exuberantly—I don't suppose 'gloriously' can be the right word—base-hearted. His characters, quite by their own lights, get into relentlessly magnetic, intricately horrible fixes that no one but his characters could deserve or come out of. America has deserved Sharpe for some time, and now at last we have him. At his best...he is far more satisfying than Kingsley Amis or any other nasty Brit novelist since Evelyn Waugh.'—Roy Blount, Jr.

Vintage Stuff

Tom Sharpe

Vintage Books
A Division of Random House
New York

First Vintage Books Edition, April 1984
Copyright © 1982 by Tom Sharpe
All rights reserved under International and Pan-American
Copyright Conventions. Published in the United States by
Random House, Inc., New York.
Originally published in Great Britain by Martin Secker &
Warburg Ltd., London, in 1982. First American Edition.

Library of Congress Cataloging in Publication Data
Sharpe, Tom.
Vintage stuff.
I. Title.
PR6069.H345V5 1984   823′.914   83-40337
ISBN 0-394-72417-8 (pbk.)

Manufactured in the United States of America

Chapter 1

The arrival of Peregrine Roderick Clyde-Browne on earth was authenticated by his birth certificate. His father was named as Oscar Motley Clyde-Browne, occupation Solicitor, and his mother as Marguerite Diana, maiden name Churley. Their address was The Cones, Pinetree Lane, Virginia Water. It was also announced in *The Times* with the additional note, 'Most grateful thanks to the staff of St Barnabas' Nursing Home.'

The thanks were premature but at the time sincere. Mr and Mrs Clyde-Browne had waited a long time for a child and were about to resort to medical help when Peregrine was conceived. Mrs Clyde-Browne was then thirty-six and her husband already forty. They were therefore understandably delighted when, after a surprisingly easy labour, Peregrine weighed in at 8 lb 5 oz at 6 a.m. on 25 March 196–.

'He's a beautiful baby,' said the Sister with greater regard for Mrs Clyde-Browne's feelings than for the facts. Peregrine's beauty was of the sort usually seen after a particularly nasty car accident. 'And such a good one.'

Here she was nearer the truth. From the moment of his birth Peregrine was good. He seldom cried, ate regularly and had just the right amount of wind to reassure his parents that he was thoroughly normal. In short, for the first five years he was a model child and it was only when he continued to be a model child through his sixth, seventh, eighth and ninth years that the Clyde-Brownes had cause to wonder if Peregrine was more model than was entirely proper for a small boy.

'Behaviour: Impeccable?' said Mr Clyde-Browne, reading his school report. Peregrine went to a very expensive preparatory school as a day-boy. 'I find that a little disturbing.'

'I can't imagine why. Peregrine has always been a very good boy and I think it does us credit as his parents.'

'I suppose so, though when I was his age nobody said my behaviour was impeccable. On the contrary . . .'

'You were an extremely naughty little boy. Your mother admitted as much.'

'My mother would,' said Mr Clyde-Browne, whose feelings for his late mother were mixed. 'And I don't much like this "Tries hard" against all the subjects. I'd rather his work was impeccable and his behaviour left something to be desired.'

'Well, you can't have everything. If he misbehaved you'd call him a hooligan or vandal or something. Be grateful he tries hard at work and doesn't get into trouble.'

So for the time being Mr Clyde-Browne left it at that and Peregrine continued to be a model child. It was only after another year of impeccable behaviour and hard trying that Mr Clyde-Browne approached the headmaster for a fuller report on his son.

'I'm afraid there's no chance of his entering for a scholarship to Winchester,' said the headmaster when Mr Clyde-Browne expressed this hope. 'In fact it's extremely doubtful if he'd get into Harrow.'

'Harrow? I don't want him to go to Harrow,' said Mr Clyde-Browne, who had a conventional opinion of Old Harrovians, 'I want him to have the best possible education money can buy.'

The headmaster sighed and crossed to the window. His was a most expensive prep. school. 'The fact of the matter is, and you must appreciate that I have had some thirty years in the teaching profession, that Peregrine is an unusual boy. A most unusual boy.'

'I know that,' said Mr Clyde-Browne, 'And I also know that every report I've had says his behaviour is impeccable and that he tries hard. Now I can face facts as well as the next man. Are you suggesting he's stupid?'

The headmaster turned his back to the desk with a deprecatory gesture. 'I wouldn't go as far as to say that,' he murmured.

'Then how far would you go?'

'Perhaps "late developer" would be more accurate. The fact of the matter is that Peregrine has difficulty conceptualizing.'

'So do I, come to that,' said Mr Clyde-Browne. 'What on earth does it mean?'

'Well, as a matter of fact . . .'

'That's the third time you've prefaced a matter of no fact whatsoever by using that phrase,' said Mr Clyde-Browne in his nastiest courtroom manner. 'Now I want the truth.'

'In short, he takes everything he's told as Gospel.'

'As Gospel?'

'Literally. Absolutely literally.'

'He takes the Gospel literally?' said Mr Clyde-Browne, hoping for a chance to vent his feelings about Religious Education in a rational world.

'Not just the Gospel. Everything,' said the headmaster, who was finding the interview almost as harassing as trying to teach Peregrine. 'He seems incapable of distinguishing between a general instruction and the particular. Take the time, for instance.'

'What time?' asked Mr Clyde-Browne, with a glazed look in his eyes.

'Just time. Now if one of the teachers sets the class some work to do and adds, "Take your own time," Peregrine invariably says "Eleven o'clock." '

'Invariably says "Eleven o'clock"?'

'Or whatever the time happens to be. It could be half past nine or quarter to ten.'

'In that case he can't invariably say "Eleven o'clock",' said Mr Clyde-Growne, resorting to cross-examination to fight his way out of the confusion.

'Well, not invariably eleven o'clock,' conceded the headmaster, 'but invariably some time or other. Whatever his watch happens to tell him. That's what I mean about him taking everything literally. It makes teaching him a distinctly unnerving experience. Only the other day I told his class they'd got to pull their socks up, and Peregrine promptly did. It was exactly the same in Bible Studies. The Reverend Wilkinson said that everyone ought to turn over a new leaf. During the break Peregrine went to work on the camellias. My wife was deeply upset.'

Mr Clyde-Browne followed his glance out of the window and surveyed the stripped bushes. 'Isn't there some way of explaining

7

the difference between metaphorical or colloquial expressions and factual ones?' he asked plaintively.

'Only at the expense of a great deal of time and effort. Besides we have the other children to consider. The English language is not easily adapted to pure logic. We must just hope that Peregrine will develop quite suddenly and learn not to do exactly what he's told.'

It was a sadder but no wiser Mr Clyde-Browne who returned to The Cones. That evening, after a heated argument with his wife, whom he blamed entirely for bringing Peregrine up too dutifully, he tried to explain to his son the hazards involved in doing exactly what he was told.

'You could get into terrible trouble, you know. People are always saying things they don't really mean and if you do what they tell you, everything they tell you, you'll end up in Queer Street.'

Peregrine looked puzzled. 'Where's Queer Street, daddy?' he asked.

Mr Clyde-Browne studied the boy with a mixture of cautious curiosity and ill-concealed irritation. Now that it had been drawn to his attention, Peregrine's adherence to the literal had about it something of the same cunning Mrs Clyde-Browne displayed when confronted by facts she preferred not to discuss. He had in mind extravagant use of the housekeeping money. Perhaps Peregrine's stupidity was as deliberate as his mother's. If so, there was still hope.

'Queer Street is nowhere. It is simply an expression meaning a bad end.'

Peregrine considered this for a moment. 'How can I go there if it's nowhere?' he asked finally.

Mr Clyde-Browne closed his eyes in silent prayer. He could appreciate the plight of the teachers who had to cope with this ghastly logic every day. 'Never mind where it is,' he said, controlling his fury with some difficulty. 'What I'm saying is, that if you don't pull yourself together . . . no, forget that.' Peregrine might go into convulsions. 'If you don't learn to make a distinction between statements of fact and mere exhortations, you'll find yourself in deep wat . . . in terrible trouble. Do I make myself plain?'

'Yes, daddy,' said Peregrine, looking at Mr Clyde-Browne's face with a critical eye that belied his father's hopes. But Mr Clyde-Browne had exhausted his repertoire of clichés. 'Then get out and don't do every damned thing you're told to,' he shouted incautiously.

Over the next few days he came to learn the full horror of Peregrine's perverse obedience. From being a model child, Peregrine became a model delinquent. He refused to pass the marmalade at breakfast when he was told to; he came home from school with a black eye precisely because the headmaster had warned the boys against fighting; he shot Mrs Worksop's cat with his airgun, thanks to his mother's injunction to be sure he didn't; and to make matters worse, told Mrs Worksop by way of inverted apology that he was glad he'd shot her pussy.

'I can't think what's got into him,' Mrs Clyde-Browne complained when she discovered that far from tidying his room as she'd asked him, Peregrine had emptied the drawers onto the floor and had practically wrecked the place. 'He's never done anything like that before. It's all most peculiar. You don't think we've got a poltergeist in the house, do you?'

Mr Clyde-Browne replied with inaudible caution. He knew only too well what they had in the house, a son with the moral discernment of a micro-processor and with an uncanny flair for misapplying logic.

'Forget what I said the other day,' he snarled, dragging Peregrine from his previously overfed pet rabbit which was now starving. 'From now on you're to do what your mother and I say. I don't care what havoc you wreak at school but I'm not having this house turned into a hellhole and the neighbours' cats shot because you're told not to. Do you understand that?'

'Yes, daddy,' said Peregrine and returned to his less disturbing model behaviour.

Chapter 2

From this discovery that their son was not as other boys were, the Clyde-Brownes drew differing conclusions. Mrs Clyde-Browne stuck to her belief that Peregrine was a genius with all a genius's eccentricities, while her husband, more practically and with far less enthusiasm for the inconveniences caused by having a pubescent prodigy about the house, consulted the family doctor, then a child psychiatrist, a consultant on educational abnormalities and finally an expert in aptitude testing. Their findings were conflicting. The doctor expressed his personal sympathy; the psychiatrist cast some unpleasant aspersions on the Clyde-Brownes' sexual life, such as it was: and the educational consultant, a follower of Ivan Illich, found fault with Peregrine's schooling for placing any emphasis at all on learning. Only the expert in aptitude testing had the practical advice Mr Clyde-Browne was seeking, and gave it as his opinion that Peregrine's best future lay in the Army, where strict obedience to orders, however insane, was highly commended. With this in mind, Mr Clyde-Browne went on to arrange for Peregrine to go to any Public School that would have him.

Here again he had trouble. Mrs Clyde-Browne insisted that her little sweetie pie needed the very best tuition. Mr Clyde-Browne countered by pointing out that if the little moron was a genius, he didn't need any tuition at all. But the chief problem lay with the Public School headmasters, who evidently found Mr Clyde-Browne's desperation almost as alarming a deterrent as Peregrine's academic record. In the end, it was only thanks to a client guilty of embezzling a golf club's funds that Mr Clyde-Browne learnt about Groxbourne, and that by way of a plea in mitigation. Since Peregrine was already fifteen, Mr Clyde-Browne acted precipitately and drove up to the school during term time.

Situated in the rolling wooded hillside of South Salop, Grox-bourne was virtually unknown in academic circles. Certainly Oxford and Cambridge claimed never to have heard of it, and what little reputation it had seemed to be limited to a few agricultural training colleges.

'But you do have a good Army entry?' Mr Clyde-Browne enquired eagerly of the retiring Headmaster who was prepared to accept Peregrine for his successor to cope with.

'The War Memorial in the Chapel must speak for our record,' said the Headmaster with mournful diffidence, and led the way there. Mr Clyde-Browne surveyed the terrible list and was impressed.

'Six hundred and thirty-three in the First War and three hundred and five in the Second,' said the Headmaster, 'I think there can be few schools in the country which have contributed their all so generously. I put our record down to our excellent sports facilities. The playing fields of Waterloo and all that.'

Mr Clyde-Browne nodded. His hopes for Peregrine's future had been vitiated by experience.

'And then again, we do have a special course for the Over-active Underachiever,' continued the Headmaster. 'Major Fetherington, M.C., runs it and we've found it a great help for the more practically endowed boy whose needs are not sufficiently met on the purely scholastic side. Naturally, it's an extra, but you might find your son benefited.'

Mr Clyde-Browne agreed privately. Whatever Peregrine's needs were, he was never going to benefit from a purely scholastic education.

They passed along the Chapel cloisters to the back of the squash court and were greeted by a volley of shots. A dozen boys with rifles were lying on the ground firing at targets in a small-bore rifle range.

'Ah, Major,' said the Headmaster to a dapper man who was slapping a swagger stick against highly polished riding boots, 'I'd like to introduce Mr Clyde-Browne whose son will be joining us next term.'

'Splendid, splendid,' said the Major, switching his swagger stick to his left arm and shaking Mr Clyde-Browne's hand while managing almost at the same time to order the boys to down rifles,

11

unload, remove bolts and apply pull-throughs. 'Your boy a keen shot?'

'Very,' said Mr Clyde-Browne, remembering the incident with Mrs Worksop's cat. 'In fact, I think he's quite good.'

'Splendid. Having pulled-through, apply an oily rag.' The boys followed his instructions and oiled barrels.

'I'll leave the Major to show you round,' said the Headmaster and disappeared. Presently, when rifles had been inspected and the little column moved off to the Armoury, Mr Clyde-Browne found himself being taken on a conducted tour of the Assault Course. A high brick wall with ropes hanging down it was succeeded by a muddy ditch, more ropes suspended from trees across a gulley, a barbed-wire entanglement, a narrow tunnel half-filled with water, and finally, built on the edge of a quarry, a wooden tower from which a tight wire hawser slanted down to a stake some thirty yards away.

'Death Slide,' explained the Major, 'Put a toggle rope in water so it won't burn, loop it over the wire, grasp firmly with both hands and away you go.'

Mr Clyde-Browne peered nervously over the edge at the rocks some fifty feet below. He could see exactly why it was called a Death Slide. 'Don't you have a great many accidents?' he asked, 'I mean what happens when they hit that iron stake at the bottom?''

'Don't,' said the Major. 'Feet touch down first and they let go. Put them through parachute landing technique first. Keep knees supple and roll over on the left shoulder.'

'I see,' said Mr Clyde-Browne dubiously, and refused the Major's offer to try it himself.

'Then there's rock-climbing. We're very good there. Lead boy goes up first and fixes the guide rope and after they've had some training we can get a squad up in two minutes.'

'Amazing,' said Mr Clyde-Browne, 'And you've never had an accident?'

'Couple of broken legs once in a while but they'd get that anyway on the rugger field. In fact, I think it's fair to say that the boys taking this course are less likely to do themselves an injury than inflict some pretty nasty ones on other people.'

They went into the gym and watched a demonstration of un-armed combat. By the time it was over, Mr Clyde-Browne had made up his mind. Whatever else Groxbourne might fail to provide, it would guarantee Peregrine's entry into the Army. He returned to the Headmaster's study well content.

'Right, well I think we'll put him in Mr Glodstone's house,' said the Headmaster, as Mr Clyde-Browne took out his cheque-book, 'Marvellous with boys, Glodstone. And as for fees . . .'

'I'll pay in advance for three years.'

The Headmaster looked at him quizzically. 'You wouldn't rather wait and see if he finds our atmosphere suits him?'

But Mr Clyde-Browne was adamant. Having got Peregrine into what approximated to a Public School, he had no intention of having him expelled. 'I've added a thousand pounds for the Chapel Restoration Fund,' he said, 'I noticed you're making an appeal.'

And having written out a cheque for ten thousand pounds, he left in an ebullient mood. He had been particularly heartened to learn that the Overactive Underachiever's Course extended into the summer holidays when Major Fetherington took the group to North Wales for 'a spot of mountaineering and cross-country compass marching'.

'It will give us a chance to get away on our own,' Mr Clyde-Browne thought happily as he drove South. But this was not the argument he used to persuade his wife, who had learned from a friend that Groxbourne was the last school she'd send her son to.

'Elspeth says it's a brutal place and the boys are nearly all farmers' sons and the teaching is appalling.'

'It's either Groxbourne or the local Comprehensive.'

'But there must be other schools . . .'

'There are. A great many, but they won't take Peregrine. Now if you want your son to mix with a lot of teenage tarts at the Comprehensive, you've merely to say the word.'

Mrs Clyde-Browne didn't. It was one of her most ingrained beliefs that only the working class sent their children to Comprehensives and Peregrine must never be allowed to pick up their deplorable habits.

'It seems such a shame we can't afford a private tutor,' she whined, but Mr Clyde-Browne was not to be deflected.

'The boy has got to learn to stand on his own feet and face up to the realities of life. He won't do that by staying at home and being mollycoddled by you and some down-at-heel unemployable posing as a private tutor.' A remark which said as much for his own view of the world's awful reality as it did for his apparent conviction that Peregrine had spent the first fifteen years of his life standing on other people's two feet or perched on one of his own.

'Well, I like that,' said Mrs Clyde-Browne with some spirit.

'And I don't,' continued her husband, working himself up into a defensive fury. 'If it hadn't been for your insistence on bringing him up like a china doll, he wouldn't be the idiot he is now. But no, it had to be "Peregrine do this and Peregrine do that" and "Don't get your clothes dirty, Peregrine." Come to think of it, it's a wonder the boy has half a mind to call his own.'

In this he was being unfair. Peregrine's peculiarities owed as much of their bias to his father as to his mother. Mr Clyde-Browne's career as a solicitor with court experience disposed him to divide the world up into the entirely innocent and the wholly guilty, with no states of uncertainty in between. Peregrine had imbibed his rigid ideas of good and bad from his father and had had them reinforced by his mother. Mrs Clyde-Browne's social pretensions and her refusal to think the worst of anyone in their circle of acquaintances, all of whom must be nice because the Clyde-Brownes knew them, had limited the range of the entirely good to Virginia Water and the entirely bad to everywhere else. Television had done nothing to broaden his outlook. His parents had so severely censored his viewing to programmes that showed cowboys and policeman in the best light, while Redskins and suspects were shown in the worst, that Peregrine had been spared any uncertainties or moral doubts. To be brave, truthful, honest and ready to kill anyone who wasn't was to be good: to be anything less was to be bad.

It was with these impeccable prejudices that he was driven up to Groxbourne and handed over to Mr Glodstone by his parents who showed truly British stoicism in parting with their son. In Mr Clyde-Browne's case there was no need for self-control, but his wife's feelings expressed themselves as soon as they had left the school grounds. She had been particularly perturbed by the housemaster.

'Mr Glodstone looked such a peculiar man,' she whimpered through her tears.

'Yes,' said Mr Clyde-Browne brusquely and refrained from pointing out that any man prepared to spend his life trying to combine the duties of a zoo-keeper, a prison warder and a teacher to half-wits could hardly be expected to look normal.

'I mean, why was he wearing a monocle in front of a glass eye?'

'Probably to save himself from seeing too clearly with the other one,' said Mr Clyde-Browne enigmatically and left her to puzzle over the remark until they got home.

'I just hope Peregrine is going to be happy,' she said as they turned into Pinetree Lane. 'If he isn't, I want you to promise me . . .'

'He'll go to the Comprehensive school,' said Mr Clyde-Browne, and put an end to the discussion.

Chapter 3

But Mrs Clyde-Browne's fears were groundless. Peregrine was perfectly happy. Unlike more sensitive boys, who found the school an intimation of hell, he was in his element. This was in large measure due to his size. At fifteen, Peregrine was almost six feet tall, weighed eleven stone and, thanks to the misguided advice of a physics teacher at his prep school who had observed that even if he did a hundred press-ups every morning, he still wouldn't understand the theory of gravity, he was also immensely strong. At Groxbourne, size and strength mattered.

Founded in the latter half of the nineteenth century by a hopelessly optimistic clergyman to bring Anglo-Catholic fervour to the local farmers' sons, the school had remained so obscure and behind the times that its traditions were those of an earlier age. There was fagging and beating and a good deal of bullying. There were also prefects, the ritual of morning and evening chapel, cold showers, draughty dormitories and wholesome, if inedible, food. In short, Groxbourne maintained the routine of its founder without achieving his ambitions. For Peregrine, these abstract considerations had no meaning. It was enough that he was too hefty to bully at all safely, that the school bell chimed at regular intervals throughout the day to tell him that a lesson had ended or lunch was about to begin, and that he never had to think what he was supposed to be doing.

Best of all, his tendency to take things literally was appreciated. In any case, no master ever encouraged him to take his time. It was always, 'Now shut up and get on with it.' And Peregrine got on with it to such an extent that for the first time in his life he found himself nearer the top of the class than the bottom.

But it was on the games field that his ability to take things literally paid off. In rugby, he hurled himself into scrums with a lack of fear that won him a place in the Junior XV and the admiration of the coach, himself a Welshman and well qualified to judge murderous tactics.

'I've never seen a youngster like him,' Mr Evans told Glodstone after a match in which Peregrine had followed instructions to the letter by putting the boot in, heeling the ball out with a fury that suggested he intended taking the opposing pack's with it, and tackling a fly-half so ferociously that the fellow was carried off the field with concussion while Peregrine claimed his shorts as a trophy.

It was the same with boxing. Peregrine brought a violence to the sport that terrified his opponents and alarmed the instructor. 'When I said, "Now let's see who can shove the other bloke's teeth through his tonsils," I didn't mean belt the blighter when he's unconscious,' he protested, after Peregrine, having knocked another boy stone-cold, proceeded to hold him against the ropes with one hand while punching him repeatedly in the mouth with the other.

Even Major Fetherington was impressed. Mr Clyde-Browne's boast that his son was a keen shot proved true. Peregrine had an unerring eye. On the small-bore range his bullets so seldom missed the bull that the Major, suspecting he was missing the target with all but one, put up a large paper screen behind it and was amazed to find he was wrong. All Peregrine's bullets hit the bull. And the Assault Course held no terrors for him. He scaled the brick wall with remarkable agility, dropped cheerfully into the muddy ditch, swung across the gully, and squirmed through the waterlogged tunnel without a qualm. Only the Death Slide caused him some problems. It wasn't that he found difficulty sliding down it, clinging to a toggle rope, but that he misunderstood the Major's instruction to return to the starting point and proceeded to climb back up the wire hawser hand over hand. By the time he was halfway up and hanging forty feet above the rocks at the bottom of the quarry, the Major was no longer looking and had closed his eyes in prayer.

'Are you all right, sir?' Peregrine asked when he reached the top. The Major opened his eyes and looked at him with a mixture of relief and fury. 'Boy,' he said, 'This is supposed to be an Assault Course, not a training ground for trapeze artists and circus acrobats. Do you understand that?'

17

'Yes, sir,' said Peregrine.

'Then in future you will do exactly what you are told.'

'Yes, sir. But you said to return to . . .'

'I know what I said and I don't need reminding,' shouted the Major and cancelled the rest of the afternoon's training to get his pulse back to normal. Two days later, he was to regret his outburst. He returned from a five mile cross-country run in the rain to discover that Peregrine was missing.

'Did any of you boys see where he got to?' he asked the little group of exhausted overactive Underachievers when they assembled in the changing room.

'No, sir. He was with us when we reached the bottom of Leignton Gorge. You remember he asked you something.'

The Major looked out on the darkening sky — it had begun to snow — and seemed to recall Peregrine asking him if he could swim the river instead of using the bridge. Since the question had been put when the Major had just stumbled over a stone into a patch of stinging nettles, he couldn't remember his answer. He had an idea it had been abrupt.

'Oh, well, if he isn't back in half an hour, we'll have to send out a search party and notify the police,' he muttered and went up to his room to console himself over a brandy with the thought that Clyde-Browne had probably drowned in the river. Twelve hours later his hopes and fears were proved to be unfounded. The police, using Alsatians, had discovered Peregrine sheltering quite cheerfully in a barn ten miles away.

'But you definitely told me to get lost, sir,' he explained when he was brought back to the school at five in the morning.

Major Fetherington fought for words. 'But I didn't mean you . . .' he began.

'And the other day you said I was to do exactly what you told me to,' continued Peregrine.

'God help us,' said the Major.

'Yes sir,' said Peregrine, and went off with the School Sister to the Sanatorium.

But if his consistency was a pain in the neck to the Major, his popularity with the boys remained high. Not only was Peregrine never bullied, but he guaranteed the safety of other new boys who could always look to him to fight for them. And thanks to his size and his looks – his battered appearance as a baby had been aggravated by boxing — not even the most frustrated sixth former found him sexually inviting. In short, Peregrine was as prodigiously a model public schoolboy as he had previously been a model child. It was this extraordinary quality that first drew the attention of Mr Glodstone to him and shaped his destiny.

Mrs Clyde-Browne had been right in her assessment of the housemaster. Mr Glodstone was peculiar. The son of a retired Rear-Admiral of such extreme right-wing views that he had celebrated the blitz on London by holding a firework display on Guy Fawkes Night, 1940, Gerald Glodstone had lost not only the presence of his father, but that of his own left eye, thanks to the patriotic if inept efforts of a gamekeeper who had aimed a rocket at his employer and missed. With the eye went Glodstone's hopes of pursuing a naval career. Rear-Admiral Glodstone went with the police to be interned on the Isle of Man where he died two year later. The subsequent punitive death duties had left his son practically penniless. Mr Glodstone had been forced to take up teaching.

'A case of arrested development,' had been the Headmaster's verdict at the time and it had proved true. Mr Glodstone's only qualifications as a teacher, apart from the fact that his late father had been Chairman of the Board of Governors at Groxbourne, had been his ability to read, write and speak English with an upper-class accent. With the wartime shortage of schoolmasters, these had been enough. Besides, Glodstone was an enthusiastic cricketer and gave the school some social cachet by teaching fencing. He was also an excellent disciplinarian and had only to switch his monocle from his glass eye to his proper one to put the fear of God up the most unruly class. By the end of the war, he had become part of the school and too remarkable a personage to lose. Above all, he got on well with the boys in a wholesome way and shared their interests. A model railway addict, he had brought his own elaborate track and installed it in the basement of the gym where surrounded by his 'chaps' he lived out in miniature his earliest ambition without the ghastly fatalities that would evidently have resulted from its fulfilment on a larger scale.

It was the same with his intellectual interests. Mr Glodstone's mental age was, as far as literature was concerned, about fourteen. He never tired of reading and re-reading the classic adventure stories of his youth and in his mind's eye, forever searching for a more orthodox hero than his father on whom to model himself, found one in each old favorite. He was by turns D'Artagnan, Richard Hannay, Sherlock Holmes, The Scarlet Pimpernel (who accounted for his monocle), and Bulldog Drummond, anyone in fiction who was a courageous and romantic defender of the old, the good and the true, against the new, the wicked and the false, as he and their authors judged these things.

In psychological terms, it could be said that Mr Glodstone suffered from a chronic identity problem, which he solved by literary proxy. Here again, he shared his enthusiasms with the boys, and if his teaching of English literature was hardly calculated to get them through O-level, let alone A, it had at least the merit of being exciting and easily understood by even the dullest fifteen-year-old. Year after year, Groxbourne turned out school leavers imbued with the unshakeable belief that the world's problems, and particularly the demise of the British Empire, stemmed from a conspiracy of unwashed Bolsheviks, Jews in high finance and degenerate Black men and Germans with hooded eyelids who tapped their fingers on their knees when at all agitated. In their view, and that of Mr Glodstone, what was needed was a dedicated band of wealthy young men who were prepared to reinforce the law by 'going outside it' to the extent of bayonetting left-wing politicians in their own cellars or, in more extreme cases, tossing them into baths filled with nitric acid. That they didn't put Bulldog Drummond's remedies into practice was largely due to lack of opportunity and the need to get up at dawn to do the milking and go to bed before the criminal world was fully awake. But above all, they were saved by their own lack of imagination and later by the good sense of their wives.

Mr Glodstone was less encumbered. His imagination, growing wilder with age, could imbue the most commonplace events with arcane significance, and successive school matrons with charms they most certainly did not possess. He was only prevented from proposing to them by an exaggerated sense of his own social standing. Instead, he was sexually self-sufficient, felt guilty about his partially enacted fantasies and did his damnedest to exorcise them by taking a cold bath every morning, summer and winter. During the holidays, he visited one or other of his numerous and, in some cases, still wealthy relatives or followed, as far as changed circumstances allowed, in the footsteps of his fictional heroes.

Thus, like Richard Hannay in *Thirty-Nine Steps*, though without the incentive of a murdered man in his rooms, he took the morning train from London to Scotland and spent several exceedingly uncomfortable nights trying to sleep in the heather, before deciding he was more likely to catch pneumonia than find adventure in such a bleak and rain-sodden part of the world. The following summer he had followed Richard Chandos' route to Austria, this time on a motorcycle, in the hope of locating The Great Well at Wagensburg, only to discover Carinthia was packed with coach-loads of tourists and German holiday makers. Mr Glodstone retreated to side roads and walked forest paths in a vain attempt to invest the area with its old magic. And so, each summer, he made another pilgrimage to the setting of an adventure story and came home disappointed but with a more fanatical gleam in his eye. One day he would impose the reality of his literary world on that of the existing one. In fact, by the time Peregrine came under his care, it was extremely doubtful if the housemaster had any idea what decade he was living in. The rolling stock and carriages of his model railway suggested the nineteen-twenties with their Wagons Lits and Pullman cars which were all pulled by steam engines.

But his proudest and most dangerous possession, acquired from a dead uncle, was a 1927 Bentley, in which, until he was asked by the Headmaster to spare the school a multiple tragedy, he terrified a few favoured boys and every other road-user by hurtling at tremendous speed along narrow country lanes and through neighbouring villages.

'But it was built for speed and eats the miles,' Glodstone protested, 'You won't find a car to equal it on the road today.'

'Mercifully,' said the Headmaster, 'and it can eat as many miles as it wants out of term time, but I'm not having the School Sanatorium turned into a mass morgue as a result of your insane driving.'

'Just as you say, Headmaster,' said Glodstone and he had kept the

Bentley in immaculate condition, locked away in his garage, awaiting the day when it would, as he put it, come into its own.

With the arrival of Peregrine Clyde-Browne at Groxbourne, that day seemed to have come closer. Mr Glodstone had found the perfect disciple, a boy endowed with the physique, courage and mental attributes of a genuine hero. From the moment he had caught Peregrine in the school bogs beating Soskins Major to a pulp for forcing a fag to wipe his arse for him, Mr Glodstone had known that his involuntary calling had not been wasted.

But, with a discretion that came from having seen what had happened to several masters in the past who had shown too early an interest in particular boys, he demonstrated his own impartiality by speaking to the House prefects. 'I want you chaps to keep an eye on Clyde-Browne,' he told them, 'we can't have him getting too big for his boots. I've known too many fellows spoilt because they're good at games and so on. Popularity goes to their heads and they begin to think they're the cat's whiskers, what!'

For the rest of the term, Peregrine's presumed ambition to be any part of the cat's anatomy was eradicated. When he wasn't doing a thousand lines for not polishing a prefect's shoes properly he was presenting his backside to the Head of House wielding a chalked cane for talking in dormitory after Lights Out, when he hadn't been, or for taking too long in the showers. In short, Peregrine was subjected to a baptism of punishment that would have caused a normally sensitive boy to run away or have a nervous breakdown. Peregrine did neither. He endured. It simply never crossed his mind that he was being singled out for special treatment. It was only when he was accused of a singularly beastly sin against Nature by the Matron, who had found blood on his pyjama trousers, that he was forced to explain.

'It's just that I got twelve strokes yesterday and eight the day before,' he said. 'A chap can't help bleeding.'

'You mean you've had twenty strokes since Tuesday?' said the Matron, utterly appalled.

'You can count them if you like,' said Peregrine matter-of-factly. 'Though actually I had sixteen last week and they're still showing so it'll be difficult to sort them out.'

Half an hour later, after his backside had been inspected by the

Matron and the doctor, Peregrine was lying face down in bed in the San. and the Headmaster had sent for Mr Glodstone. Since he was rather more progressive than his predecessor and held strong views on corporal punishment, and had been waiting to have a row with Glodstone, the meeting was acrimonious.

'Do you realize we could be sued for damages for what's been done to that poor boy?' he demanded.

'I don't see how,' said Glodstone, lighting his pipe nonchalantly. 'Clyde-Browne hasn't complained, has he?'

'Complained? No, he hasn't. Which only goes to show how brutally you run your house. The poor boy's clearly too terrified to say anything for fear he'll get another thrashing if he does.'

Mr Glodstone blew a smoke ring. 'Is that what he says?'

'No, it isn't. It's what I say and what I mean —'

'If he doesn't say it, I don't see how you can argue that he means it,' said Mr Glodstone. 'Why don't you ask him?'

'By God, I will,' said the Headmaster, rising to the bait, 'though I'm not having him intimidated by your presence. I'll speak to him alone and you'll kindly wait here while I do.'

And leaving Mr Glodstone to browse through his personal correspondence with a curiosity the Housemaster would have found disgusting in one of his 'chaps', he marched off to the San. By the time he returned, Glodstone had put some more wood on the fire, together with two unopened envelopes for the hell of it, and the Headmaster was forced to temporize. Peregrine had refused to complain about his treatment and, in spite of the Headmaster's pleading, had said he was jolly happy in Gloddie's house and anyway, chaps ought to be beaten.

'What did I tell you?' said Glodstone, and sucked noisily on his pipe. 'Boys appreciate a firm hand. And Clyde-Browne's made of the right stuff.'

'Perhaps,' said the Headmaster morosely. 'But whatever stuff he's made of, I don't want any more of it beaten this term. It may interest you to know that his father is a leading solicitor and has paid his son's fees in advance. A man in his position could bring a court action that would bankrupt the school.'

'Just as you say, Headmaster,' said Glodstone and took his leave, while the Headmaster went back distraughtly to his depleted correspondence and considered desperate measures for getting rid of the ghastly Glodstone.

Outside the study, the Housemaster knocked his pipe out into a bowl of hyacinths and returned to his rooms. There he selected one of his favourite books, *Mr Standfast* by John Buchan, and took it up to the San.

'Thought you might like something to read, old chap,' he said to the back of Peregrine's head.

'Thank you very much, sir,' said Peregrine.

'And jolly good show on your part not letting the side down,' continued Mr Glodstone. 'So when you've finished that, tell Matron and I'll bring you another.'

The literary infection of Peregrine had begun.

Chapter 4

It continued. By the time he was allowed out of the Sanatorium, Peregrine had finished all the Adventures of Richard Hannay and was well into Bulldog Drummond's. He went home for the holidays with several volumes from Glodstone's library, a letter from the Headmaster explaining that he intended to abolish corporal punishment and apologizing for Peregrine having to be beaten at all, an excellent report on his term's work and a positively glowing testimony from Mr Glodstone. Mr Clyde-Browne read the Headmaster's letter with mixed feelings and didn't show it to his wife. In his opinion there was a great deal to be said for beating Peregrine, and in any case, it seemed to suggest that the brute had at last taken it into his head not to do what he was told. Mr Clyde Browne took that as a good sign. His views of the excellent report and Glodstone's testimony were different.

'He seems to be doing extremely well at his work,' said Mrs Clyde-Browne, 'He's got an Alpha for every subject.'

'One hesitates to think what the Betas must be like,' said Mr Clyde-Browne, who was surprised to learn that any of the masters at Groxbourne knew enough Greek to use Alpha.

'And Mr Glodstone writes that he has shown remarkable character and is a credit to the House.'

'Yes,' said Mr Clyde-Browne, 'He also says Peregrine is a born leader and that's a downright lie if ever I heard one.'

'You just don't have any faith in your own son.'

Mr Clyde-Browne shook his head. 'I have every faith in him except when it comes to leading. Now if that damn fool housemaster thinks . . . oh, never mind.'

'But I do mind. I mind very much, and I'm thankful that Peregrine has at last found someone who appreciates his true gifts.'

'If that's all he does appreciate,' said Mr Clyde-Browne with rather nasty emphasis.

'And what exactly does that mean?'

'Nothing. Nothing at all.'

'It does, or you wouldn't have said it.'

'I just find the letter peculiar. And I seem to remember that you found Mr Glodstone peculiar yourself.'

Mrs Clyde-Browne bridled. "If you're thinking what I think you're thinking, you've got a filthier mind than even I would have supposed.'

'Well, it's been known to happen,' said Mr Clyde-Browne, among whose guiltier clients there had been several seedy schoolmasters.

'Not to Peregrine,' said Mrs Clyde-Browne adamantly, and for once her husband had to agree. When next day, on the pretence of having to mow the lawn in December, he questioned Peregrine on the subject, it was clear that he took a robust attitude towards sex.

'Onanism? What's that?' he shouted above the roar of the lawn-mower.

Mr Clyde-Browne adjusted the throttle. 'Masturbation,' he whispered hoarsely, having decided that auto-eroticism would meet with the same blank look.

'Master who?' said Peregrine.

Mr Clyde-Browne dredged his mind for a word his son would understand and decided not to try 'self-abuse'. 'Wanking,' he said finally with a convulsive spasm. 'How much wanking goes on at school?'

'Oh, wanking,' Peregrine shouted as the lawn mower destroyed Mr Clyde-Browne's cover by stopping, 'well, Harrison's are a lot of wankers and Slymne's go in for brown-hatting, but in Gloddie's we –'

'Shut up,' yelled Mr Clyde-Browne, conscious that half the neighbours in Pinetree Lane were about to be privy to what went on in Gloddie's, 'I don't want to know.'

'I can't see why you asked then,' bawled Peregrine, still evidently under the impression that the lawnmower was purely incidental to the discussion. 'You asked if there was a lot of wanking and I was telling you.'

Mr Clyde-Browne dragged lividly at the mower's starting cord.

'Anyway, Gloddie's don't if that's what you're worried about,' continued Peregrine, oblivious of his father's suffering. 'And when Matron thought I'd been shafted, I told her –'

Mr Clyde-Browne wrenched the lawnmower into life again and drowned the rest of the explanation. It was only later in the garage, and after he'd warned his son that if he raised his voice above a whisper, he'd live to regret it, that Peregrine finally established his innocence. He did so in language that appalled his father.

'Where the hell did you learn the term "brown-hatter"?' he demanded.

'I don't know. Everyone uses it about Slymne's.'

'I don't use it,' said Mr Clyde-Browne. 'And what's slime got to do with it. No, don't tell me, I can guess.'

'Slymne's a shit,' said Peregrine. Mr Clyde-Browne turned the statement over in his mind and found it grammatically puzzling and distinctly crude.

'I should have thought it was bound to be,' he said finally, 'though why you have to reverse the order of things and use the indefinite article into the bargain, beats me.'

Peregrine looked bewildered. 'Well, all the other chaps think Slimey's wet and he's sucking up to the Head. He wears a bow tie.'

'Who does?'

'Mr Slymne.'

'Mr Slymne? Who the hell is Mr Slymne?'

'He's the geography master and there's always been a feud between his house and Gloddie's ever since anyone can remember.'

'I see,' said Mr Clyde-Browne vaguely. 'Anyway, I don't want you to use foul language in front of your mother. I'm not paying good money to send you to a school like Groxbourne for the privilege of having you come home swearing like a trooper.'

But at least Mr Clyde-Browne was satisfied that Mr Glodstone's extraordinary enthusiasm for his son was not obviously based on sex, though what cause it had he couldn't imagine. Peregrine appeared to be as obtuse as ever and as unlikely to fulfil the Clyde-Brownes' hopes. But he seemed to be happy and rudely healthy. Even his mother was impressed by his eagerness to go back to school at the end of the holidays, and began to revise her earlier opinion of Groxbourne.

'Things must have changed with the new headmaster,' she said, and by the same process which saw no bad in her acquaintances because she knew them, she now conferred some distinction on Groxbourne because Peregrine went there. Even Mr Clyde-Browne was relatively satisfied. As he had predicted, Peregrine stayed on in the summer holidays and allowed his parents to have an unencumbered holiday by going on Major Fetherington's Fieldcraft and Survival Course in Wales. And at the end of each term, Peregrine's report suggested that he was doing very well. Only in Geography was he found to be wanting, and Peregrine blamed that on Mr Slymne. 'He's got it in for everyone in Gloddie's,' he told his father, 'you can ask anyone.'

'I don't need to. If you will insist on calling the wretched man Slimey, you deserve what you get. Anyway, I can't see how you can be doing so well in class and fail O-levels at the same time.'

'Gloddie says O-levels don't matter. It's what you do afterwards.'

'Then Mr Glodstone's notion of reality must be sadly wanting,' said Mr Clyde-Browne. 'Without qualifications you won't do anything afterwards.'

'Oh, I don't know,' said Peregrine, 'I'm in the First Eleven and the First Fifteen and Gloddie says if you're good at sports –'

'To hell with what Mr Glodstone says,' said Mr Clyde-Browne, and dropped the subject.

His feelings for Glodstone were but a faint echo of those held by Mr Slymne. He loathed Glodstone. Ever since he had first come to Groxbourne some fifteen years before, Slymne had loathed him. It was a natural loathing. Mr Slymne had, in his youth, been a sensitive man and to be christened 'Slimey' in his first week at the school by a one-eyed buffoon with a monocle who professed openly that a beaten boy was a better boy had, to put it mildly, rankled. Mr Slymne's view on punishment had been humane and sensible. Glodstone and Groxbourne had changed all that. In a desperate attempt to gain some respect and to deter his classes from calling him Slimey to his face, he had devised punishments that didn't include beating. They ranged from running ten times to the school gates and back, a total distance of some five miles, to learning Wordsworth's *Prelude* off by heart and, in extreme cases, missing games. It was this last method that brought things to a head. Groxbourne might not be noted for its academic standards but rugby and cricket were another matter, and when boys who were fast bowlers or full-backs complained that they couldn't play in school matches because Mr Slymne had put them on punishment, the other masters turned on him.

'But I can't have my authority undermined by being called nicknames to my face,' Slymne complained at a staff meeting convened after he had put six boys in the First Eleven on punishment two days before the Bloxham match.

'And I'm damned if I'm going to field a side consisting of more than half the Second Eleven,' protested the infuriated cricket coach, Mr Doran. 'As it is, Bloxham is going to wipe the floor with us. I've lost more practice time in the nets this term than any summer since we had the mumps epidemic in 1952, and then we were in quarantine and couldn't play other schools, so it didn't matter. Why can't you beat boys like any decent master?'

'I resent that,' said Mr Slymne. 'What has decency to do with beating –'

The Headmaster intervened. 'What you don't seem to understand, Mr Slymne, is that it is one of the occupational facts of teaching life to be given a nickname. I happen to know that mine is Bruin, because my name is Bear.'

'I daresay,' said Mr Slymne, 'But Bruin's a pleasant name and doesn't undermine your authority. Slimey does.'

'And do you think I like being called the Orangoutang?' demanded Mr Doran, 'Any more than Glodstone here enjoys Cyclops or Matron's flattered by being known as Miss World 1914?'

'No,' said Mr Slymne, 'I don't suppose you do, but you don't get called Orangoutang to your face.'

'Precisely,' said Mr Glodstone. 'Any boy foolish enough to call me Cyclops knows he's going to get thrashed so he doesn't.'

'I think beating is barbaric,' maintained Mr Slymne, 'It not only brutalizes the boys –'

'Boys are brutal. It's in the nature of the beast,' said Glodstone.

29

'But it also brutalizes masters who do it. Glodstone's a case in point.'

'I really think there's no need to indulge in personal attacks,' said the Headmaster, but Mr Glodstone waved his defence aside with a nasty smile.

'Wrong again, Slymne. I don't beat. I know my limitations and I leave it to the prefects in my house to do it for me. An eighteen-year-old has an extremely strong right arm.'

'And I suppose Matron gets boys to do her dirty work for her when she's called Miss World 1914,' said Slymne, fighting back.

Major Fetherington spoke up. 'She doesn't need to. I remember an incident two or three years ago involving Hoskiss Minor. I think she used a soap enema – or was it washing-up liquid? Something like that. He was off games for a week anyway, poor devil.'

'Which brings us back to the main point of contention,' said the Headmaster. 'The Bloxham match is the high point in our sporting calendar. It is of social importance for the school too. A great many parents attend and we'd be doing ourselves no good in their eyes if we allow ourselves to lose it. I am therefore overriding your ban, Mr Slymne. You will find some less time-consuming means of imposing your will on the boys. I don't care how you do it, but please bear in mind that Groxbourne is a games-playing school first and foremost.'

'But surely, Headmaster, the purpose of education is to –'

'Build character and moral fibre. You'll find our purpose set out in the Founder's Address.'

From that moment of defeat, Mr Slymne had suffered further humiliations. He had tried to get a job at other, more progressive, schools, only to learn that he was regarded as totally unsuitable precisely because he had taught at Groxbourne. Forced to stay on, he had been despised by the boys and was made an object of ridicule in the common-room by Mr Glodstone who always referred to him as 'our precious little conscientious objector.' Mr Slymne fought back more subtly by raising the level of geography teaching above that of any other subject and, at the same time, exercising his sarcasm so exclusively on boys from Glodstone's house that they failed their O-levels while other boys passed.

But the main thrust of his revenge was confined to Glodstone himself and over the years had developed into almost as demented an obsession as Glodstone's lust for adventure. Mr Slymne's was more methodical. He observed his enemy's habits closely, made notes about his movements, watched him through binoculars from his room in the Tower, and kept a dossier of boys to whom Glodstone spoke most frequently. Originally, he had hoped to catch him out fondling a boy – Slymne had bought a camera with a telescopic lens to record the event incontrovertibly – but Glodstone's secret sex life remained obstinately concealed. He even failed to rise to the bait of several gay magazines which Mr Slymne had ordered in his name. Glodstone had taken them straight to the Headmaster and had even threatened to call the police in if he received any more. As a result, Mr Slymne and the entire school had had to sit through an unusually long sermon on the evils of pornography, the detrimental effects on sportsmen of masturbation, referred to in the sermon as 'beastliness', and finally the cowardly practice of writing anonymous letters. The sermon ended on the most sinister note of all. 'If any of this continues, I shall be forced, however unwillingly, to refer these matters to the police and the long arm of the law!'

For the first time in his agnostic life, Mr Slymne prayed to God that the sex-shop owner in Soho to whom he had sent his order wouldn't solicit Mr Glodstone's custom again, and that the Headmaster's threat wasn't as all-inclusive as it had sounded. It was a view evidently shared by the boys, whose sex life over the next few days became so restricted that the school laundry was forced to work overtime.

But it was thanks to this episode that Mr Slymne first glimpsed Mr Glodstone's true weakness. 'The damned scoundrel who sent that stuff ought to have known I only read decent manly books. Rider Haggard and Henty. Good old-fashioned adventure yarns with none of your filthy modern muck like *Forever Amber*,' Glodstone had boasted in the common-room that evening, 'What I say is that damned poofters ought to have their balls cut off, what!'

'Some of them appear to share your opinion, Glodstone,' said the Chaplain, 'I was reading only the other day of an extraordinary case where a man actually went through some such operation and turned himself into a woman. One wonders . . .'

31

But Slymne was no longer listening. He put his coffee-cup down and went out with a strange feeling that he had found the scret of Glodstone's success and his popularity with the boys. The wretched man was a boy himself, a boy and a bully. For a few extraordinary seconds things reversed themselves in Mr Slymne's mind; the boys were all adults and the staff were boys, boys grown larger and louder in their opinions and the authority they wielded but still small, horrid boys themselves in their innermost being. It was as though they had been stunted in perpetual adolescence, which explained why they were still at school and hadn't dared the risks and dangers of the outside world. As he crossed the quad with this remarkable insight, as curious in its transposition of his previous beliefs as one of the negatives held up to the light in his darkroom, Mr Slymne felt a sudden relief. He was freed from the responsibilities of his career. He was no longer a schoolmaster, no longer an elderly thirty-eight, he was eighteen, no, fifteen, and entitled to a fifteen-year-old's ebullient spirits and unfeeling harshness, but with the marvellous difference that he had years of adult experience and knowledge on which to rely in his war with Glodstone. He would destroy the bully before he had finished.

With something approaching gaiety, Mr Slymne climbed the steps in the Tower to his room two at a time and added the findings that Glodstone only read adventure yarns to his dossier on the man. Downstairs, there came the sound of fighting in the dormitory. Mr Slymne rose from his desk, descended the stairs and ten minutes later had changed the whole pattern of his life by beating three boys without a qualm.

Chapter 5

'Heard about Slimey's conversion?' Major Fetherington said at breakfast the next morning. Glodstone peered over the *Daily Express*.

'Don't tell me he's joining the Church. God help his parishioners.'

'No such luck. The fellow's finally come round to a proper way of dealing with boys. Beat three little blighters last night for pillow-fighting in dorm.'

Mr Glodstone put down his paper and glared at the Major with his gimlet eye. 'You're joking, of course.'

'Damned if I am. Cleaves, Milshott and Bedgerson. Saw their backsides this morning when they were changing for early PT. A nicer set of welts too you couldn't wish for.'

'Extraordinary. Didn't think the runt had it in him,' said Glodstone, and turned back to his paper only slightly puzzled.

But when Mr Slymne came in five minutes later, Glodstone was genuinely startled. 'Good God,' he said loudly, 'Never thought I'd live to see the day when you'd join us for breakfast, Slymne.'

Slyme helped himself to bacon and eggs and smiled almost cordially. 'Thought it would make a change,' he said, 'One tends to get stuck in a rut. I'm thinking of taking up jogging too.'

'Just don't do yourself an injury,' said Glodstone unpleasantly. 'We wouldn't know how to get along without your conscientious objections. But then I hear you don't have any now. Beat some boys last night, eh?'

'They asked for it and they got it,' said Mr Slymne, managing to ignore the sarcasm.

'Nothing like consistency,' said Glodstone, and stalked out of the dining-room. That morning his classes suffered from his short temper and were set essays to write while Glodstone brooded.

Slymne's change of behaviour was disconcerting. If the damned fellow could suddenly alter his habits and start beating and take up jogging, Glodstone felt hard done by. Slymne had always been a comforting standard of wetness against which Glodstone could measure his own forthright and manly behaviour. Damn it, the next thing the wretched Slymne would do was get married. Glodstone, staring out of the window, felt a new wave of resentment boiling up inside him at the thought. Adventure had eluded him. So had romance. And he was growing older.

'Might not be a bad thing to marry some woman after all,' he muttered to himself, but apart from a distant cousin with no money, who had once proposed to him on Valentine's Day, there were no women of his social background he could think of who would do. There were some divorced mothers, of course, whose presence at the beginning of term or on Open Day had excited him, but their visits were too brief for him to get to know them. Anyway, they were hardly his sort. Glodstone dismissed them from his thoughts until he remembered La Comtesse de Montcon. He had never met her, but Anthony Wanderby, her son by a previous marriage, was in his House and while Glodstone disliked the little blighter – he was a typical American spoilt brat in the Housemaster's eyes and always malingering – he appreciated the crested envelopes and notepaper on which La Comtesse wrote to him from her château in France. Glodstone had endowed La Comtesse – in his too-frequent mentions of her in the staff-room he stuck to the French – with all those qualities of beauty and nobility he had never encountered outside his books, but which had to exist somewhere. Certainly the château existed. Glodstone had looked it up in his Michelin map for Périgord and found it apparently standing above the river, La Boose, a tributary of the Dordogne. A narrow road ran down beside the river and the hillsides opposite were coloured green which meant they were forested. It had often occurred to him to take the Bentley and find some excuse for dropping in but . . . Anyway, there was no point in pining over her. There was doubtless some damned Frog, Monsieur Le Comte, in attendance.

But that evening, after a restless day, he went up to his rooms early and sat sucking a pipe, studying the map again and turning over La Comtesse's brief letters to him. Then he folded them carefully away and replaced them in the cigar-box he kept in his desk before knocking out his pipe on the window sill and turning in.

'Damn Slymne,' he muttered as he lay in the darkness.

He would have damned him far more had he seem Mr Slymne move from the roof of the chapel opposite and descend the circular steps holding his camera carefully with his left hand while feeling the wall with his right. He paused at the bottom, made sure the quad was empty, and crossed to the Tower with the camera and 300mm lens concealed under his jacket. Ten minutes later, after locking himself in his bathroom and pulling the dark blind over the window, he had loaded the developing tank.

For Peregrine, the strange contortions of character in Glodstone and Slymne were too complex to be noticeable. He took them as usual quite literally at face value and since Glodstone's face with its neat moustache, monocle and glass eye gave the impression of strength and authority, while Slymne's didn't, he despised the latter. Besides, he enjoyed a man-to-man friendliness with Glodstone as a result of his enthusiastic reading of every book in his library, to the present where he was allowed to help to polish the Bentley on wet Sunday afternoons. There in the garage with rain pattering on the glass cupola above them (the place had once been a coachhouse with a few old bridles still hanging on the walls) he imbibed the code of the English gentleman which was Glodstone's special mania. He had already merged Richard Hannay, Bulldog Drummond and every other upstanding hero, including James Bond, into a single figure in his mind and had conferred their virtues on Mr Glodstone. In fact, his reading had gone further than Gloddie's which stopped around 1930. James Bond was one such character. Glodstone wasn't too sure about Bond.

'The thing is,' he told Peregrine one afternoon when they had unstrapped the bonnet of the Bentley and were polishing the great engine, 'The thing is with Bond that he's not your everyday decent chap who gets caught up in an adventure quite by chance. He's a sort of paid government employee and anyway his attitude to women's pretty rotten and sordid. And he's always flying about and gambling and generally living it up. Not a gentleman, what?'

'No sir,' said Peregrine and struck Bond off his list.

35

Glodstone sat down on the running-board and took out his pipe. 'I mean to say, it's his job to deal with crime. The damned fellow is a professional. He's told what to do and he has official backing. Now the real thing isn't like that. It happens accidentally. A chap is driving along and he stops for a breather and he sees murder done and naturally he has to do something about it, and by Jove he does. Takes the swine on outside the law and if he gets caught that's the luck of the draw. And another thing is, he's as fit as a fiddle and he sticks to the countryside which he knows like the back of his hand and your genuine crooks don't. That's the way it really is.'

In the presence of the Bentley, Peregrine's feelings were almost religious. Mr Glodstone's clichés opened up an idyllic world where simple chaps made simple decisions and crooks were simply crooks and got what was coming to them. It corresponded exactly with his own view of life; one day he'd be lucky enough to see murder done and would do something about it.

But apart from these occasional visions of the future, he was occupied with games, with the Major's OU course of shooting, doing the assault course, swimming in cold rivers and rock-climbing in Wales during the summer holidays and generally fitting himself for the Army career his father had decided on for him. In schoolwork, he remained a failure. Each year he took his O-levels and failed. It was the only cloud on his simple horizon. There were others gathering.

On the evening after his spell on the chapel roof, Mr Slymne locked himself in his bathroom, set up his enlarger and printed the negatives. They showed Glodstone holding an envelope and placing it in a cigar box. But the 8 × 10 prints were not big enough to tell him more. Mr Slymne turned the enlarger round, put several books on the baseboard and focused on the bathroom floor. This time the negative was so enlarged that the print only included Glodstone's hand, the lower part of his face and the envelope. As it appeared in the developing dish Slymne bent over it eagerly. There was something on the back of the envelope, he could see that now, but it was only when he had transferred the print to the fixer and turned the light on that he recognized in spite of the grain the blob as a crest. A crest? Slymne's thoughts turned to Glodstone's background. The man was always boasting about his family but there'd never been any mention of a family crest, and Glodstone was just the sort of fellow to have made a big thing about it.

If it wasn't his own, what was he doing with crested envelopes? And why keep them in a cigar box?

Anyway, he had learnt something new to add to the dossier. Mr Slymne took the print and was about to wash it when his cautious mind considered the dangers if it were found. It would be extremely awkward having to think of an excuse for photographing Glodstone from the chapel roof. Far better to destroy them now. He tore the photographs into strips of soggy paper and flushed them down the lavatory. The negatives went too. As he washed the dishes and cleared away, Mr Slymne pondered his next move. It might be possible to provoke Glodstone into some discussion on heraldry. He would have to do it tactfully.

In the event, he had to do nothing more than listen. Two days later, he was passing his house room when he heard two boys.

'Tambon says it's a bloody great castle like the sort of thing you see on telly with towers and everything,' said a boy Slymne recognized to be Paitter.

'I bet he sucked up to Wanderby to get himself invited,' said Mowbray. 'He's always doing that and Wanderby's a grotty snob. Just because his mother's a countess and he gets letters with crests, he thinks he's going to marry a royal.'

'Anyway, the countess is a real old cow according to Tambon. He was scared stiff of her. You ask him what it was like.'

A group of boys clattering down the staircase forced Slymne to move. He hurried along to the staff-room deep in thought. Was it pure coincidence that Glodstone kept crested envelopes in a cigar box and that he had a boy in his house whose mother was a countess and used crested notepaper? And if it wasn't, what did it portend? Probably nothing, but it would be worth looking into. For a moment he considered bringing the subject of Wanderby up in Glodstone's presence and watching his reaction. But Slymne's mind, honed by the misery of so many years of insult and dislike, had a new edge of cunning to it. He must do nothing to arouse the slightest glimmer of suspicion in Glodstone. Besides, there was a simple way of finding out if there was any connection between

Glodstone and Wanderby's mother. Slymne bided his time.

His opportunity came at half-term.

'I'm taking a group of chaps over to the railway museum at York,' Glodstone announced one evening. 'Never like to see boys left here when their parents don't pitch up to take them out.'

'Giving the Bentley an airing, eh,' said the Major. 'The Head won't like it, old boy.'

'Not going to give him a chance to dislike it. Hired a charabanc for the trip.'

'A charabanc. Now there's a word that's gone out of fashion,' said the Chaplain.

'I stick to the old ways, Padre,' said Glodstone, rubbing his pipe against the side of his nose to give it a greasy shine. 'They are still the best.'

Mr Slymne noted the archaism. It was another of the irritating facets of Glodstone's character that he seemed to ignore that the world had changed. But it was good to know that Glodstone would be away when the school was almost empty. Very good.

And so, when the parents had been and the coach with Glodstone's steam-engine enthusiasts had left, Mr Slymne slipped quietly along the corridor that connected his house with Gloddie's, carefully checking that each study was empty and that no one was about, and arrived at the door of Glodstone's rooms. For a moment he hesitated and listened but there were none of the usual sounds of the school. He was safe but his heart was beating palpably fast. Two deep breaths to quieten it and he was inside the room and the door was shut behind him. He crossed to the desk. The cigar box had been in a drawer on the left-hand side. Slymne tried the top one and found only exercise books and a broken pipe. The box was in the second. Keeping below the level of the window, he knelt and opened it. The envelopes were inside with the letters. With sudden decisiveness Slymne reached for the bottom one, took it out, examined the crest on the back and noted the French stamp, and put it carefully into the inside pocket of his jacket. Then he shut the drawer and hurried back to his room.

There he took out the letter and read it through with a growing sense of anti-climax. It was simply a short note written in a large flowing hand informing Mr Glodstone that Anthony would be a week late in returning to school because his father was in Paris and would be flying back to the States on September 10th. The letter was signed 'Yours sincerely, Deirdre de Montcon.' Mr Slymne sat staring at it trying to think why Glodstone would want to keep a business letter so carefully in a cigar box and bring it out with the almost reverential look he had seen on his face through the telescopic lens. Perhaps he ought to look at the other letters in the box. They might reveal a more intimate relationship. He would do that when he took this letter back but in the meantime he would photograph it. First he measured the envelope and made a note of its exact dimensions. Then fitting the 55mm Micro lens to his Nikon, he photographed both the letter and the envelope and finally, moving in to within a few inches, photographed the address on the notepaper and the crest on the back of the envelope. That done, he put the letter and envelope in his pocket and slipped back to Glodstone's room, all the time listening for any sound that might indicate there was anyone about. But the school was still silent and the musty smell Slymne always associated with its emptiness during the holidays seemed to pervade the place.

Inside Glodstone's room he checked the letters in the cigar box, replaced the one at the very bottom and was no wiser. Why on earth did Glodstone bring these letters out and handle them as if they were precious? Slymne looked round the room for a clue. The photograph of Rear-Admiral Glodstone on the quarter deck of H.M.S. *Ramillies* told him nothing. Nor did a water-colour of a large square Victorian house which Slymne supposed to be Glodstone's family home. A pipe-rack, another photograph of Glodstone at the wheel of his Bentley, the usual bric-á-brac of a bachelor schoolmaster, and shelves filled with books. An amazing number of books. Slymne had had no idea Glodstone was such an omnivorous reader. He was about to cross to a bookshelf when a sound outside halted him. Someone was coming up the stairs.

Slymne moved. With understandable swiftness, he was through the door of Glodstone's bedroom and wedged up against the washbasin behind it when someone entered the study. Slymne held his breath and was conscious of a horrible weakness. Who the hell could be about when the school was supposed to be empty? And how in God's name was he to explain his presence hiding in the bedroom? For a moment he supposed it might be the woman who cleaned Glodstone's room and made his bed. But the bed was made and whoever was in the study was putting a book back on a shelf. Several minutes passed, another book was withdrawn, there was silence and the sound of the door opening and shutting again. Slymne slumped against the wall with relief but stayed there for five more minutes before venturing out.

On the desk he found a sheet of paper and a message written in neat but boyish script. 'Dear sir, I've returned *Rogue Male*. It was just as good as you said. I've borrowed *The Prisoner of Zenda*. I hope you don't mind. Clyde-Browne.'

Slymne stared at the message and then let his eyes roam round the room. The books were all adventure stories. He ran along a shelf containing Henty and Westerman, Anthony Hope, A. E. W. Mason, all of Buchan. Everywhere he looked there were adventure stories. No wonder the beastly man had boasted that he only read decent manly stuff. Taking a book from a side table, he opened it: 'The castle hung in the woods on the spur of a mountainside, and all its walls could be seen, except that which rose to the North.'

It was enough. Slymne had found the connecting link between Glodstone's treasure of mundane letters from the Comtesse de Montcon, his Bentley and his belligerent datedness.

As evening came, and with it the sounds of cars and boys' voices, Slymne sat on in the darkness of his room letting his mind loose on a scheme that would use all Glodstone's adolescent lust for violent adventure and romance, lure him into a morass of misunderstanding and indiscretion. It was a delightful prospect.

Chapter 6

For the rest of the term, Slymne soaked himself in adventure stories. It was a thoroughly distasteful task but one that had to be done if his plan was to work. He did his reading secretly and, to maintain the illusion that his interests lay in an entirely different direction, he joined the Headmaster's Madrigal Singers, bought records of Tippett and Benjamin Britten and, ostensibly to hear Ashkenazy playing at the Festival Hall, drove down to London.

'Slimey's trying to worm his way into the Head's good graces by way of so-called music,' was Glodstone's comment, but Slymne's activities in London had nothing to do with music. Carefully avoiding more fashionable stationery shops, he found a printer in Paddington who was prepared to duplicate La Comtesse de Montcon's notepaper and crested envelopes.

'I'll have to see the original if you want it done exactly,' he told Slymne, who had produced photographs of the crest and printed address. 'And it'll cost.'

'Quite,' said Slymne, uncomfortably supposing that the man took him for a forger or blackmailer or both. The following week, he found an excuse to be in the Secretary's office when the mail came, and was able to filch Wanderby's letter from his mother. That Saturday, on the grounds that he had to visit a London dentist about his gum trouble, Slymne was back at the printer's with the envelope he had carefully steamed open. He returned to Groxbourne with a lump of cotton wool stuck uncomfortably in his mouth to suggest some dental treatment. 'I'm afraid you'll have to do without me. Dentist's orders,' he explained thickly to the Headmaster. 'Not allowed to sing for the time being.'

'Dear me, well we'll just have to do our best in your absence,' said the Headmaster, with the later comment to his wife that at least they couldn't do worse.

Next day, Wanderby's lost letter was found, rather muddied, in the flowerbed outside the Secretary's office and the postman was blamed.

By the end of term, Slymne had completed his preliminary preparations. He had collected the envelopes and notepaper and had deposited most of them in a locked tin box at his mother's house in Ramsgate for the time being. He had renewed his passport and taken out travellers' cheques. While the rest of the staff dispersed for the Easter holidays, Mr Slymne took the cross-Channel ferry to Boulogne and hired a car. From there he drove to the Belgian frontier before turning south at a small border crossing near Armentières. The place was carefully chosen. Even Slymne had memories of old men croaking '*Mademoiselle d'Armentières, parlez-vous?*' in remembrance of their happy days of slaughter in the First World War, and the name would arouse just the right outdated emotions he required in Glodstone. So must the route. Slymne stopped frequently to consult his maps and the guidebooks to find some picturesque way through this industrial grimness, but finally gave up. Anyway, it would heighten the romance of the wooded roads and valleys further south and the slag-heaps and coal-mines had the advantage of lending the route a very convincing reality. If one wanted to enter France unobserved, this was the way to come. And so Slymne kept to side roads, well away from autoroutes and big towns during his daytime driving, only moving into a hotel in a city at night. All the time he made notes and made sure he was maintaining the spirit of Glodstone's reading without bringing him too closely in touch with the real world.

For that reason he avoided Rouen and crossed the Seine by a bridge further south, but indulged himself on Route 836 down the Eure before back-tracking to Ivry-la-Bataille and noting an hotel there and its telephone number. After that, another diversion by way of Houdan and Faverolles to Nogent-Le-Roi and Chartres. He was hesitant about Chartres, but one look at the Cathedral reassured him. Yes, Chartres would inspire Glodstone. And what about Château Renault just off the road to Tours? It had been four miles outside Château Renault that Mansel and Chandos had gassed Brevet in his own car. Slymne decided against it and chose the minor road to Meung-sur-Loire as being more discreetly surreptitious. He would have to impress on Glodstone the danger of crossing rivers in big towns. Slymne made a note 'Bridge bound to be watched,' in his notebook and drove on.

It took him ten days to plan the route and, to be on the safe side, he stayed clear of the countryside round the Château Carmagnac with one exception. On the tenth night he drove to the little town of Boosat and posted two letters in separate boxes. To be precise, he posted envelopes, each with a crest on the back and with his own address typed onto a self-adhesive label on the front. Then he turned north and retraced his route to Boulogne, checking each mark he had made on his maps against the comments in his notebook and adding more information.

By the time he sailed for Folkestone, Mr Slymne was proud of his work. There were some advantages to be had from a degree in geography after all. And the two envelopes were waiting for him at his mother's house. With the utmost care, he prised off the self-adhesive labels and steamed open the lightly gummed flaps. Then he set to work with an ink-pad to obliterate the date on the postmark while leaving Boosat clearly visible. For the next three days, he pored over the photograph of the Comtesse's letter to Glodstone and traced again and again her large flowing handwriting. When he returned to Groxbourne, even the Comtesse herself would have found difficulty in saying which of the letters she had written without reading their contents. Mr Slymne's skills had come into their own.

It was more than could be said for Peregrine Clyde-Browne. The discrepancy between his school report and his failure to pass any subject at O-level apart from the maths which, because it allowed of no alternatives to right and wrong, he had managed to scrape through with a grade C, had finally convinced Mr Clyde-Browne that sending his son to Groxbourne might have had the advantage of keeping the brute out of the house for most of the year, but that it certainly hadn't advanced the chances of getting him into the Army. On the other hand, he had paid the fees for three years, not to mention his contribution to the Chapel Restoration Fund, and it infuriated him to think that he had wasted the money.

'We're almost certain to be lumbered with the cretin at the end of the summer term,' he grumbled, 'and at this rate, he'll never get a job.'

'I think you're being very hard on him. Dr Andrews says he's probably a late developer.'

'And how late is late? He'll be fifty before he knows that Oui is French for Yes and not an instruction to go to the toilet. And I'll be ninety.'

'And in your second childhood,' retorted Mrs Clyde-Browne.

'Quite,' said her husband. 'In which case you'll have double problems. Peregrine won't be out of his first. Well, if you want to share your old age with a middle-aged adolescent, I don't.'

'Since I'm spending my own middle-age with a bad-tempered and callous –'

'I am not callous. I may be bad-tempered but I am not callous. I am merely trying to do the best for your . . . all right, our son while there's still time.'

'But his reports say –'

But Mr Clyde-Browne's patience had run out. 'Reports? Reports? I'd as soon believe a single word of a Government White Paper as give any credence to those damned reports. They're designed to con parents of morons to go on shelling out good money. What I want are decent exam results.'

'In that case you should have taken my advice in the first place and had Peregrine privately tutored,' said Mrs Clyde-Browne, knitting with some ferocity.

Mr Clyde-Browne wilted into a chair. 'You may be right at that,' he conceded, 'though I can't imagine any educated man staying the course. Peregrine would have him in a mental home within a month. Still, it's worth trying. There must be some case-hardened crammer who could programme him with enough information to get his O-levels. I'll look into it.'

As a result of this desperate determination, Peregrine had spent the Easter holidays with Dr Klaus Hardboldt, late of the Army Education Corps. The doctor's credentials were of the highest. He had drilled the Duke of Durham's son into Cambridge against hereditary odds and had had the remarkable record of teaching eighteen Guards officers to speak pidgin Russian without a lisp.

'I think I can guarantee your son will pass his O-levels,' he told Mr Clyde-Browne. 'Give me anyone for three weeks of uninterrupted training and they will learn.'

Mr Clyde-Browne had said he hoped so and had paid handsomely. And Dr Hardboldt had lived up to his promise. Peregrine had spent three weeks at the Doctor's school in Aldershot with astonishing results. The Doctor's methods were based on his intimate observations of dogs and a close connection with several chief examiners.

'Don't imagine I expect you to think, because I don't,' he explained the first morning. 'You are here to obey. I require the use of only one faculty, that of memory. You will learn off by heart the answers to the questions which will be set you in the exam. Those of you who fail to remember the answers will be put on bread and water; those who are word perfect will get fillet steak. Is that clear?'

The class nodded.

'Pick up the piece of paper in front of you and turn it over.'

The class did as they were told.

'That is the answer to the first question in the Maths paper you will be set. You have twenty minutes in which to learn it off by heart.'

At the end of twenty minutes, Peregrine could remember the answer. Throughout the day, the process continued. Even after dinner it resumed and it was midnight before Peregrine got to bed. He was wakened at six next morning and required to repeat the answers he had learnt the day before to a tape recorder.

'That is known as reinforcement,' said the Doctor. 'Today we will learn the answers to the French questions. Reinforcement will be done tomorrow before breakfast.'

Next day, Peregrine went hungrily into the classroom for geography and was rewarded with steak at dinner. By the end of the week, only one boy in the class was still incapable of remembering the answers to all the questions in History, Geography, Maths, Chemistry, Biology and English Literature.

Dr Hardboldt was undismayed. 'Sit, sir,' he ordered when the boy fell off his chair for the third time, owing to semi-starvation. The lad managed to get into a sitting position. 'Good dog,' said the

Doctor, producing a packet of Chocdrops. 'Now beg.'

As the boy put up his hands, the Doctor dropped a Chocdrop into his mouth. 'Good. Now then Parkinson, if you can obey that simple instruction, there's not the slightest doubt you can pass the exam.'

'But I can't read,' whimpered Parkinson, and evidently tried to wag his tail.

Doctor Hardboldt looked at him grimly. 'Can't read? Stuff and nonsense, sir. Any boy whose parents can afford to pay my fees must be able to read.'

'But I'm dyslexic, sir.'

The Doctor stiffened. 'So,' he said. 'In that case we'll have to apply for you to take your O-levels orally. Take this note to my secretary.'

As Parkinson wobbled from the room, the Doctor turned back to the class. 'Is there any other do . . . boy here who can't read? I don't want any shilly-shallying. If you can't read, say so, and we'll have you attended to by the hypnotist.'

But no one in the class needed the attentions of the hypnotist.

The second week was spent writing down verbatim the answers to the questions and in further reinforcement. Peregrine was woken every so often during the night and interrogated. 'What is the answer to question four in the History paper?' said the doctor.

Peregrine peered bleary-eyed into the ferocious moustache. 'Gladstone's policy of Home Rule for Ireland was prevented from becoming law because Chamberlain, formerly the radical Mayor of Birmingham, split the Liberal party and . . .'

'Good dog,' said the doctor when he had finished and rewarded him with a Chocdrop.

But it was in the third week that reinforcement became most rigorous. 'A tired mind is a receptive mind,' the doctor announced on Sunday evening. 'From now on, you will be limited to four hours sleep in every twenty-four, one hour in every six being allocated for rest. Before you go to sleep, you will write down the answers to one exam paper and, on being woken, will write them down again before going on to the next subject. In this way, you will be unable to fail your O-levels even if you want to.'

After seven more days of conditioning, Peregrine returned to his parents exhausted and with his brain so stuffed with exam answers that his parents had their own sleep interrupted by an occasional bark and the sound of Peregrine automatically reciting the doctor's orders. They were further disturbed by Dr Hardboldt's insistence that Peregrine be prevented from returning to Groxbourne until after he had sat his exams. 'It is absolutely essential that he isn't exposed to the confusion of other methods of teaching,' he said. 'Nothing is more damaging to an animal's learning ability than contradictory stimuli.'

'But Peregrine isn't an animal,' protested Mrs Clyde-Browne. 'He's a delicate, sensitive –'

'Animal,' said her husband, whose views on his son coincided entirely with the Doctor's.

'Exactly,' said Dr Hardboldt. 'Now where most teachers go wrong is in failing to apply the methods used in animal training to their pupils. If a seal can be taught to balance a ball on its nose, a boy can be taught to pass exams.'

'But the questions are surely different every year,' said Mr Clyde-Browne.

Dr Hardboldt shook his head. 'They can't be. If they were, no one could possibly teach the answers. Those are the rules of the game.'

'I hope you're right,' said Mrs Clyde-Browne.

'Madam, I am,' said the Doctor. 'Time will prove it.'

And time, as far as Peregrine was concerned, did. He returned to Groxbourne a month late and, with the air of a sleepwalker, took his O-level exams with every sign that this time he would succeed. Even the Headmaster, glancing through the papers before sending them off to the external examiners, was impressed. 'If I hadn't seen it with my own eyes I wouldn't have believed it possible,' he muttered, and immediately wrote to the Clyde-Brownes to assure them that they could go ahead with their plans to enter Peregrine for the Army.

Mr Clyde-Browne read the letter with delight. 'He's done it. By golly, he's done it,' he whooped.

'Of course he has,' said Mrs Clyde-Browne, 'I always knew he was gifted.'

Mr Clyde-Browne stopped whooping. 'Not him . . .' he began and decided to say no more.

Chapter 7

But Peregrine's future was being decided by more subtle influences than those of the military Doctor. Mr Glodstone had spent the holidays in search, as he put it, 'of some damned woman' to marry. 'The thing is one doesn't want to marry beneath one,' he confided to Major Fetherington over several nightcaps of whisky in his rooms.

'Absolutely,' said the Major, whose wife had died of boredom ten years before. 'Still, if there's lead in your pencil, you've got to make your mark somewhere.'

Glodstone glanced at him dubiously. The Major's metaphor was too coarse for his romantic imagination. 'Perhaps, but love's got to be there too. I mean, only a cad would marry a girl he didn't love, don't you think?'

'Suppose so,' said the Major, enjoying the whisky too much to argue from his own experience. 'Still, a fellow's got to think of the future. Knew a chap once, must have been eighty if he was a day, keen tennis-player in his time, married a woman he happened to be sitting next to in the Centre Court at Wimbledon. Splendid match. Died in her arms a fortnight later desperately in love. Never can tell till you try.'

Glodstone considered the moral of this example and found it hardly illuminating. 'That sort of thing doesn't happen to me,' he said and put the cap back on the whisky bottle.

'The trouble with you,' said the Major, 'is that you've got champagne tastes and a beer income. My advice is to lower your sights. Still, you never know. Chance has a funny way of arranging things.'

For once Mr Slymne would have shared Glodstone's unspoken disagreement. He was leaving as little as possible to chance. Having discovered Glodstone's wildly romantic streak, he was determined to exploit it, but there were still problems to cope with. The first concerned Sports Day. La Comtesse de Montcon might put in an appearance, and if the wretched woman turned out to be as formidable as the conversation he had overheard in the house-room suggested, all his preparations would be wasted. Glodstone would hardly go to the aid of a woman who was manifestly capable of looking after herself. No, it was vital that the image in Glodstone's imagination should be that of a poor, defenceless, or to be exact, a rich defenceless sylph-like creature with an innocence beyond belief. Slymne had a shrewd idea that La Comtesse was more robust. Any mother who could send her son to Groxbourne had to be. Slymne checked his dossier and found that Tambon had said 'The countess is a real old cow,' and was reassured. He also surreptitiously took a look at the Visiting Parents' Book in the Bursar's office and found no evidence that La Comtesse had ever visited the school.

But to be on the safe side, he used a geography lesson to ask all those boys whose mothers were coming to Sports Day to put up their hands. Wanderby didn't. Having dealt with that problem, Slymne concentrated on the next one; how to phrase his letter to Glodstone. In the end he decided on the direct approach. It would appeal to Glodstone's gallantry more effectively than anything too subtle. On the other hand, there had to be more definite instructions as well. Slymne penned the letter, tracing La Comtesse's handwriting again and again for practice, and then on a weekend visit to London, spent the night in a hotel room making a number of direct-dialled calls to France. By the time he returned to Groxbourne, he was ready to provide the instructions. Only one uncertainty remained. Glodstone might have made arrangements for his summer holidays already. In which case, the timing of the letter would be vital. And Wanderby's own movements in the holidays might prove awkward too. Again Slymne made use of a geography lesson to find out where the boy was spending the summer.

'I'm going to Washington to stay with my father and his girl friend,' Wanderby announced brashly. Mr Slymne was delighted and used the statement in the Common Room that evening to good advantage.

'I must say we have some pretty peculiar parents,' he said loudly,

'I was discussing time zones with 2B this morning and that American boy, Wanderbury, suddenly said his father's got a mistress in Washington.'

Glodstone stopped sucking his pipe. 'Can't you even remember the names of the boys you teach?' he asked angrily. 'It's Wanderby. And what's all this about his father having a mistress?'

Slymne appeared to notice Glodstone for the first time. 'In your house, isn't he? Typical product of a broken home. Anyway, I'm merely repeating what he said.'

'Do you make a habit of poking your nose into the boy's family affairs in your lessons?'

'Certainly not. As I said, I was discussing time zones and jet-lag and Wandleby –'

'Wanderby, for God's sake,' snapped Glodstone.

'– volunteered the information that he was going to Washington at the end of term and that his father –'

'All right, we heard you the first time,' said Glodstone and finished his coffee hurriedly and left the room. Later that evening as he crossed the quad, Slymne was pleased to notice Glodstone sitting at his desk by the window with a cigar box beside him. The crack about the broken home and Wanderby's father having a mistress would enhance Glodstone's romantic image of La Comtesse. That night, Slymne completed the task of writing out her instructions and locked the letter away in his filing cabinet.

It was to remain there for another five weeks. The summer term dragged on. Sports Day came and went, cricket matches were won or lost and Glodstone's melancholy grew darker with the fine weather and the liveliness of youth around him. He took to polishing the Bentley more frequently and it was there in the old coach-house one evening that he asked Peregrine what he was going to do when he left.

'Father's got me down for the Army. But now I've got O-levels, he's talking about my going into a bank in the City.'

'Not your sort of life I would have thought. Dashed dull.'

'Well, it's on account of my maths,' said Peregrine. 'That and Mother. She's all against my going into the Army. Anyway, I've got a month free first because I'm going on the Major's course in Wales.

It's jolly good fun doing those night marches and sleeping out in the open.'

Glodstone sighed at the remembrance of his youth and came to a sudden decision. 'Damn the Head,' he muttered, 'let's take the old girl out for a spin. After all, it is your last term and you've done more than your fair whack in keeping her shipshape and Bristol fashion. You go off down to the school gates and I'll pick you up there in ten minutes.'

And so for an hour they bowled along country lanes with the wind in their faces and the great exhaust murmuring gently behind them.

'You drive jolly well,' said Peregrine, as they swung round a corner and headed through an overhang of oaks, 'and she goes like a dream.'

Beside him, Glodstone smiled. 'This is the life, eh. Can't beat a vintage Bentley. She's a warhorse just raring to go.'

They came to a village and on the same impulse that had carried him so far, Glodstone stopped outside a pub. 'Two pints of your best bitter, landlord,' said Glodstone loudly, provoking the man into enquiring if Peregrine was eighteen.

'No . . .' said Peregrine but his answer was drowned by the boom of Glodstone's voice.

'Of course he is. Damnation, man, you don't imagine I'd bring an under-age drinker into your place?'

'I've known it happen,' said the barman, 'so I'll make it one bitter and a lemonade shandy and you can take your glasses outside to a table.'

'We can do better than that and take our custom elsewhere,' said Glodstone and stalked out of the pub. 'That's the trouble with the damned world today, people don't know their place any more. In my father's day, that fellow would have lost his licence and no mistake. Anyway, with a manner like that, the beer was probably flat.'

They drove on to the next village and stopped again. This time Glodstone lowered his voice and they were served. As they sat on a bench outside admiring their reflections in the shining waxed coachwork of the great car and basking in the comments it caused, Glodstone cheered up.

'You can say what you like but there's nothing to touch a pint of the best British bitter,' he said.

'Yes,' said Peregrine, who had hardly touched his beer and didn't much like it anyway.

'That's something you won't find in any other country. The Hun swills lager by the gallon and the Dutch have their own brew which isn't bad but it's got no body to it. Same with the Belgians, but it's all bottled beer. Mind you, it's better than the Frog muck. Charge the earth for the stuff too but that's the French all over. Dashed odd, when you come to think of it, that the wine-drinking countries have never been a match for the beer ones when it comes to a good scrap. Probably something in the saying they've got no guts and no stomach for a fight.'

Peregrine drank some more beer to mark his allegiance while Glodstone spouted his prejudices and the world shrank until there was only one decent place to be, and that was sitting in the summer twilight in an English village drinking English beer and gazing at one's reflection in the coachwork of an English car that had been made in 1927. But as they drove back to the school, Glodstone's melancholy returned. 'I'm going to miss you,' he said. 'You're my sort of chap. Dependable. So if there's anything I can ever do for you, you've only to ask.'

'That's jolly good of you, sir,' said Peregrine.

'And another thing. We can forget the "sir" bit from now on. I mean, it's the end of term and all that. All the same, I think you'd better hop out when we get to the school gates. No need to give the Head any reason to complain, eh?'

So Peregrine walked back up the avenue of beeches to the school while Glodstone parked the Bentley and morosely considered his future. 'You and I are out of place here, old girl,' he murmured, patting the Bentley's headlight affectionately, 'we were born in a different world.'

He went up to his room and poured himself a whisky and sat in the darkening twilight wondering what the devil he was going to do with himself during the holidays. If only he'd been younger, he'd be inclined to join Major Fetherington's walkabout in Wales. But no, he'd look damned silly now and anyway the Major didn't like anyone poaching on his own private ground. It was a fairly desperate Glodstone who finally took himself off to bed and spent half an hour reading *The Thirty-Nine Steps* again. 'Why the hell can't something challenging come my way for once?' he thought as he switched out the light.

A week later it did. As the last coach left for the station and the cars departed, Slymne struck. The School Secretary's office was conveniently empty when he tucked the envelope addressed to G. P. Glodstone, Esq., into the pigeonhole already jammed with Glodstone's uncollected mail. Slymne's timing was nicely calculated. Glodstone was notorious for not bothering with letters until the pigeonhole was full. 'A load of bumpf,' he had once declared. 'Anyone would think I was a penpusher and not a schoolmaster.' But with the end of term, he would be forced to deal with his correspondence. Even so, he would leave it until the last moment. It was in fact three days before Glodstone took the bundle of letters up to his room and shuffled through them and came to the envelope with the familiar crest, an eagle evidently tearing the entrails from a sheep. For a moment Glodstone gazed almost rapturously at the crest before splitting the envelope open with a paper-knife. Again he hesitated. Letters from parents were too often lists of complaints about the treatment of their sons. Glodstone held his breath as he took it out and laid it flat on the desk. But his fears were unfounded.

'Dear Mr Glodstone,' he read, 'I trust you will forgive me writing to you but I have no one else to turn to. And, although we have never met, Anthony has expressed such admiration for you – indeed maintains you are the only gentleman among the masters at Groxbourne – that I feel you alone can be trusted.' Glodstone re-read the sentence – he had never suspected the wretched Wanderby of such perception – and then continued in a ferment of excitement.

'I dare express nothing in a letter for fear that it will be intercepted, except that I am in the greatest danger and urgently need help in a situation which is as hazardous as it is honourable. Beyond that I cannot go in writing. Should you feel able to give me that assistance I so desperately require, go to the left-luggage office at Victoria Station and exchange the enclosed ticket. I can say no more but know you will understand the necessity for this precaution.'

The letter was signed, 'Yours in desperation, Deirdre de Montcon. P.S. Burn both the letter and the envelope at once.'

Glodstone sat transfixed. The call he had been awaiting for over thirty years had finally come. He read the letter several times and then, taking the left-luggage ticket, which he put into his wallet, he ceremoniously burnt the letter in its envelope and as an extra precaution flushed the ashes down the lavatory. Seconds later, he was packing and within the half hour the Bentley rolled from the coach-house with a rejuvenated Glodstone behind the wheel.

From the window of his rooms in the Tower, Slymne watched him leave with a different excitement. The loathsome Glodstone had taken the bait. Then Slymne too carried his bags down to his car and left Groxbourne, though less hurriedly. He would always be one step ahead of his enemy.

Chapter 8

It was late afternoon by the time Glodstone parked the Bentley in a street near Victoria Station. He had driven down in a state of euphoria interspersed with occasional flashes of insight which told him the whole affair was too good to be true. There must be some mistake. Certainly his judgement of Wanderby had been wholly wrong. What had the letter said? 'Maintains that you are the only gentleman among the masters.' Which was true enough, but he'd hardly expected Wanderby to have recognized it. Still, the boy's mother was La Comtesse, and he evidently knew a gentleman when he saw one.

But for the most part, Glodstone had spent the drive concentrating on ways of reaching the Château Carmagnac as speedily as possible. It would depend on what message he found at the left-luggage office, but if he took the Weymouth to Cherbourg ferry, he could drive through the night and be there in twenty-four hours. He had his passport with him and had stopped at his bank in Bridgnorth to withdraw two thousand pounds from his deposit account and change them into travellers' cheques. It was the sum total of his savings but he still had his small inheritance to fall back on. Not that money counted in his calculations. He was about to embark on the expedition of his dreams. He was also going alone. It was at this point that a feeling of slight disappointment crept over him. In his fantasies, he had always seen himself accompanied by one or two devoted friends, a small band of companions whose motto would be that of The Three Musketeers, 'All for one and one for all.' Of course when he was young it had been different, but at fifty Glodstone felt the need for company. If only he could have taken young Clyde-Browne with him – but there was no time for that now. He must act with speed.

But the message he found waiting for him at the left-luggage office changed his opinion. He had been rather surprised to find that it was in fact a piece of luggage, a small brown suitcase. 'Are you sure this is the article?' he asked the attendant rather incautiously.

'Listen, mate, it's yours isn't it? You gave me the ticket for it and that's the luggage,' said the man and turned away to deal with another customer. Glodstone glanced at a label tied to the handle and was satisfied. Neatly typed on it was his own name. He walked back to the car with a new sense of caution and twice stopped at a corner to make sure he was not being followed. Then with the case on the seat beside him he drove to the flat of an aged aunt in Highgate which he was forced to use when he was in London. In keeping with his background, Glodstone would have much preferred his club, The Ancient Automobile, but it didn't run to rooms.

'Well I never, if it isn't Gerald,' said the old lady, rather gratuitously in Glodstone's opinion, 'and you didn't even write to say you were coming.'

'I didn't have time. Urgent business,' said Glodstone.

'It's a good thing your room is still ready just as you left it, though I'll have to put a hot-water bottle in to air the sheets. Now you just sit down and I'll make a nice pot of tea.'

But Glodstone was in no mood for these domestic details. They clashed too prosaically with his excitement. All the same, his aunt disappeared into the kitchen while he went up to his room and opened the suitcase. Inside it was stuffed with French newspapers and it was only when he had taken them all out that he found the second envelope. He ripped it open and took out several sheets of notepaper. They were all crested and the handwriting was unmistakably that of La Comtesse.

'Dear Mr Glodstone, Thank you for coming thus far,' he read. 'It was to be expected of you but, though I would have you come to my aid, I fear extremely you do not appreciate the dangers you will face and I would not put you at your peril without fair warning. Desperate as my situation is, I cannot allow you to come unprepared. Those about me are wise in the ways of crime whereas you are not. This is perhaps to your advantage but for your own sake and for mine, be on your guard and come, if you can, armed, for this is a matter of life and death and murder has already been done.'

'Your tea is ready, dear,' the old lady called from her cluttered sitting-room.

'All right, I'll be there in a minute,' said Glodstone irritably. Here he was about to engage in a matter of life and death and with murder already done, and aged aunts who called him dear and served tea were distinctly out of place. He read on. 'I enclose the route you must follow. The ports are watched and on no account must you appear to be other than an English gentleman touring through France. It is vital therefore that you take your time and trust no one. The men against whom you are set have agents among the gendarmerie and are themselves above suspicion. I cannot state their influence too highly. Nor dare I catalogue their crimes in writing.' This time the letter was signed 'Yours in gratitude, Deirdre de Montcon,' and as before the postscript ordered him to burn both letter and envelope.

Glodstone turned to the other page. It was typewritten and stated that he was to cross from Dover to Ostend on the early morning ferry on the 28th of July and drive to Iper before passing the frontier into France the following day. Thereafter his route was listed with hotels at which 'rooms have been booked for you.' Glodstone read down the list in amazement. Considering the terrible dangers La Comtesse was evidently facing, her instructions were quite extraordinarily explicit. Only when he turned the page was there an explanation. In her own handwriting she had written, 'Should I have need to communicate with you, my messages will be waiting for you in your rooms each night. And now that I have written this by hand, please copy and then burn.'

Glodstone reached in his pocket for a pen, only to be interrupted by his aunt.

'Your tea's getting cold, dear.'

'Damn,' said Glodstone, but went through to the sitting-room and spent an extremely impatient half an hour listening to the latest family gossip. By the time Aunt Lucy got on to the various diseases her grandnieces and nephews had been suffering from, Glodstone was practically rabid. 'Excuse me, but I have some really pressing business to attend to,' he said, as she launched into a particularly clinical account of the symptoms his cousin Michael had contracted, or more precisely expanded, as a result of mumps.

'Balls,' continued Aunt Lucy implacably.

'I beg your pardon,' said Glodstone, whose attention had been fixed on La Comtesse's instructions.

'I was saying that his –'

'I simply must go,' said Glodstone and rather rudely left the room.

'What a very peculiar boy Gerald is,' muttered the old lady as she cleared away the tea things. Her opinion was confirmed some forty minutes later when she discovered the hallway was filling with smoke.

'What in heaven's name are you doing in there?' she demanded of the door to the lavatory which seemed to be the source of the fire.

'Nothing,' choked Glodstone, wishing to God he hadn't been so conscientious in following La Comtesse's instructions to burn all evidence. The letter and his itinerary had gone easily enough, but his attempt to screw the envelope into a ball and catch the flood had failed dismally. The envelope remained obstinately buoyant with the crest plainly visible. And the cistern had been no great help either. Built for a more leisurely age, it filled slowly and emptied no faster. Finally Glodstone had resorted to the French newspapers. They were incriminating too and by crumpling them up around the sodden envelope he might get that to burn as well. In the event, he was proved right, but at considerable cost. The newspapers were as fiery as their editorials. As flames shot out of the pan, Glodstone slammed the lid down and was presently tugging at the chain to extinguish what amounted to an indoor bonfire. It was at this point that his aunt intervened.

'Yes, you are,' she shouted through the door, 'You've been smoking in there and something's caught fire.'

'Yes,' gasped Glodstone, finding this a relatively plausible explanation. Nobody could say that he hadn't been smoking. The damned stuff was issuing round the edges of the lid quite alarmingly. He seized the towel from behind the door and tried to choke the smoke off before he suffocated.

'If you don't come out this minute I shall be forced to call the fire brigade,' his aunt threatened but Glodstone had had enough. Unlocking the door, he shot, gasping for air, into the hall.

His aunt surveyed the smoke still fuming from beneath the seat. 'What on earth have you been up to?' she said, and promptly extinguished the smouldering remnants of *Le Monde* with a basin of water from the kitchen before examining the fragments with a critical eye.

'You've been a bachelor too long,' she declared finally. 'Your Uncle Martin was found dead in the lavatory with a copy of *La Vie Parisienne* and you've evidently taken after him. What you need is a sensible wife to take care of your baser needs.'

Glodstone said nothing. If his aunt chose to draw such crude conclusions it was far better that she do so than suspect the true nature of his enterprise. All the same, the incident had taken a measure of the immediate glamour out of the situation. 'I shall be dining out,' he said with some hauteur and spent the evening at his club planning his next move. It was complicated by the date of his cross-channel booking, which was set for the 28th. He had five days to wait. Then there was the question of obtaining arms. The letter had definitely said 'Come armed,' but that was easier said than done. True, he had a shotgun at a cousin's farm in Devon but shotguns didn't come into the category of proper arms. He needed a revolver, something easy to conceal in the Bentley, and he could hardly go into a gunsmith in London and ask for a .38 Smith & Wesson with a hundred cartridges. The thing to do would be to approach some member of the underworld. There must be plenty of people selling guns in London. Glodstone didn't know any and had not the foggiest notion where to look for them. It was all very disconcerting and he was about to give up the notion of going armed when he remembered that Major Fetherington kept revolvers and ammunition in the School Armoury. In fact there were several old ones there. And he knew where the Major kept the keys. It would be a simple matter to take one and he could have it back before the beginning of next term. With a more cheerful air, Glodstone ordered a brandy before returning to his aunt's flat. Next morning he was on the road again and by lunchtime back at Groxbourne.

'Fancy you coming back so soon,' said the School Secretary. 'The galloping Major's back too, only he isn't galloping quite so much. Been and gone and sprained his ankle.'

'Damnation,' said Glodstone horrified at this blow to his plan, 'I mean, poor fellow. Where is he?'

'Up in his rooms.'

Glodstone climbed the staircase to the Major's rooms and knocked.

'Come in, whoever you are,' shouted the Major. He was sitting in an armchair with one leg propped up on a stool. 'Ah, Gloddie, old boy. Good to see you. Thought you'd shoved off.'

'I had to come back for something. What on earth happened? Did you slip on some scree in Wales?'

'Never got to bloody Wales. Glissaded on a dog-turd in Shrewsbury and came a right purler, I can tell you. All I could do to drive that damned minibus back here. Had to cancel the OU course and now I've got old Perry on my hands.'

'Peregrine Clyde-Brown?' asked Glodstone with rising hope.

'Parents off in Italy somewhere. Won't be back for three weeks and he's been trying to phone some uncle but the chap's never in. Blowed if I know what to do with the lad.'

'How long is that ankle of yours going to take to mend?' asked Goldstone, suddenly considering the possibility that he might have found just the two people he would most like to have with him in a tight spot.

'Quack's fixed me up for an X-ray tomorrow. Seems to think I may have fractured my coccyx.'

'Your coccyx? I thought you said you'd sprained your ankle.'

'Listen, old man,' said the Major conspiratorially. 'That's for public consumption. Can't have people going round saying I bought it where the monkey hid the nuts. Wouldn't inspire confidence, would it? I mean, would you trust a son of yours to go on a survival course with a man who couldn't spot a dog-pat when it was staring him in the face?'

'Well, as a matter of fact I don't . . .' began Glodstone, only to be interrupted by the Major who was shifting his posterior on what appeared to be a semi-inflated plastic lifebelt. 'Another thing. The

60

Head don't know, so for Lord's sake don't mention a word. The blighter's only too anxious to find an excuse for closing the OU course down. Can't afford to lose my job.'

'You can rely on me,' said Glodstone. 'Is there anything I can get you?'

The Major nodded. 'A couple of bottles of whisky. Can't ask Matron to get it for me. Bad enough having her help me to the loo, and then she hangs about outside asking if I need any help. I tell you, old boy, everything they say about passing razor blades is spot-on.'

'I'll see to the whisky,' said Glodstone, not wishing to pursue this line of conversation any further. It was obvious that the Major was a broken reed as far as the great adventure was concerned. He went downstairs in search of Peregrine. He had no difficulty. The sound of shots coming from the small-arms range indicated where Peregrine was. Glodstone found him using a .22 to puncture the centre of a target. For a moment he watched with delight and then stepped forward.

'Gosh, sir, it's good to see you,' said Peregrine enthusiastically and scrambled to his feet, 'I thought you'd left.'

Glodstone switched his monocle to his good eye. 'Something's turned up. The big show,' he said.

Peregrine looked puzzled. 'The big show, sir?'

Glodstone looked cautiously round the range before replying. 'The call to action,' he said solemnly. 'I can't give any details except to say that it's a matter of life and death.'

'Gosh, sir, you mean –'

'Let's just say I've been asked to help. Now, as I understand it, your folks are in Italy and you've nothing on.'

For a moment Peregrine's literal mind struggled with the statement before he caught its meaning. 'No, sir, I've been trying to phone my uncle but I can't get through.'

'In which case you won't be missed. That's number one. Number two is we've three weeks in which to do the job. I take it you've got a passport.'

Peregrine shook his head. Glodstone polished his monocle thoughtfully. 'In that case we'll have to think of something.'

'You mean we're going abroad?'

'To France,' said Glodstone, 'that is, if you're game. Before you answer, you must know that we'll be acting outside the law with no holds barred. I mean, it won't be any picnic.'

But Peregrine was already enthralled. 'Of course I'm game, sir. You can count me in.'

'Good man,' said Glodstone and clapped him on the shoulder. 'Now as to a passport, I have an idea. Didn't Mr Massey take the fifth-form French to Boulogne last year?'

'Yes sir.'

'And Barnes had flu and couldn't go. If I'm not wrong, the Bursar said he'd kept his temporary visitor's passport back. It could be he still has it in his office.'

'But I don't look a bit like Barnes.'

Glodstone smiled. 'You will by the time you cross,' he said, 'We'll see to that. And now for weapons. You don't by any chance have the key to armoury, do you?'

'Well, yes sir. The Major said I could keep my eye in so long as I didn't blow my head off.'

'In that case, we'll pay the gunroom a visit. We need to go armed and two revolvers won't be missed.'

'They will, sir,' said Peregrine. 'The Major always checks the guns.'

'I can't see him doing it in his present condition,' said Glodstone. 'Still, I don't like going unprepared.'

For once Peregrine had the answer. 'There's a smashing shop for replica guns in Birmingham, sir. I mean if we –'

'Splendid,' said Glodstone. 'The Major wants some whisky. We can kill two birds with one stone.'

That evening the substitutions were made and two .38 Webleys with several hundred rounds of ammunition were stored in cardboard boxes beneath the seats of the Bentley. And the problem of the passport had been solved too. Glodstone had found Barnes's in the Bursar's office.

'Now it remains to convince the Major that you're going to your uncle's. Tell him you're catching the ten o'clock train and I'll pick you up at the bus-stop in the village. We don't want to be seen leaving the school together. So hop along to his room and then turn in. We've got a long day ahead of us tomorrow.'

Glodstone went up to his rooms and sat on in the evening sunlight studying his route on the map and sipping pink gins. It was nine before he remembered the Major's Scotch and took him the two bottles.

'Bless you, old lad,' said the Major, 'You'll find a couple of glasses in the cupboard. Saved my life. And Perry's off to his uncle's tomorrow.'

'Really?' said Glodstone. 'Anyway, your very good health.'

'Going to need it by the feel of things. Bloody nuisance being cooped up here with no one much to chat to. Are you staying around for long?'

Glodstone hesitated. He was fond of the Major and the whisky coming on top of his pink gins had added to the intoxication he felt at the prospect of his adventure. 'Strictly between these four walls,' he said, 'and I do mean strictly, the most extraordinary thing's happened and . . .' He hesitated. The Countess had asked for the utmost secrecy but there was no harm in telling the Major and if anything went wrong, it would help to have someone know. 'I've had a summons from La Comtesse de Montcon, Wanderby's mater. Apparently she's in terrible trouble and needs me . . .'

'Must be,' said the Major unsympathetically, but Glodstone was too drunk to get the message. By the time he'd finished, Major Fetherington had downed several stiff whiskies in quick succession and was looking at him peculiarly. 'Listen, Gloddie, you can't be serious. You must have dreamt this up.'

'I most certainly haven't,' said Glodstone. 'It's what I've been waiting for all my life. And now it's come. I always knew it would. It's destiny.'

'Oh, well, it's your pigeon. What do you want me to do?'

'Nothing. I know how you're placed and all that. But do remember, you're sworn to secrecy. No one, but no one, must know. I want your hand on that.'

'If you say so,' said the Major. 'Shake a paw. No names, no pack-drill and all that. You can rely on me. All the same . . . Pass the bottle. So you're crossing to Ostend?'

'Yes,' said Glodstone and got up unsteadily. 'Better get some shut-eye.' He wove to the door and went downstairs. On the way, he met the Matron and ignored her. She held no attractions for him now. La Comtesse de Montcon wanted him and the great romance of his life had begun. He crossed the quad. A light was burning in Peregrine's dormitory but Glodstone didn't see it.

'Fuck me,' said the Major, unfortunately just as the Matron entered.

Peregrine shut the book and turned out the light. He had just finished *The Day of the Jackal*.

Chapter 9

In Ramsgate, Slymne hardly slept. Away from Groxbourne and in the saner atmosphere of his mother's house, Slymne could see considerable weaknesses in his plan. To begin with, he had forged two letters from the Countess and if Glodstone hadn't followed instructions to burn the confounded things and actually produced them to her, things could become exceedingly awkward. The woman might well call the police in and they would probably find his fingerprints on the letters. At least Slymne supposed they could, with modern methods of forensic science, and even if they didn't there was still the matter of the hotel bookings. As far as he could see, this was his most fatal mistake. He should never have made the bookings by telephone from England. If the calls were traced the police would begin looking for motive and from there to his own progress across France during the Easter holidays . . . Slymne preferred not to think of the consequences. He'd lose his job at the school and Glodstone would gloat over his exposure. In fact he could see now that the whole thing had been a ghastly mistake, a mental aberration that was likely to wreck his career. So, while Glodstone and Peregrine drove to London next day and booked into separate rooms, one with a bathroom, Slymne concentrated on means of stopping the scheme he had so successfully started. Possibly the best way would be to send a telegram to the school purporting to come from the Countess and countermanding the instructions. Slymne decided against it. For one thing they always phoned telegrams before sending the printed message and the School Secretary would take the call, and for another Glodstone had probably left no forwarding address. To make absolutely certain, Slymne took the opportunity, while his mother was out shopping, to put a large wad of cotton wool very uncomfortably in his mouth to disguise his voice and phone the school. As he anticipated the Secretary answered.

'No, Mr Slymne,' she said, to his horror, 'you've just missed him. I mean he was here till yesterday but he's gone now and you know what he's like about letters anyway. I mean they pile up in his pigeonhole even in term-time and he never does leave a forwarding address. Is there anything I can tell him if he comes back again?'

'No,' said Slymne, 'and my name isn't Slymne. It's . . . it's . . . er . . . Fortescue. Just say Mr Fortescue phoned.'

'If you say so, Mr Fortescue, though you sound just like one of the masters here. He had ever such bad toothache the term before last and –'

Slymne had put the phone down and removed the wad of cotton wool. There had to be some way of stopping Glodstone. Perhaps if he were to make an anonymous phone call to the French Customs authorities that Glodstone was a drug smuggler, they would turn him back at the frontier? No, phone calls were out, and in any case there was no reason to suppose the French Customs officials would believe him. Worse still, the attempt might provoke Glodstone into some more desperate action such as crossing the frontier on foot and hiring a car once he was safely in France and driving straight to the Château. Having opened the Pandora's box of Glodstone's adolescent imagination it was going to prove exceedingly difficult to close the damned thing. And everything depended on Glodstone having burnt those incriminating letters. Why hadn't he considered the possibility that the man might keep them as proof of his *bona fides*? The answer was because Glodstone was such a fool. But was he? Slymne's doubts increased. Putting himself in Glodstone's shoes, he decided he would have kept the letters just in case the whole thing was a hoax. And again, now that he came to think of it, the instruction to burn every piece of correspondence was distinctly fishy and could well have made Glodstone suspicious. As his doubts and anxieties increased, Slymne decided to act.

He packed a bag, found his passport, took the file containing the photographs of the Countess's letter, together with several sheets of crested notepaper and envelopes, and was ready to leave when his mother returned from her shopping.

'But I thought you said you were going to stay at home this

summer,' she said. 'After all, you had a continental holiday at Easter and it's not as though you can afford to go gallivanting about . . .'

'I shall be back in a few days,' said Slymne. 'And I'm not gallivanting anywhere. This is strictly business.'

He left the house in a huff and drove to the bank for more travellers' cheques. That afternoon, he was in Dover and had joined the queue of cars waiting for the ferry when he was horrified to see Glodstone's conspicuous green Bentley parked to one side before the barrier to the booking office. There was no doubt about it. The number plate was GUY 444. The bastard was disregarding the Countess's instructions and was leaving earlier than he was meant to. Crossing to Calais and sending a telegram from the Countess addressed to Glodstone care of the Dover–Ostend ferry was out of the question. And Slymne was already committed to taking the Calais ferry himself. As the queue of cars slowly moved through Customs and Immigration and down the ramp into the ship, Slymne's agony increased. Why the hell couldn't the man have done what he was told? And further awful implications were obvious. Glodstone's suspicions had been aroused and while he was still committed to the 'adventure', he was following an itinerary of his own. More alarming still, he was travelling on the same ship and might well recognize Slymne's Cortina on the car deck. With these fears plaguing him, Slymne disappeared into the ship's toilet where he was prematurely sick several times before the ship got under way. Very furtively, he went up on deck and stared at the retreating quay in the hope that the Bentley would still be there. It wasn't. Slymne drew the obvious conclusion and spent the rest of the voyage in a corner seat pretending to read the *Guardian* and hiding his face from passers-by. He was therefore in no position to observe a young man with unnaturally black hair who leaned over the ship's rail and was travelling under a temporary passport made out in the name of William Barnes.

In the end, unable to stand the suspense, Slymne slipped down to the car deck as soon as the French coast was sighted and made a hurried inventory of the cars. Glodstone's Bentley was not among them. And when he drove off the ship at Calais and followed the *Toutes Directions* signs, he was even more confused. Presumably

Glodstone was crossing on the next ferry. Or was he going to Boulogne or even sticking to his original instructions to travel by Ostend? Slymne turned into a side road and parked beneath a block of flats, and, having considered all the permutations of times of ferry crossings and destinations, decided there was only one way to find out. With a sense of doom, Slymne walked back to the office and was presently asking the overworked clerk in broken French if he could trace a Monsieur Glodstone. The clerk looked at him incredulously and replied in perfect English.

'A Mr Glodstone? You're seriously asking me if I can tell you if a Mr Glodstone has crossed, is crossing or intends to cross from Dover to Calais, Dover to Boulogne, or Dover to Ostend?'

'Oui,' said Slymne, sticking to his supposedly foreign identity, 'je suis.'

'Well you can suis off,' said the clerk, 'I've got about eight hundred ruddy cars crossing on the hour by the hour and thousands of passengers and if you think –'

'Sa femme est morte,' said Slymne, 'C'est très important . . .'

'His wife's dead? Well, that's a different matter, of course. I'll put out a general message to all ferries . . .'

'No, don't do that,' Slymne began but the man had already disappeared into a back office and was evidently relaying the dreadful news to some senior official. Slymne turned and fled. God alone knew how Glodstone would respond to the news that he was now a widower when he'd never had a wife.

With a fresh sense of despair Slymne scurried back to his car and drove wildly out of Calais with one over-riding intention. Whether Glodstone arrived at Calais or Boulogne or Ostend he would still have to come south to reach the Château Carmagnac, and with any luck would stick to the route he'd been given. At least Slymne hoped to hell he would, and since it was the only hope he had he clung to it. He might be able to head the swine off and the best place to start would be at Ivry-La-Bataille. The place had the sort of romantic picturesqueness that would most appeal to Glodstone and the hotel he had booked him into there was Highly Recommended in the Guide Gastronomique. As he drove through the night, Slymne prayed that Glodstone's stomach would prove his ally. He need not have been so concerned. Glodstone was still in Britain and had worries of his own. They mostly concerned Peregrine and the discrepancy between his appearance, as altered by dyeing his hair dark brown, and that of William Barnes as depicted on his passport. The transformation had taken place in the London hotel. Glodstone had sent Peregrine out with instructions to get some dye from a chemist and had told him to get on with it. It had been a bad mistake. Peregrine had been booked into the hotel an unremarkable blond and had left it sixteen hours and ten towels later, looking, in Glodstone's opinion, like something no bigoted Immigration Officer would let out of the country, never mind allow in.

'I didn't tell you to take a bath in the blasted stuff,' said Glodstone surveying the filthy brew in the tub and the stained towels. 'I told you to dye your hair.'

'I know, sir, but there weren't any instructions about hair.'

'What the hell do you mean?' said Glodstone who wished now that he had supervised the business instead of protecting his reputation as a non-consenting adult by having tea in the lounge. 'What did it say on the bottle?'

'It was a powder, sir, and I followed what they said to do for wool.'

'Wool?'

Peregrine groped for a sodden and practically illegible piece of paper. 'I tried to find hair but all they had down was polyester/cotton mixtures, heavy-duty nylon, acetate, rayon and wool, so I chose wool. I mean it seemed safer. All the other ones said to simmer for ten minutes.'

'Dear Lord,' said Glodstone and grabbed the paper. It was headed 'DYPERM, The Non-Fade All-Purpose Dye.' By the time he had deciphered the instructions, he looked despairingly round the room again. 'Non-Fade All-Purpose' was about right. Even the bathmat was indelibly dyed with footprints. 'I told you to get hair-dye, not something suitable for ties, batik and macramé. It's a miracle you're still alive. This muck's made for blasted washing-machines.'

'But they only had stuff called Hair Rinse at the chemist and that didn't seem much use so I –'

'I know, I know what you did,' said Glodstone. 'The thing is, how the devil do we explain these towels . . . Good God! It's even stained the shower curtains, and they're plastic. I wouldn't have believed it possible. And how on earth did it get up the wall like that? You must have been spraying the filth all over the room.'

'That was when I had a shower afterwards, sir. It said rinse thoroughly and I did in the shower and some got in my mouth so I spat it out. It tasted blooming horrible.'

'It smells singularly foul too,' said Glodstone gloomily. 'If you'll take my advice, you'll empty that bath and try and get the stain off the enamel with some Vim, and then have another bath in clean water.'

And retreating to the bar for several pink gins, he left Peregrine to do what he could to make himself look less like something the Race Relations Board would find hard to qualify. In the event DYPERM didn't live up to its promise and Peregrine came down to dinner unrecognizable but at least moderately unstained except for his hair and eyebrows.

'Well, that's a relief,' said Glodstone. 'All the same, I think it best to get you on the most crowded ferry tomorrow and hope to hell you'll pass in a crowd. I'll tell the manager here you had an accident with a bottle of ink.'

'Yes, sir, and what do I do when I get to France?' asked Peregrine.

'See a doctor if you fell at all peculiar,' said Glodstone.

'No, I mean where do I go?'

'We'll buy you a rail ticket through to Armentières and you'll book into the hotel nearest the station and be sure not to leave it except to go to the station every two hours. I'll try to make it across Belgium as fast as I can. And remember this, if you are stopped at Calais, my name must not be mentioned. Invent some story about always wanting a trip to France and pinching the passport yourself.'

'You mean lie, sir?'

Glodstone's fork, halfway to his mouth, hovered a moment and returned to his plate. Peregrine's peculiar talent for taking everything he was told literally was beginning to unsettle him. 'If you must put it like that, yes,' he said with an awful patience. 'And stop calling me "sir". We're not at school now and one slip of the tongue could give the game away. From now on I'll call you Bill and you can address me as . . . er . . . Patton.' 'Yes, si . . . Patton,' said Peregrine.

Even so, it was a worried Glodstone who went to bed that night and who, after an acrimonious discussion with the hotel manager on the matter of towels, took the Dover road next morning with Peregrine beside him. With understandable haste, he booked him as William Barnes on the ferry and by train to Armentières and then hurried away before the ship sailed. For the rest of the day, he lay on the cliff above the terminal scanning returning passengers through his binoculars in the hope that Peregrine wouldn't be among them. In between whiles, he checked his stores of tinned food, the camping gas stove and saucepan, the picnic hamper and the two sleeping-bags and tent. Finally, he taped the revolvers to the springs below the seats and, unscrewing the ends of the tent-poles, hid the ammunition inside them. And as the weather was good, and there was no sign of Peregrine being dragged ashore by Immigration Officers, his spirits rose.

'After all, nothing ventured, nothing gained,' he replied tritely to a gull that shrieked above him. In the clear summer air he could see faint on the horizon the coastline of France. Tomorrow he'd be there. That evening, while Peregrine struggled to explain to the desk clerk that he wanted a room at the hotel in Armentières and Slymne drove desperately towards Ivry-La-Bataille, Glodstone dined at a country pub and then went down to the ferry terminal to confirm his booking to Ostend next morning.

'Did you say your name was Glodstone, sir?' enquired the clerk.

'I did,' said Glodstone, and was alarmed when the man excused himself and went to another office with an odd look on his face. A more senior official with an even odder look came out.

'If you'll just come this way, Mr Glodstone,' he said mournfully and opened the door of a small room.

'What for?' said Glodstone, now throughly worried.

'I'm afraid I have some rather shocking news for you, sir. Perhaps if you took a seat . . .'

'What shocking news?' said Glodstone, who had a shrewd idea what he was in for.

'It concerns your wife, sir.'

'My wife?'

'Yes, Mr Glodstone. I'm sorry to have to tell you –'

'But I haven't got a wife,' said Glodstone, fixing the man with his monocle.

'Ah, then you know already,' said the man. 'You have my most profound sympathy. I lost my own three years ago. I know just how you must feel.'

'I very much doubt if you do,' said Glodstone, whose feelings were veering all over the place. 'In fact, I'd go as far as to say you can't.'

But the man was not to be denied his compassion. The years behind the booking counter had given him the gift of consoling people. 'Perhaps not,' he murmured, 'As the Bard says, marriages are made in heaven and we must all cross that bourne from which no traveller returns.'

He cast a watery eye at the Channel but Glodstone was in no mood for multiple misquotations. 'Listen,' he said, 'I don't know where you got this idea that I'm married because I'm not, and since I'm not, I'd be glad to hear how I can have lost my wife.'

'But you are Mr G. P. Glodstone booked for the Ostend boat tomorrow morning?'

'Yes. And what's more, there isn't any Mrs Glodstone and never has been.'

'That's odd,' said the man. 'We had a message from Calais just now for a Mr Glodstone saying his wife had died and you're the only Mr Glodstone on any of the booking lists. I'm exceedingly sorry to have distressed you.'

'Yes, well since you have,' said Glodstone, who was begining to find the message even more sinister than the actual death of any near relative, 'I'd like to hear who sent it.'

The man went back into the office and phoned through to Calais. 'Apparently a man came in speaking French with a strong English accent and wanted to find out on which ferry you were crossing,' he said. 'He wouldn't speak English and the clerk there wouldn't tell him where you were landing, so the man said to tell you your wife had died.'

'Did the clerk describe the man?'

'I didn't ask him and frankly, since . . .'

But Glodstone's monocle had its effect and he went back to the phone. He returned with the information that the man had disappeared as soon as he'd delivered the message.

Glodstone had made up his mind. 'I think I'll change my booking,' he said. 'Is there any space on tonight's ferries?'

'There's some on the midnight one, but –'

'Good. Then I'll take it,' said Glodstone, maintaining his authority, 'and on no account is that fellow to be given any information about my movements.'

'We don't make a habit of handing out information of that sort,' said the man. 'I take great exception to the very idea.'

'And I take exception to being told that a wife I don't have has just died,' said Glodstone.

At midnight, he took the ferry and was in Belgium before dawn. As he drove out of the docks, Glodstone kept his eyes skinned for any suspicious watchers but the place was dark and empty. Of one thing, Glodstone was now certain. La Comtesse had not been exaggerating the brilliant criminal intelligence he was up against. That they knew he was coming was proof enough of that. There was also the terrible possibility that the message had been a warning.

'If they touch one hair of her head,' Glodstone muttered ferociously and adjusted his goggles as the Bentley ate the miles towards Iper and the obscure frontier crossing beyond it.

Chapter 10

'Gosh, it's good to see you, sir . . . I mean Patton, sir,' said Peregrine when the Bentley drew up outside the railway station that morning. Glodstone peered at him from behind his one-eyed goggles, and had to admit that he was fairly pleased to see Peregrine. He was terribly tired, had had no sleep for twenty-four hours and the border crossing Slymne had chosen for him had been so obscure that he'd spent several hours trying to find it.

'I'll get some breakfast while you fetch your kit from the hotel,' he said, 'I don't want to be delayed here too long. So step lively. You see, they know I'm coming but that you're with me they do not know.'

And with this strangely accurate remark, Glodstone climbed down and entered a café where, to his disgust, he was forced to make do with café au lait and croissants. Half an hour later the Bentley, which had attracted a disconcerting number of vintage car buffs around it, was once more on the road.

'We've stolen a march on them so far,' said Glodstone, 'but there's no doubt they know La Comtesse has been in communication with me. Which goes to show she has been badly served. And so, from now on, we must be on our guard and keep our eyes open for anything suspicious.' And he recounted the story of the man who had visited the booking office at Calais and had left the warning message. 'Which means they may be holding her against our coming.'

'Your wife?' asked Peregrine. 'I didn't know you had one.' For a moment Glodstone took his eye off the road to glare at him and looked back just in time to avoid crushing a herd of cows that was blocking the way.

'La Comtesse, you oaf,' he shouted as the car screeched to a halt.

'Oh, her,' said Peregrine. 'In that case, why did they say your wife was dead?'

To vent his fury and avoid actual violence, Glodstone sounded the horn. Ahead of them, the cows mooched on their way unperturbed. 'Because,' said Glodstone, with barely controlled patience, 'not even the most brazen swine would walk up to a booking clerk and say "Tell Mr Glodstone that if he comes any further La Comtesse will die." The last thing they want to do is bring the police in.'

'No, I suppose they don't. Still –'

'And another thing,' continued Glodstone before Peregrine could send his blood pressure up any further by his obtuseness, 'the fellow enquired which ferry I was taking, which tells me this: they don't know I was crossing via Ostend. At least they didn't last night and it will take them time to find out and by then we must have reached the Château. It's surprise that counts, so we'll press on.'

'When those cows get out of the way,' said Peregrine. 'You don't suppose they're blocking the road on purpose?'

For a few seconds Glodstone eyed him incredulously. 'No,' he said, 'I don't.'

Presently they were able to drive on. As they drove, Glodstone's mind wrestled with the problem of hotels. La Comtesse had arranged the bookings to enable her to communicate with him en route and if he avoided them and pushed on there was the danger that he might miss a vital message. Against that there was the need for speed. In the end, Glodstone compromised and when they reached Gisors, where he had been scheduled to spend the first night, he sent Peregrine in to cancel the room.

'Explain that I've been taken ill and won't be coming,' he said, 'and if there are any messages for me, collect them.' He parked the Bentley out of sight round the corner and Peregrine went into the hotel. He was back in five minutes. 'The manager spoke English,' he said.

'So the blighter should. After all we've saved them from the Hun in two World Wars and a fat lot of thanks we've had for it. Bloody butter mountains and wine lakes and the confounded Common Market,' said Glodstone, who had been looking forward to a short nap. 'And no message or letter for me?'

Peregrine shook his head and Glodstone started the Bentley again. All day, the great car ate the miles and a vast quantity of petrol, but Glodstone pushed along the side roads of Slymne's tortuous route. It was afternoon by the time they came to Ivry-La-Bataille and Glodstone was able to totter into the hotel and remove his goggles. 'I believe you have a room reserved for me. The name is Glodstone,' he said in French that was a shade less excruciating than Slymne's and infinitely more comprehensible than Peregrine's.

'But yes, monsieur. Number Four.'

Glodstone took the key and then paused. 'Has any message come for me?'

The clerk looked through a stash of envelopes until he came to the familiar crest. 'This was delivered this afternoon, monsieur.'

Glodstone took the letter and tore it open. Five minutes later the key to his room was back on the board and Glodstone had left. 'You can stop bringing the baggage in,' he told Peregrine, 'La Comtesse has sent a message.'

'A message?' said Peregrine eagerly.

'Shut up and get in,' said Glodstone casting a suspicious eye round the street, 'I'll explain while we go.'

'Well?' said Peregrine when they were clear of the little town.

'Take a good look at that,' said Glodstone and handed him the letter.

'It's from the Countess asking you on pain of her death not to come,' he said when he had read it through.

'In that case why was it delivered by a man with an English accent who refused to speak English? In short, our friend who left the warning at Calais. And another thing, you've only to compare her handwriting with that of the earlier letters to see that the devils have tortured her into writing it.'

'Good Lord, you mean –' began Peregrine. But Glodstone's mind has already fabricated a number of new conclusions. 'Just this, that they know the route we're following and where we're going to stay the night, which may be to their liking but doesn't suit my book.'

'Which book?' asked Peregrine, browsing through a mental library from *The Thirty-Nine Steps* to The Day of the Jackal with more insight into the workings of Glodstone's mind than he knew.

Glodstone ignored the remark. He was too busy planning a new strategy. 'The thing is to put yourself in the other fellow's shoes,' he said, 'I'm sure we're being watched or waited for. And they know we've had that message yet we're going on. And that will give them pause for thought. You see, we've been warned off twice now. I think it's time we played their game. We'll turn back at Anet and head for Mantes and there we'll spend the night. Tomorrow we'll rest up and tour the sights and then tomorrow night we'll take the road again as soon as it is dark and drive for Carmagnac.'

'I say, that will confuse them,' said Peregrine as the Bentley turned left across the Eure and headed north again.

But Slymne was already confused. Having driven all night to reach Ivry-La-Bataille, he hadn't dared stay there but had gone on to Dreux. There in a hotel he had penned the letter from La Comtesse and had slept briefly before returning with the ominous message for Glodstone to pick up. After that, he had watched the road from a track and had seen the Bentley go by. With a muttered curse he started his Ford Cortina and followed at a discreet distance in time to see the Bentley cross the bridge and turn a little later onto the Mantes road. For a few minutes Slymne was delighted before it dawned on him that, if Glodstone had intended to give up the expedition, there would have been no need for him to have left the hotel or to have taken the road south in the first place. The natural thing to do would have been to spend the night in Ivry-La-Bataille and head back towards Calais next morning. But Glodstone hadn't done the natural thing and moreover, to complicate matters, he wasn't alone. There had been another passenger in the Bentley. Slymne hadn't been able to glimpse his face but evidently Glodstone had persuaded some other damned romantic to join him on his adventure. Another bloody complication. With a fresh sense of exasperation, he followed the Bentley and wondered what to do next. At least the great car wasn't difficult to spot and was in fact extremely conspicuous while his own Cortina was relatively anonymous and could easily match the Bentley for speed.

As they reached the outskirts of Mantes, Slymne made another plan. If Glodstone left the town travelling north, well and good, but if he turned south, Slymne would drive for the Château and be ready to take action before Glodstone could get to see the Countess.

What action he would take he had no idea, but he would have to think of something. In the event, he was forced to think of other things. Instead of leaving Mantes, the Bentley pulled up outside a hotel. Slymne turned into a side street. Five minutes later, the Bentley had been unloaded and then driven into the hotel garage.

Slymne shuddered. Obviously Glodstone was spending the night but there was no telling when he would leave next morning and the idea of staying awake in case the blasted man decided to make a dawn start was not in the least appealing. Slymne wasn't remaining where he was in a sidestreet. Glodstone might, and, by all the laws of nature, must be exhausted but he was still capable of taking a stroll round the neighbourhood before going to bed and would, if he saw it, immediately recognize the Cortina. Slymne started the car and drove back the way he had come before stopping and wondering what the hell to do the next. He couldn't send yet another message from the Countess. Unless the old cow possessed second sight she couldn't know where Glodstone had got to, and anyway letters didn't travel several hundred miles in a couple of hours.

Slymne consulted the map and found no comfort in it. All roads might lead to Rome, but Mantes was a contender when it came to roads leading from it. There was even a motorway running into Paris which they had driven under on the way into town. Slymne dismissed it. Glodstone loathed motorways and if he did turn south again his inclination would be to stick to minor roads. By watching the intersection on the outskirts of the town he would be in a position to follow if Glodstone took one. But the 'if' was too uncertain for Slymne's liking and in any case following was insufficient. He had to stop the idiot from reaching the Château with those damning letters.

Slymne drove on until he found a café and spent the next hour gloomily having supper and cursing the day he had ever gone to Groxbourne and even more vehemently the day he had set up this absurd plan. 'Must have been mad,' he muttered to himself over a second brandy and then, having paid the bill, went back to his car and consulted the map again. This time his attention was centred on the district round the Château. If Glodstone continued on his infernal mission he would have to pass through Limoges and Brive or find some tortuous byroads round them. Again Slymne considered Glodstone's peculiar psychology and decided that the latter course would be more likely. So that put paid to any attempt to stay ahead of the brute. He would have to devise some means of following him.

But for the moment he needed sleep. He found it eventually in a dingy room above the café where he was kept awake by the sound of a jukebox and by obsessive thoughts that Glodstone might already have left his hotel and be driving frantically through the night towards Carmagnac. But when he got up groggily at six and, after drinking several black coffees, walked back into town he was reassured by the sight of the Bentley being washed down by a young man with black hair who looked strangely familiar.

Slymne, passing on the other side of the street, did not linger but went into the first clothing shop he could find and emerged wearing a beret and the blue jacket he supposed would make him look like a typical French peasant. For the rest of the day Slymne lurked round corners, in cafés that commanded a view of the hotel, in shop doorways even further down the street, but Glodstone put in no appearance.

He was in fact faced with almost the same dilemma as Slymne. Having driven for twenty-four hours without sleep, he was exhausted and his digestion had taken a pounding from rather too many champignons with his steak the night before. In short, he was in no condition to do any sightseeing and was having second thoughts about La Comtesse's letter. 'Clearly the swine forced her to write it,' he told Peregrine,' and yet how did they know we would be staying at Ivry-La-Bataille?'

'Probably tortured her until she told them,' said Peregrine. 'I mean, they're capable of anything.'

'But she is not,' said Glodstone, refusing to believe that even a helpless heroine, and a Comtesse at that, would give in to the most fiendish torture. 'There's a message for us here if we could read it.'

Peregrine looked at the letter again. 'But we've already read it. It says . . .'

'I know what it seems to say,' snapped Glodstone, 'What I want to know is what it's trying to tell us.'

'To go back to England and if we don't she'll be —'

79

'Bill, old chap,' interrupted Glodstone through clenched teeth, 'what you don't seem to be able to get into that thick head of yours is that things are seldom what they appear to be. For instance, look at her handwriting.'

'Doesn't look bad to me,' said Peregrine, 'it's a bit shaky but if you've just been tortured it would be, wouldn't it? I mean if they used thumbscrews or red-hot pokers –'

'Dear God,' said Glodstone, 'what I'm trying to tell you is that La Comtesse may have written in a trembling hand with the intention of telling us she is still in trouble.'

'Yes,' said Peregrine, 'and she is, isn't she? They're going to kill her if we don't go back to Dover. She says that.'

'But does she mean it? And don't say Yes . . . Well, never mind. She wrote that letter under duress. I'm sure of it. More, if they could murder her with impunity, why haven't they done so already. Something else is different. In all her previous messages, La Comtesse has told me to burn the letter but here she doesn't. And there's our cue. She means us to go on. We're going to draw their fire. We'll leave as soon as it's dark and take the road we would have gone if we'd never read this letter.'

Glodstone got up and went down the corridor to the bathroom with a box of matches. He returned to the room with a fresh wave of euphoria seething up inside him to find Peregrine staring out of the window.

'I say, Patton,' he whispered, 'I'm sure we're being watched. There's a Frenchie on the corner and I swear I've seen him before somewhere.'

'Where?' asked Glodstone peering down into the street.

'I don't know. He just looks like someone I know.'

'I don't mean that,' said Glodstone, 'I mean where is he now?'

'He's gone,' said Peregrine, 'but he's been hanging about all day.'

'Good,' said Glodstone with a nasty smile. 'Two can play that game. Tonight we'll be followed and so we'll go armed. I'd like to hear what our watcher has to tell us. And let me know if you spot him again.'

But Slymne did not put in another appearance. He had had an appalling day and his feeling about thriller-writers was particularly violent. The sods ought to try their hands at skulking about French towns pretending to be peasants and attempting to keep a watch on a hotel before they wrote so glibly about such things. His feet were sore, the pavements hard, the weather was foully hot and he had drunk more cups of black coffee than were good for his nervous system. He had also been moved on by several shopkeepers who objected to being stared at for half an hour at a time by a shifty man wearing dark glasses and a beret. He'd also had the problem of avoiding the street outside the hotel and this meant that he had to walk down a back-alley, along another street and up a third to vary the corners from which he watched. All in all Slymne made a rough calculation that he must have trudged fifteen miles during the course of the day. And for all his pains he had learnt nothing except that Glodstone hadn't left the hotel, or if he had, he hadn't used the Bentley.

And it was the Bentley that most interested Slymne. As he wandered the streets or stared so menacingly into shop windows his mind, hyped by too much caffeine, tried to devise ways of following the car without keeping it in sight. In books it was quite simple. Reality was something else again. So were boys. On the other hand, if he could only bring the Bentley to a halt in some lonely spot, Glodstone would have to leave the car and go for help. Slymne remembered the time when an enterprising fourteen-year-old at Groxbourne had stuffed a potato up the exhaust pipe of the Art master's car to such good effect that the man had had to have it towed away and the engine stripped before anyone had found out what was wrong. And there had been talk of another master's car which had been wrecked before the War by adding sugar to its petrol tank. Inspired by these memories, Slymne went into a café and ordered a calvados. Under its influence, and that of a second, he reversed his order of priorities. If Glodstone started south again, Slymne could stay ahead of him by sticking to the main roads. But not in the Cortina. One glimpse of its number plate would give the game away.

Slymne left the café in search of a garage where he could hire a car. Having found one, he moved his luggage from the Cortina to a Citroën, bought two kilos of sugar, another kilo of nails, several large cans of oil at different garages, and parked near the hotel. If

81

Glodstone left that night, he was in for a nasty surprise. Wearily he looked at his watch. It was nine o'clock. He would give Glodstone until midnight. But at ten-thirty the Bentley's bonnet poked cautiously from the garage, paused for a moment and then swung south. Slymne let it go and when it had turned the corner started the car and moved after it. Five minutes later he watched it turn onto the Anet road. Slymne put his foot down, doing ninety on the N183, and before Glodstone could have entered the Forêt de Dreux, the Citroën was six kilometres ahead of him.

Chapter 11

In the event, he need not have hurried. Glodstone was taking his time. Twice he had turned down side roads and switched off his lights.

'Because,' he said, 'I want to give them a chance to go by. They've been waiting to see what we're going to do and they'll follow. But they won't know which road we've taken and they'll have to look.'

'Yes, but when they don't find us, won't they watch the roads ahead?' asked Peregrine who was enjoying himself unstrapping the revolvers from their hiding places beneath the seats.

Glodstone shook his head. 'They may later on, but for the moment they'll assume we're travelling fast. I mean they would if they were in our shoes. But we'll move slowly. And France is a big country. If we lose them here they'll have a thousand roads to search much further south. And here, I think, they come.'

'How do you know?' whispered Peregrine as a Jaguar shot past the side road. Glodstone started the Bentley.

'Because French headlights are yellow and those were white,' he said, 'and if I'm not mistaken, our Englishman at Calais is the link man. He's probably above suspicion too. Some wealthy member of the Bar whose Club is White's and who moves in the best circles. Now a Jag may be a shade too flashy in London but it'll do very well in France for speed.'

And with this pleasing invention Glodstone drove the Bentley out into the road and turned sedately after the disappearing tail lights.

In the Forêt de Dreux, Slymne completed his preparations. He had chosen the end of a long straight with a tight corner on it for his ambush, had parked his car on a track well out of sight round the bend, and was ready to swill a can of oil on the road as soon as he saw the Bentley's headlights. It was a desperate measure but Slymne was a desperate and partially drunk man and the memory of being called Slimey had inspired him with a grim determination. Glodstone had to be stopped, and quickly. As he waited, Slymne made some further calculations. The Bentley would slow before the bend, would then hit the oil slick and skid. Slymne considered its next move and decided that a log in the road would help. He found a fallen branch and had just put it down when the headlights appeared. Slymne emptied the can of oil and crossed the road to be on the safe side. There he lay in the forest waiting for his man.

In the event, he was proved wrong. It was less a man than an entire family, Mr and Mrs Blowther from Cleethorpes and their two children, who were enjoying the privilege afforded by straight French roads of travelling at a hundred miles an hour in their brand-new Jaguar when they hit the oil slick. For a moment they continued on their way. It was a brief respite. A second later the car slewed sideways. Mr Blowther, under the misapprehension that both his front tyres had blown, slammed his foot on the brake. The Jaguar spun like a whirling dervish before encountering the branch and then somersaulted through the air. As it landed on its roof and with a crescendo of breaking glass and tearing metal shot upside down round the corner, Slymne knew he had made a ghastly mistake and was running for the car. Or trying to. After the brilliance of the now shattered headlights, the forest was pitch-black and filled with an extraordinary number of hollows, barbed bushes and invisible trees. As he came abreast of the wrecked car the Blowthers, still miraculously alive, were crawling from the windscreen and giving vent to their outraged feelings. Mr Blowther, convinced that the fallen branch had caused the catastrophe, was particularly vehement about fornicating French foresters and flaming firtrees, and only stopped when Mrs Blowther more maternally began moaning about saving the children.

'Save? Save?' yelled her husband still too deafened to hear at all clearly, 'Of course we'll have to save. It'll take ten years to save enough to buy another effing Jag. You don't think that crumpled conglomeration of craftsmanship was comprehensively covered? All we had was third-party insurance and for your beastly benefit, the only third party is that fractured flipping fir-tree.'

In the bushes the authentic third party shuddered. Not only had he wrecked the wrong car but he had just remembered the oil cans. He had left them in the wood and his fingerprints would be all over the things. Under cover of Mr Blowther's demented alliteration, Slymne slipped back into the forest rather more successfully now that his eyes weren't blinded by the headlights and had reached the cans when the Bentley appeared. Slymne slid into the undergrowth and prayed it would emulate the Jaguar. But his hopes were dashed by Mr Blowther who scampered round the corner and was endeavouring to flag down the Bentley when he encountered the oil slick. For a moment, he waved frantically before losing his foothold and slumping down on the road. By the time he had got to his feet four times, had fallen three and had rolled into the ditch, he was not a sight to inspire confidence. Even Slymne could see that. Glodstone could evidently see more. He brought the Bentley to a halt and stared at Mr Blowther suspiciously.

'Don't make another move,' he called out. 'You see we've got you covered.'

Mr Blowther took umbrage. 'Move?' he shouted. 'You must be out of your bleeding mind. I can't even shuffle without falling arse over elbow. And as for being covered, I don't know what you think I am now but the way it feels to me I'm a human Christmas tree. That flaming holly –'

'That's enough of that,' shouted Glodstone, for whom Mr Blowther's North country accent was further proof that he was a gangster and the whole thing an elaborate trap. 'Now get your hands above your head and walk backwards. And remember, one false step and you're a dead man.'

Mr Blowther stared into the darkness behind the great headlamps incredulously. 'Listen, mate,' he said, 'If you think I'm going to stick my hands in the air and try to walk anywhere on this grease pan and not be a dead man, you've got another think coming.'

'I shall count to ten,' said Glodstone grimly, 'One, two . . .' But Mr Blowther had had enough. He had been through a terrible car crash and was now in the middle of a second inexplicable nightmare. He moved. To be precise he slid sideways and landed on his shoulder before rolling back into the ditch. As he went the Bentley started forward into the oil and, skidding this way and that, disappeared round the corner. Thanks to this veering and the erratic swing of the headlamps, Glodstone was spared the sight of the wrecked Jaguar among the trees and of the distraught Mrs Blowther searching in the debris for her handbag and a handkerchief with which to blow the nose of a little Blowther. All his energies were concentrated on keeping the Bentley on the road.

'By God,' he said, when the car finally steadied itself, 'that was a damned near thing. It only goes to show the sort of swine we're up against.'

'Do you think they'll come after us?' asked Peregrine hopefully, toying with a revolver.

'Certain to,' said Glodstone, 'But we'll give them a run for their money. There's a crossroads coming up and I'm going to go left. From now on we'll drive straight through the night.'

Behind them, Slymne was struggling with two empty oil cans and his conscience. From Mr Blowther's vehement opinions and Mrs Blowther's complaints about using foul language in front of the children, he had gathered that, although he had been responsible for wrecking a very fine motor car, the occupants had somehow managed to escape unhurt. It was small consolation. The police would undoubtedly be called to the scene and it would be extremely difficult to explain his presence there or his possession of the oil cans, two kilos of sugar and a large quantity of nails. Worse still, he had the crested notepaper and the notes he had made for Glodstone's premeditated adventure in his suitcase. In the circumstances it seemed wisest to make himself scarce as quickly as possible.

Under cover of the Blowthers' acrimony, he stumbled back to the Citroën, put the cans in the boot and, driving without lights, followed the road by the gap of night sky between the trees. Ten miles further on, he wiped the oil cans clean of fingerprints, dumped them over a bridge into the river and buried his handkerchief in a ditch. To make doubly sure, he poured the sugar into the river too and drove on another mile before disposing of the nails. Finally he burnt the rest of the notepaper and the envelopes, and drove back to Mantes considering extradition treaties. For the first time in his life, Slymne was definitely against them. He was also very much against remaining in France. Whatever Glodstone might find when he reached the Château and even if he still had the forged letters in his possessions, Slymne and no intention of spending time in a French prison for destroying a car and endangering life. It seemed best to leave the Citroën at the garage and drive like hell for Calais in his own Cortina. With any luck, he would be across the Channel and safely home in Ramsgate before the police had made any headway in their investigations. And so Slyme drove quietly into Mantes and spent the rest of the night trying to get some sleep in the forecourt of the rent-a-car garage. At eight that morning, he was on the road for Calais.

Far to the south, the Bentley was still covering ground. Glodstone finally pulled into the side of a very minor road and yawned.

'We seem to have lost them,' said Peregrine, who had spent the night peering over the back of the car in the hope of taking a shot at their pursuers.

'Not the only thing we've lost,' said Glodstone gloomily looking at the map. 'I suppose we can find where we are when we come to the next town. All the same, we're not out of the wood yet.'

'Aren't we?' said Peregrine, too literally for Glodstone's taste. 'I mean we can see for miles around and they don't know where we are.'

Glodstone took out a pipe and lit it. 'But they know where we're heading,' he said, 'And if I were in their shoes I'd concentrate my forces on the roads leading to the Château. I mean I wouldn't waste my time any further afield when it is obvious where we're going.'

He laid the map out on the grass and knelt beside it. 'Now here's the Château and as you see it's devilish conveniently placed. Five roads lead into Boosat but only one leads from the village and past the Château. The drive must come from that road and by the look of the ground I'd say it goes up here. But first it has to cross the river and that means a bridge. That shows they've only to watch the road from Boosat to the north and Frisson to the south and guard the bridge to have us neatly in a trap. In short, if we drive there we're entering a killing ground. And so we won't. Instead, we'll go south on this road here to Florial. It's about twenty miles away with empty country in between and no connecting road to Boosat. If we can find a base somewhere there we can travel on foot to these heights overlooking the Château. They may be guarded but I doubt it. All the same, we'll have to move cautiously and take our time. And now

87

let's have some breakfast. After that we'll lie up for the day and get some rest.'

Peregrine climbed back into the Bentley and fetched the camping-gas stove and the picnic hamper and, when they had breakfasted, Glodstone unrolled a sleeping bag. 'We'll take it in turns to keep watch,' he said, 'and remember, if anyone stops, wake me. And stop toying with those damned revolvers. Put them away. The last thing we want is to draw attention to ourselves.'

While Glodstone lay on the far side of the Bentley and slept, Peregrine kept vigil. But the road was little more than a track and the country flat and quiet and nothing passed. Seated on the running-board, Peregrine basked in the morning sun and was intensely happy. In a less literal person, the thought might have crossed his mind that his dreams had come true; but Peregrine had accepted dreams as reality from his earliest childhood and had no such gap to bridge. All the same, he was excited, and endowed the countryside around him with dangers it didn't obviously possess. Unlike Glodstone, whose heroes were romantic and born of nostalgia, Peregrine was more modern. Seated on the running-board, he was not Bulldog Drummond and Richard Hannay, he was Bond and The Jackal; a man licensed to kill. Even a cow which peered at him over a gateway seemed to sense its danger and retreated to browse more safely further afield.

So the morning passed with Glodstone snoring in his sleeping bag and Peregrine eyeing the world for lethal opportunities. The afternoon was left to Glodstone. Leaning on the gate and sucking his pipe, he planned his campaign. Once the base was found, they would need enough supplies of food to keep them off the roads and away from towns for several weeks if necessary. He took out a notebook and made a list, and then, deciding that their purchases should be made as far from the Château as possible, he woke Peregrine and they drove on to the next town. By the time they left it the back of the Bentley was filled with tinned food, bottles of Evian water, a comprehensive first-aid kit and a quite extraordinarily long strand of nylon rope.

'And now that we are well prepared,' said Glodstone, stopping to study the map again, 'we'll make a detour so far to the south that no one will suspect our destination. If anyone should ask, we're on a mountaineering holiday in the Pyrenees.'

'With all these torches and candles I'd have thought potholing would be more likely,' said Peregrine.

'Yes, we'd better get them out of sight. What else? We'll need a good supply of petrol to see us there and out again without using local garages. And that requires two jerrycans as a reserve.'

That night, they took the road again but this time their route was further east and through wider and more barren country than any they had seen before. By four in the morning Glodstone was satisfied they had come sufficiently far to turn towards the Château again without risk.

'They'll be watching the north-south roads,' he said, 'but we are coming from the east and besides, the Floriac road is off the beaten track.'

It was. As the sun rose behind them, they breasted a hill and looked down into a shallow wooded valley beyond which a panoply of oaks and ancient beeches rose to a crested range before falling again. Glodstone brought the Bentley to a halt and took out the binoculars. But there were no signs of life on the road below them and no habitation of any sort to be detected among the trees.

'Well, now we have our route in and out secure and if I'm not mistaken, there's a track down there that might prove useful.' He let in the clutch and the Bentley slipped forward almost silently. When they came to the junction, Glodstone stopped. 'Go and take a look at that track,' he said, 'see if it's been used lately and how far it leads into the woods. By my reckoning it points towards the Château Carmagnac.'

Peregrine got down, crossed the road and moved through the trees with a silent expertise he had learnt from Major Fetherington on the Survival Course in Wales. He returned with the news that the track was almost overgrown with grass and ended in a clearing.

'There's an old sawmill there but it's all tumbled down and no one has been down there for ages.'

'How can you tell?' asked Glodstone.

'Well if they have, they didn't use a car,' said Peregrine. 'There are two trees down across the path and they'd have had to move them to get past. It's not difficult because they're not heavy but I'd swear they had been like that for a couple of years.'

'Splendid. And what about turning-room?'

'Plenty up by the sawmill. There's an old lorry rusting outside the place and you can put the Bentley in a shed behind it.'

'It sounds as though it will do for the moment,' said Glodstone and presently the Bentley was stealing up the track. As Peregrine had said, it was overgrown with tall grass and the two fallen trees were light enough to move aside and then replace. By the time they reached the disused sawmill, Glodstone was convinced. An atmosphere of long disuse hung over the crumbling buildings and rusty machinery.

'Now that we're here, we'll use the track as seldom as possible and for the rest we'll move on foot. That's where we'll score. The sort of swine we're up against aren't likely to be used to fieldcraft and they don't like to leave their cars. Anyway, we came here unobserved and for the moment they'll be occupied watching the roads for a Bentley. I'd say they'll do that for two days and then they'll start to think again. By that time we'll have proved the ground and be ready to take action. What that action will be I don't know, but by nightfall I want to be in a position to observe the Château.'

While Peregrine unloaded the stores from the Bentley and put them in neat piles in what had evidently been the manager's office, Glodstone searched the other buildings and satisfied himself that the place was as deserted as it seemed. But there was nothing to indicate that the sawmill had been visited since it had closed down. Even the windows of the office were unbroken and a calendar hanging on the wall and portraying a presumably long-dead kitten and a bowl of faded flowers was dated August 1949.

'Which suggests,' said Glodstone, 'that not even the locals come here.'

Best of all was the large shed behind the ancient lorry. Its corrugated iron doors were rusted on their hinges but by prising them apart it was possible to berth the Bentley under cover and when the doors had been shut there was nothing to show that the place was inhabited again.

'All the same, one of us had better sleep beside the car,' said Glodstone, 'and from now on, we'll carry arms. I doubt if we'll be disturbed but we're in the enemy's country and it's foolish to be unprepared.'

On that sober note he took his sleeping bag through to the office while Peregrine settled down beside the Bentley with his revolver gleaming comfortingly in a shaft of sunlight that came through a slit in the door.

Chapter 12

It was mid-afternoon before Glodstone was prepared to leave for the Château.

'We've got to be ready for every eventuality and that means leaving nothing to chance,' he said, 'and if for any reason we're forced to separate, we must each carry enough iron rations to last us a week.'

'I can see why they're called iron rations,' said Peregrine as Glodstone stuffed another five cans of corned beef into his rucksack. Glodstone ignored the remark. It was only when he had finished and was trying to lift his own rucksack that its relevance struck him at all forcefully. By then each sack contained ten cans of assorted food, a flashlight with two sets of spare batteries, extra socks and shirts, a Calor-gas stove, ammunition for the revolvers, a Swiss army knife with gadgets for getting stones out of horses' hooves and, more usefully, opening bottles. On the outside was a sleeping bag and groundsheet beneath which hung a billycan, a water bottle, a compass and a map of the area in a plastic cover. Even the pockets were jammed with emergency supplies: in Peregrine's case four bars of chocolate, while Glodstone had a bottle of brandy and several tins of pipe tobacco.

'I think that's everything,' he said before remembering the Bentley. He disappeared into the garage and came out ten minutes later with the sparking plugs.

'That should ensure nobody steals her. Not that she's likely to be found but we can't take risks.'

'I'm not sure we can take all this lot,' said Peregrine who had only just managed to get his rucksack onto his back and was further burdened by a long coil of nylon rope round his waist.

'Nonsense. We may be in the field for some time and there's no use shirking,' said Glodstone and immediately regretted it. His rucksack was incredibly heavy and it was only by heaving it onto a rusting oil drum that he was able to hoist the damned thing onto his back. Even then he could hardly walk, but tottered forward involuntarily propelled by its weight and by the knowledge that he mustn't be the first to shirk. Half an hour later he was thinking differently and had twice stopped, ostensibly to take a compass bearing and consult the map. 'I'd say we are about fifteen miles to the south-east,' he said miserably. 'At this rate we'll be lucky to be there before dark.'

But Peregrine took a more optimistic line. 'I can always scout ahead for an easier route. I mean fifteen miles isn't really far.'

Glodstone kept his thoughts to himself. In his opinion fifteen miles carrying over half a hundredweight of assorted necessities across this diabolically wooded and hilly country was the equivalent of fifty on the flat, and their failure to find any sort of path, while reassuring in one way, was damnably awkward in another. And Peregrine's evident fitness and the ease with which he climbed steep banks and threaded his way through the forest did nothing to help. Glodstone struggled on, puffing and panting, was scratched and buffeted by branches of trees and several times had to be helped to his feet. To make matters worse, as the leader of the expedition he felt unable to complain, and only by staying in front could he at least ensure that Peregrine didn't set the pace. Even that advantage had its drawbacks in the shape of Peregrine's revolver.

'Put that bloody thing away.' Glodstone snapped when he fell for the second time. 'All I need now is to be shot in the back.'

'But I'm only holding it in case we're ambushed. I mean, you said we've got to be prepared for anything.

'I daresay I did but since no one knows we're here and there isn't a semblance of a path, I think we can safely assume that we aren't going to be waylaid,' said Glodstone and struggled to his feet. Twenty minutes and four hundred yards of wooded hillside later, they had reached the top of a ridge and were confronted by a dry and rocky plateau.

'The Causse de Boosat,' said Glodstone again taking the opportunity to consult the map and sit on a boulder. 'Now if anyone does see us we've got to pretend we're hikers on a walking tour and we're heading for Frisson.'

'But Frisson is over there,' said Peregrine, pointing to the south.

'I know it is but we'll make out we've lost the way.'

'Bit odd, considering we've got maps and compasses,' said Peregrine. 'Still if you say so.'

'I do,' said Glodstone grimly and heaved himself to his feet. For the next hour they trudged across the stony plateau and Glodstone became increasingly irritable. It was extremely hot and his feet were beginning to hurt. All the same, he forced himself to keep going and it was only when they came to a dry gully with steep sides that he decided to revise his tactics.

'No good trying to reach the Château tonight,' he said, 'and in any case this looks like a suitable site for a cache of foodstuffs. We'll leave half the tins here. We can always comes back for them later on if we need them.' And unhitching his rucksack he slumped it to the ground and began to undo his bootlaces.

'I shouldn't do that,' said Peregrine.

'Why not?'

'Major Fetherington says you only make your feet swell if you take your boots off on a route march.'

'Does he?' said Glodstone, who was beginning to resent Major Fetherington's constant intrusion even by proxy. 'Well, it so happens all I'm doing is pulling my socks up. They've wrinkled inside the boots and the last thing I want is to get blisters.' For all that, he didn't take his boots off. Instead he unstrapped the sleeping-bag, undid his rucksack and took out six tins. 'Right, now we'll dig a hole and bury the emergency supplies here.'

While Peregrine quarried a cache in the side of the gully, Glodstone lit his pipe and checked the map again. By his reckoning they had covered only six miles and had another nine to go. And nine more miles across this confoundedly stony ground in one day would leave him a cripple.

'We'll go on for another hour or two,' he said when Peregrine had finished stowing the tins in the hole and covered them with soil. 'Tomorrow morning we'll make an early start and be in a good position to spy out the land round the Château before anyone's up and about.'

For two hours they tramped on across the causse, encountering

94

nothing more threatening than a few scrawny sheep, one of which Peregrine offered to shoot.

'It would save using any of the tins and I don't suppose anyone would miss just one sheep,' he said. 'The Major's always telling us to live off the land.'

'He wouldn't tell you to go around blasting away at sheep if he were with us now,' said Glodstone. 'The shot would be heard miles away.'

'I could always slit its throat,' said Peregrine, 'nobody would hear anything then.'

'Except a screaming bloody sheep,' said Glodstone, 'and anyway it's out of the question. We'd still have to cook it and the smoke would be spotted.'

But Peregrine wasn't convinced. 'We could roast bits of it over the Calor-gas stoves and that way –'

'Listen,' said Glodstone, 'we've come here to rescue the Countess, not to butcher sheep. So let's not waste time arguing about it.'

Finally they found a hollow with several thorn trees and bushes in it and Glodstone called a halt. 'We can't be more than three miles from the river and from there we'll be able to view the Château,' he said as they unrolled their sleeping-bags and put a billycan of water on a stove. Above them, the evening sky was darkening and a few stars were visible. They ate some sardines and baked beans and made coffee, and Glodstone, having added some brandy to his, began to feel better.

'Nothing like the open-air life,' he said, as he climbed into his sleeping bag and put his dentures in the empty coffee-cup.

'Hadn't one of us better stay on guard?' asked Peregrine, 'I mean we don't want to be taken unawares.'

Glodstone groped for his false teeth. 'In the first place, no one knows we're here,' he said when he'd managed to find them and get them back in his mouth, 'and in the second, we've come the devil of a long way today and we're going to need all our strength when we reach the Château.'

'Oh, I don't know. We've only come about twelve miles and that's not all that far. I don't mind taking the first watch and I can wake you at midnight.'

'I shouldn't if I were you,' said Glodstone, and put his teeth back into the mug. He lay down and tried to make himself comfortable. It wasn't easy. The ground in the hollow was uneven and he had to sit up again to dislodge several stones that had wedged themselves under his sleeping-bag. Even then he was unable to get to sleep but lay there conscious that his hip seemed to be resting on a small mound. He shifted sideways and finally got it settled but only at the expense of his right shoulder. He turned over and found his left shoulder on a stone. Once more he sat up and pushed the thing away, upsetting the coffee mug in the process.

'Damn,' he mumbled and felt around for his teeth. As he did so, Peregrine, who had been peering suspiciously over the edge of the hollow, slid down towards him.

'Don't move another inch,' said Glodstone indistinctly.

'Why not?'

'Because I've mislaid my bloody dentures,' Glodstone mumbled, aware that his authority was being eroded by this latest admission of a physical defect and terrified that Peregrine would step on the damned things. In the end, he found the top plate resting against something that felt suspiciously like sheep droppings. Glodstone shoved it hurriedly back into the mug and made a mental note to wash it carefully in the morning before having breakfast. But the bottom plate was still missing. He reached across for his torch and was about to use it when Peregrine once more demonstrated his superior fieldcraft and his night vision by whispering to him not to turn it on.

'Why the devil not?' asked Glodstone.

'Because there's something moving around out there.'

'Probably a blasted sheep.'

'Shall I slip out and see? I mean if it's one of the swine and we captured him, we could make him tell us how to get into the Château and what's going on there.'

Glodstone sighed. It was a long, deep sigh, the sigh of a man whose bottom plate was still missing while the other was in all probability impregnated with sheep dung and who was faced with the need to explain that it was extremely unlikely that one of the 'swine' (a term he regretted having used so freely in the past) was wandering about on a barren plateau at dead of night.

'Listen,' he hissed through bare gums, 'even if it is one of them,

96

what do you think they're going to think when the . . . er . . . blighter doesn't turn up in the morning?'

'I suppose they might think –'

'That we're in the neighbourhood and have got him and he's told us he knows. So they'll be doubly on the *qui-vive* and –'

'On the what?'

'On the lookout, for God's sake. And the whole point of the exercise is that we take them by surprise.'

'I don't see how we're going to do that,' said Peregrine. 'After all they know we're coming. That oil trap in the forest –'

'Told them we're coming by road, not across country. Now shut up and get some sleep.'

But Peregrine had slid quietly back up the bank and was peering intently into the night. Glodstone resumed the search for his teeth and finally found them covered in sand. He dropped them into the mug and transferred this to a safer spot inside his rucksack. Then he wormed down into his sleeping bag again and prayed that Peregrine would let him get some rest. But it still took him some time to fall asleep. A lurking feeling that he had made a mistake in bringing Peregrine with him nagged at his mind. He was no longer a young man and there was something about Peregrine's fitness and his blasted fieldcraft that irritated him. In the morning, he'd have to make it quite clear who was in charge.

In fact it was only an hour or so later when he was woken. The weather had changed and it had began to drizzle. Glodstone stared bleakly from his one eye into a grey mist and shivered. He was stiff and cold and doubly aggravated to see that Peregrine had covered his own sleeping-bag with his ground-sheet and pools of water had gathered in the folds. In Glodstone's case it had soaked through the bag itself and the bottom half felt decidedly damp.

'Stay in here any longer and I'll go down with pneumonia,' he muttered to himself and, crawling out, put on a jersey, wrapped the groundsheet round his shoulders and lit the stove. A cup of coffee with a bit of brandy in it would take off the chill. Blearily, he filled the billycan with water and had put his top dentures in his mouth before being reminded by their earthy taste and something else where they had been. Glodstone spat the things out and rinsed them as best he could. Presently, huddled under the groundsheet, he was sipping coffee and trying to take his mind off his discomfort by planning their stategy when they reached the Château. It was rather more difficult than he had foreseen. It had been all very well to drive across France, eluding pursuit, but now that they were so close to their goal he began to see snags. They couldn't very well march up to the front door and ask for the Countess. In some way or other they would have to let her know they were in the vicinity and were waiting for her instructions. And this would have to be done without giving the game away to anyone else. The phrase brought him up short. 'The *game* away'? In the past he had always thought of the great adventure as a game but now in the cold, wet dawn, squatting in a hollow in a remote part of France, it had a new and rather disturbing reality about it, one involving the genuine possibility of death or torture and something else almost as alarming. For one brief moment, Glodstone sensed intuitively the unlikelihood that he should have been asked to rescue a Countess he had never met from villains occupying her own Château. But a raindrop dribbling down his nose into his coffee-cup put an end to this insight. He was there in the hollow. He had received her letters and two attempts had been made, at Dover and again in the forest of Dreux, to stop his coming. Those were undeniable facts and put paid to any doubts about the improbability of the mission. 'Can't have this,' he muttered, and stood up. Over the edge of the hollow drifts of light rain shifted across the plateau obscuring the horizon and giving the broken terrain the look of No-Man's-Land as he had seen it in photographs taken in the Great War. He turned and prodded Peregrine. 'Time to be moving,' he said and was horrified to find the barrel of a revolver pointing at him.

'Oh, it's you,' said Peregrine, who was all too evidently a light sleeper and one who woke instantly, 'I thought –'

'Never mind what you bloody thought,' snapped Glodstone, 'Do you have to sleep with the damned gun? I could have been shot.'

Peregrine scrambled out. 'I didn't have it cocked,' he said without any attempt at apology, 'it was just in case anyone attacked us in the night.'

'Well, they didn't,' said Glodstone. 'It would have been a dashed sight more helpful if you'd let me know it was raining. As it was, I got soaked.'

'But you told me I wasn't to wake you. You said –'

'I know what I said but there's a difference between blathering on about sheep being people and letting me get pneumonia.'

'Actually it was a pig,' said Peregrine. 'When you started snoring it started moving this way and I thought I'd better go out and head it off.'

'All right, let's get some breakfast,' said Glodstone. 'The one good thing about this drizzle is that we'll be able to approach the Château without being seen, especially if we move off as soon as possible.'

But getting anywhere near the Château proved easier said than done. They had covered a couple of miles when the plateau ended on the edge of a deep ravine whose sides were thick with thorny undergrowth. Glodstone looked over and hesitated. There was no question of fighting their way down it. 'I think we'd better head round to the north,' he said but Peregrine was consulting his map.

'If I'm right,' he said, adopting an expression Glodstone considered his own and consequently resented, 'we're too far to the north already, the Château lies three miles south-south-west from here.'

'What makes you so sure?' said Glodstone, once more feeling that Peregrine was getting the upper hand.

'I counted the paces.'

'The paces?'

'We've come about three thousand yards and if we'd been going in the right direction we should have come to these woods by now.'

'What woods?' said Glodstone looking round wearily.

'The ones on the map,' said Peregrine, 'they're marked green and the river is just beyond them.'

Glodstone peered at the map and was forced to agree that they were woods opposite the Château. 'Must be something wrong with my compass,' he said. 'All right, you lead the way but for God's sake go carefully and don't hurry. We can't afford to take any chance of being spotted now.' And having tried to ensure that Peregrine wouldn't march off at some godawful speed he plodded along behind him. This time there was no mistake and an hour later they had entered the woods marked on the map. They sloped away from the plateau and then rose to a ridge.

'The river must be on the other side,' said Peregrine, 'We have only to get to the top and the Château should be opposite us.'

'Only,' muttered Glodstone, disentangling his sodden trousers from a bramble bush. But Peregrine was already pushing ahead, weaving his way through the undergrowth with a cat-like stealth and litheness that Glodstone couldn't emulate. Before they had reached the ridge, he had twice had to retrieve his monocle from bushes and once, when Peregrine suddenly froze and signalled to him to do the same, had stood awkwardly with one foot poised over a pile of twigs.

'What the devil are we waiting for?' he asked in a hoarse whisper. 'I can't stand here like a damned heron on one leg.'

'I could have sworn I heard something,' said Peregrine.

'Another bloody sheep, I daresay,' muttered Glodstone but Peregrine was immune to sarcasm.

'You don't get sheep in woods. They're ruminants. They eat grass and –'

'Have two blasted stomachs. I know all that. I didn't come all this way to listen to a lecture on animal physiology. Get a move on.'

'But you said –'

Glodstone put his foot down to end the discussion and, shoving past Peregrine, blundered on up the hill. As he crested the rise, he stopped for a moment to get his breath back only to have it taken away again by the view ahead. Like some holy shrine to which he had at last come, the Château Carmagnac stood on a pinnacle of rock half a mile away across the Gorge du Boose. Even to Glodstone the Château exceeded a life-time's devotion to the unreal. Towers and turrets topped by spire-like roofs were clustered around an open courtyard which seemed to overhang the river. An ornate stone balustrade topped the cliff and to the south, beneath the largest tower, was an archway closed by a massive pair of gates.

Then, realizing that he might be seen from its windows, he dropped to the turf, and, reaching for his binoculars, scanned the place in an ecstasy mixed with anxiety, as if the Château was some mirage which might at any moment disappear. But the glasses only magnified his joy. Everything about the Château was perfect. Window-boxes of geraniums hung from the first floor as did a stone balcony; a tiny belvedere perched on a slim promontory above the cliff; orange trees in tubs stood on either side of the steps leading down from doors set in a round tower whose walls were pierced at intervals to indicate the passage of a staircase that circled up it. In short, all was as Glodstone would have had it. And as he looked, the sun broke through the clouds and the spires and the flagstones of the courtyard gleamed silver in its light.

Glodstone put down the binoculars and studied the surrounding landscape. It was rather unpleasantly at odds with the Château itself and while the latter had a festive air about it, the same couldn't be said for its environs. To put it bluntly, the country was as bleak and barren as the Château was ornamental. A few rather desiccated walnut trees had been planted, and presumably irrigated ever since, to provide an avenue for the portion of the drive closest to the main gates but for the rest the Château was surrounded by open ground which afforded no cover. And the drive itself was formidable. Cut into the rock to the south of the Château, it writhed its way up the cliff in a series of extraordinary bends which suggested a truly maniacal desire for the spectacular on the part of its designer. Finally, to make the approach by road still more secure, a wooden bridge without a guard rail spanned the river.

'Dashed cunning,' Glodstone muttered. 'There's no way of crossing that bridge without signalling your coming.' As if to prove the truth of this observation, a van turned off the road below them and rattled slowly across the planks before grinding its way in bottom gear up the quarried drive. Glodstone watched it reach the walnut trees and disappear round the rear of the Château. Then he turned hopefully to the north in search of an easier way up. True, the slope was less perpendicular than the cliff but the few stunted thorn trees managing to grow among the rocks afforded little cover. And the rocks themselves seemed untrustworthy, to judge by the number that had rolled down and now formed a barrier along the river bank. Last but by no means least in the list of natural hazards was the river itself. It swirled round the base of the cliff with a dark and malevolent turbulence that suggested it was both deep and subject to dangerous currents.

'Well, we've had a preliminary look at the place,' he told Peregrine. 'What we need now is to establish a base camp out of sight

101

and get something warm inside us while we consider the next move.'

They crawled back off the ridge and found a suitable space among the bracken. There, while Peregrine heated up some baked beans on the stove, Glodstone sat on his rucksack sucking his pipe and pondered what to do.

Chapter 13

For the rest of the day Glodstone lay in the sun drying himself out and keeping a close watch on the Château.

'They're bound to have some system for watching the roads,' he told Peregrine, 'and for signalling when someone suspicious puts in an appearance and once we find out what that is we can bypass it.'

'Yes, but we're not on the road,' said Peregrine. 'I should have thought the simplest thing would be to swim the river and shin up the cliff . . . What's the matter?'

'Nothing,' said Glodstone when he could bring himself to speak, 'And when do you propose we do this? In broad bloody daylight?'

'Well, no, we'd have to do it after dark.'

Glodstone gnawed on the stem of his pipe and tried to control himself. 'Listen,' he said finally, 'if you're seriously suggesting that we try to climb what amounts to the north face of the Eiger, on a miniature scale, in pitch darkness, you must have less between the ears than I thought you had. We've come here to save the Countess, not to commit bloody suicide. Why do you think the Château is walled on three sides but there's only a balustrade above the river?'

Peregrine considered the question thoughtfully, 'I don't suppose it's very safe to build a high wall on top of a cliff,' he said, 'I mean you never know with cliffs, do you? I've an auntie in Dorset and she's got a bungalow near some cliffs and she can't sell it because some of the other bungalows are slipping over and -'

'To hell with your blasted aunt,' said Glodstone, savaging a can of corned beef with a tin-opener. 'The reason there's no wall on this side is because they don't have to protect it. Only a blithering idiot would try to scale that precipice.'

'Clive did,' said Peregrine unabashed.

'Clive? What on earth are you talking about now?'

'When he captured Quebec. He sailed his -'

'Wolfe, for God's sake. Can't you get anything right?'

'All right, Wolfe then. I never was much good at history.'

'So I've noticed,' said Glodstone, skewering bits of corned beef into the billycan. But Peregrine hadn't finished.

'Anyway, it's not really a cliff. And we wouldn't have to start at the bottom. There's a ledge near the top and we could get onto it from the drive.'

'Which they've left unguarded just to make things easier for us, I suppose,' said Glodstone.

'We could always make our way round to the south and climb up there,' Peregrine continued. 'That way we'd be coming down the drive from the top instead of the other way round. They'd never expect us to do that.'

'I'll grant you that,' said Glodstone, absentmindedly putting the billycan on the Calor-gas stove and lighting it, 'and if I were in their shoes I wouldn't expect anyone to do such an asinine thing either.'

'Then once we're on that ledge –' He stopped and stared at the smoking billycan. 'I say, I've never seen corned beef cooked like that before. Shouldn't you stir it round a bit?'

Glodstone wrenched the pan off the stove and burnt his hand in the process. 'Now look what you've made me do,' he said lividly.

'I didn't make you do it,' said Peregrine, 'all I said was –'

'Once we were on that bloody ledge. That's what you said. Well, let's get something straight. We're not going anywhere near that ledge. That cliff is unclimbable and there's an end to the matter.'

'What I meant was I didn't tell you to fry that corned beef like that. Major Fetherington always taught us to put cans in hot water and heat them that way. You open them first, of course, otherwise they might explode.'

'And doubtless he also taught you to climb cliffs in the middle of the fucking night too,' said Glodstone, resorting to foul language as a safety value against exploding himself.

'Well, actually, yes,' said Peregrine. 'Mind you, we used tampons.'

'You used what?' demanded Glodstone, momentarily diverted from his burnt hand by the extraordinary vision this conjured up.

'Steel things you hammer into the rock,' said Peregrine.

'For your information they're called crampons. Otherwise known as climbing-irons.'

'That's not what the Major calls them. He said always to call them tampons because if you didn't ram them into some bleeding crack really tight you'd end up looking like a jam-rag yourself. I don't know what he meant by that.'

'I do,' said Glodstone miserably.

These revelations of the Major's revolting teaching methods were having an adverse effect on his morale. He had come on an adventure to rescue a noble lady and already the idyll was turning into an unnerving and sordid experience. To get some temporary relief he told Peregrine to shut up, crawled back to the lookout and went through the notes he'd made on the occupants of the Château as he had observed them during the day in an attempt to discern some sinister pattern to their movements.

The van he had seen drive up at 7 a.m. had left twenty minutes later; at 8 a young man in a track suit had come out onto the terrace, had run round it thirty-eight times and had then touched his toes fifty times, done twenty-two press-ups, had lain on his back and raised his feet in the air too erratically for Glodstone to keep count, and had finally wandered exhaustedly back to the door in the round tower on the right under the watchful eye of a portly woman in a floral dressing-gown who had appeared on the balcony above. Glodstone had switched his own observations to her but she had disappeared before he could deduce anything very sinister from her appearance except that she seemed to be wearing haircurlers. At 8.30 an old man with a watering-can had ambled from the gate tower and had made some pretence of watering several flower-beds, which considering the rain there had been through the night, Glodstone found distinctly suspicious.

But it was only at 10 that Glodstone's interest was genuinely aroused. A group of men came out onto the terrace engaged in heated argument. They were joined presently by the woman he had seen on the balcony. Training the binoculars on her, he hoped she wasn't the Countess. His image of her had been more petite and vulnerable. On the other hand, the men lived up to his expectations.

'That's as unpleasant a bunch as I've seen in a long while,' he told

Peregrine, handing him the binoculars. 'Take a good look at the bald-headed bastard with the moustache and the co-respondent shoes.'

'The what?'

'The . . . the two-tone shoes. It's my guess he's the leader of the gang.'

'He seems to be having a row with a swine in a grey suit.'

'Probably because they lost us on the road. I wouldn't like to cross his path.'

Peregrine thought this over. 'But we're bound to,' he said at last. 'That's what we've come for, isn't it?'

'Yes,' said Glodstone, 'Yes, it is. I just meant . . . Never mind. I'm just pointing him out as a particularly nasty piece of goods.'

'It's a pity we didn't bring a rifle,' said Peregrine a few minutes later. 'I could have picked a couple of them off from here with no trouble.'

'Doubtless. And given our position away into the bargain. For goodness' sake, try to understand we mustn't do anything to put the Countess's life in danger. When we strike we're only going to get the one chance. Miss it and she's done for.'

'I'd have done for some of them too. Anyway, I don't miss.'

'Thank God we didn't bring a rifle,' said Glodstone. 'And now let's go and have some lunch. They're going in and I'm feeling peckish myself.'

They crawled back to the dell and settled down to a meal of stale French bread and over-ripe Camembert washed down with vin très ordinaire. 'You'd think they'd have some sentries posted,' said Peregrine as Glodstone lit his pipe.

'No doubt they have. But not here. They'll be on the roads or on the far side of the Château. It's nice and flat over there and it's the direction they'd expect an attack to come from.'

'I wouldn't. I'd –'

'I don't want to know,' said Glodstone, 'I'm going to take a kip and I'd advise you to do the same. We've got a long night ahead of us.'

He climbed into the sunlight and lay looking up at the cloudless sky. If it hadn't been for Peregrine's lust for action and preferably for killing people at the drop of a hat, he'd have been perfectly happy. He'd have to keep him under control. With this thought in mind he drifted off to sleep. But when he awoke it was to find Peregrine squinting up the barrel of a revolver.

'It's nice and clean and I've oiled them both.'

Glodstone asserted his authority. 'Look,' he said, 'tonight's expedition is simply a recce. It's highly unlikely we're going to find an easy way in. We're going to check every avenue . . . Yes, I know there's only one fucking avenue of walnut trees. Just keep your trap shut and listen. We're going to see how many ways there are of getting into the place. And only when we've worked out a definite and foolproof plan will we act. Get that clear in your head.'

'If you say so,' said Peregrine. 'All the same I'd have thought we –'

'I am not interested in what you think. I'm in charge and those are my orders.' And without waiting for an answer, Glodstone went back to the lookout. That ought to keep the stupid bastard quiet, he thought. It did.

Later that night they set out. Peregrine was grimly silent. 'We're going up-river,' Glodstone told him, 'I've an idea we'll find some shallows there.'

Peregrine said nothing but when half an hour later they scrambled down the hillside and crossed the road to the water's edge it was obvious that Glodstone had been mistaken. The Boose ran darkly past and curved away towards the cliff at the top of which the Château loomed weirdly against the starlit sky. Not even Glodstone's imagination could endow the place with anything more romantic than grim menace and when a car swept round the bend in the road above them, its headlights briefly illuminating the river, he was frankly shocked. Dark swirls of water indicated that the Boose was both deep and fast-flowing.

'Well, at least one thing is clear,' he said. 'We know now why they're not watching this side. It's too well protected. The river sees to that.'

Beside him, Peregrine merely grunted.

'And what's that supposed to mean?' asked Glodstone.

'You told me to keep my trap shut and just listen,' said Peregrine. 'Those were your orders and that's what I'm doing.'

'And I suppose you don't agree with me?' said Glodstone.

'About what?'

'That it's impossible to get across here,' said Glodstone and immediately regretted it.

'I could swim across easily enough if that's what you mean.'

'It's not a risk I'm prepared to allow you to take. We'll have to try further on.'

But though they stumbled along the bank for half a mile the river grew wider and less inviting. Glodstone had to admit defeat. 'We'll just have to look for another route downstream in daylight tomorrow,' he said.

'I don't see why you won't let me swim across with the rope,' said Peregrine. 'I could tie it to something on the other side and you could haul yourself over on it.'

'And what about the guns and the equipment in the rucksacks? They'd get soaked.'

'Not necessarily. Once you're over I can come back and get them. The Major –'

But Glodstone had had enough of Major Fetherington's methods. 'If you get across.'

'I shall,' said Peregrine and taking the coil of rope and winding it round his waist he waded into the river.

Left to himself, Glodstone sat disconsolately in the darkness. To conjure up some courage he concentrated his thoughts on the Countess. She had warned him that the affair would be hazardous and she had obviously been telling the truth. On the other hand she had taken a terrible risk herself in writing to him. Above all she had appealed to him as a gentleman, and gentlemen didn't flinch in the face of a mere river. After all, his father had fought at Jutland and a maternal great-uncle had assisted in the bombardment of Alexandria in 1881. There had even been a Midshipman Glodstone at Trafalgar. With such a nautical tradition in the family he couldn't fail in his duty now. And in any case it would never do to show the slightest fear in front of Peregrine. The brute was cocky enough as it was.

All the same, he was decidedly disappointed when Peregrine returned with the news that there was nothing to it. 'A bit of a current, that's all, but it's all right if you swim upstream and anyway you'll have the rope.'

Glodstone took off his boots and, tying the laces together, looped them across his shoulders. The main thing was to act quickly and not to think. Even so, he hesitated as he took hold of the wet rope. 'You're absolutely certain you saw nothing suspicious over there? The last thing we want is to walk into a trap.'

'I didn't see anything except rocks and things. And anyway you said they're not watching this side because –'

'I know what I said. You don't have to keep repeating it all the time. Now as soon as I'm over I'll give a tug on the rope as a signal. Have you got that straight?'

'Yes,' said Peregrine, 'but shouldn't I get the rope taut and tied to something?'

Glodstone didn't hear him. He had already plunged into the river and was experiencing to the full what Peregrine had described as 'a bit of current'. To Glodstone's way of thinking – not that he had much opportunity for thought – the lout didn't know a current from a maelstrom. And as for swimming upstream . . . Desperately fighting to keep his head above water and failing (tying his boots round his neck had been a ghastly mistake, the bloody things had filled with water and acted as sinkers), holding his breath when he went under and spouting when he came up, Glodstone clung to the rope for dear life and was swept downstream at a rate of knots. Only the rope saved him and just as he knew he was drowning, he banged into a rock, found himself bobbing in some slightly less turbulent water, and his feet touched ground. For a moment he lay there before scrambling up onto a rock ledge. It was still below water but it served as a seat and when the water had drained from his eye he saw that he was at the base of the cliff. He hadn't much use for cliffs but in the circumstances they were infinitely preferable to the swirling river. Glodstone edged himself away from it and stood up. As he did so he gave a tug on the rope.

Upstream, Peregrine responded. He'd been having some difficulty getting his hands on the cord in the darkness but had finally found it. And now came the signal that Glodstone was safely across. Peregrine dragged on the rope. So, for a moment, did Glodstone, but the imminent prospect of being hauled back into that infernal torrent combined with his inability to stand upright on the slimy rock proved too much for him. With a groan he slumped down and let go. He knew now with a terrible certainty that he should never have brought Peregrine. 'The bloody moron,' he muttered, before realizing that his only hope lay in the moron realizing what had happened. It was a faint hope but he clung to it as desperately as he did to the rock. As usual he was wrong. Peregrine was busy devising a method of carrying the guns and rucksacks across without getting them wet. On their way up the river he had noticed what looked like a rubbish tip. Worming his way along the bank he made a number of other interesting discoveries, among them an ancient bedstead, a rotted garden frame, several plastic sacks filled with garbage, something that felt and smelt like a dead dog and finally an old oil drum. This was just what he needed. He dragged it back and was about to put the rucksacks in when it dawned on him that it wouldn't float upright unless weighted down. After searching around for some rocks he climbed back to the road and brought down a painted concrete block which marked the verge. He dumped it in and tying the drum to the rope, let it out. The thing stayed upright. Only then did he put the guns and rucksacks in and, wedging the thing against the bank, undid the rope from the tree.

Five minutes later he was on the opposite bank. 'I've got everything ready to pull across,' he whispered. There was no reply. Crouching down he stared up the rocky hillside and was wondering where Glodstone had got to when something moved and a boulder rolled down to his left followed by a cascade of small stones. Evidently Glodstone had gone ahead to recce, and as usual was making a bad job of it. Presumably he'd be back in a minute or two and in the meantime the equipment had to be brought across.

Setting his back against the slope and bracing his feet against a large rock, Peregrine grasped the rope and began to haul. For a moment the oil drum seemed to resist his efforts and them with a surge it was out into the mainstream and swirling away almost as fast as Glodstone. Certainly it followed the same course, and Glodstone, who had just taken his sodden pipe out and was sucking it morosely, was suddenly aware that a new and possibly more dangerous element than the river itself had entered his limited domain. With a metallic thud the drum slammed into the rock he was crouching on and it was only by throwing himself to one side that he avoided having his legs crushed. Then as he glared at this latest threat, the thing moved away upstream leaving him to ponder on its purpose. Clearly whatever it was that had attempted to kill him couldn't be making headway against the current unless it was being pulled . . . Glodstone got the message but it was too late to grab the drum. In any case the notion that Peregrine's idea of trying to rescue him consisted of letting heavy metal objects batter the ledge he was on suggested that the lout was insane. Standing well back against the cliff he waited for the next attempt. It never came.

Having pulled the drum up the bank Peregrine hurriedly unloaded it, untied the rope and stowed it on the rocks. Only then did he begin to wonder what to do next. If Glodstone had gone ahead he would presumably come back or send a signal for Peregrine to join him. But as the minutes went by and nothing happened a new and more ominous thought came to mind. Perhaps Glodstone had walked into a trap. He'd said they wouldn't be watching this side of the Château because it was too well protected but that was just the opposite of what Major Fetherington had taught. 'Remember this,' he had said, 'the one place you don't expect the enemy to attack is the one they'll choose. The secret of strategy is to do what your opponent least expects.' But Glodstone hadn't seen it that way. On the other hand, why hadn't they waited to capture him too? Again Peregrine found an easy answer: the swine had thought Glodstone was on his own and didn't know there were two of them. Besides, his fieldcraft was hopeless and you could hear him coming a mile off. And he'd definitely got across because there had been that tug on the rope.

With all the stealth of a dangerous predator Peregrine put the coil over his shoulder, stuffed one revolver in his belt, cocked the other one and began the slow ascent of the hillside. Every few yards he stopped and listened but apart from a goat that scurried off across the rocks he heard and saw nothing suspicious. At the end of twenty minutes he had reached the top and was standing in the dry moat under the walls of the Château itself. To his left was the cliff while to his right was a corner tower. For a moment he hesitated. The notion of climbing in by way of the cliff still appealed to him but it was too easy now. He was about to move round the tower when he found what he wanted to make a genuinely dangerous entry. A metal strip ran down the wall of the tower. A lightning conductor. Shoving his hands behind it, he pulled but the copper strip held. Five minutes later he had reached the top of the tower and was on the roof. He crawled forward and peered down into the courtyard. It was empty but a few windows on the first floor were still alight and opposite him under the archway that led to the main gates a lamp shone down on the cobbles. That put paid to his idea of letting himself down on the rope. He'd be seen too easily.

He got up and moved across the roof towards the tower, and saw a square box-shaped trap protruding from the lead. Kneeling down beside it, he eased the top up and peered down into the darkness. It was obviously a means of access to the roof but what was below? Shoving it still further over, he lay down and put his head through the opening. Silence. Nothing stirred below and after listening carefully he took out his torch and flashed it briefly down. He was looking into a corridor but, best of all, some metal rungs were set into the wall. Peregrine switched off the flashlight, swung his legs over the edge and, hanging onto the top rung, eased the cover back over the trap. Then he climbed down and moving with the utmost caution, crept along the passage to a door at the end. Again he waited with every sense alert for danger but the place was silent. He opened the door and by the light shining through a slit window found himself at the head of a curved turret staircase.

Keeping close to the outer wall, he went down until he came to another door. Still silence. He opened it a fraction and saw a long corridor at the end of which a light was shining on a landing. Peregrine closed the door and went on down. If Glodstone was imprisoned anywhere it would be in an underground cell. Perhaps the Countess would be there too. Anyway it was the first place to look. Peregrine reached the ground floor and, ignoring the door into the courtyard, followed the steps down below ground. Here everything was pitch-dark and after taking the precaution of waiting and listening again, he switched on his torch. The base of the turret had brought him to the junction of two tunnels. One led off to his right under the east wing while the other disappeared into the distance below the main body of the Château. Peregrine chose the latter and was halfway along it when through an open doorway on one side he heard the murmur of voices. That they didn't come from the room itself was obvious. It was rather that people in the room above could be heard down there. He flashed his torch briefly and saw that the place had once been a kitchen.

An old black iron range stood in the chimney breast and in the middle of the room a large wooden table stood covered with dust. Beyond it was a large stone sink and a window and a door which led out into a sunken area. To one side of the sink, a chain hung down over the walled lip of what seemed to be a well. A wooden lid covered it now. Peregrine crossed the room, lifted the lid and shone the torch down and very faintly saw, far below, its reflected light. It might come in handy for a hiding place in an emergency but in the meantime he was more interested in the voices. The sound of them came, he realized, from what looked like a small lift-shaft set into the wall at the far end of the kitchen. Peregrine switched off his torch and stuck his head through the opening. Two men in the room above were engaged in heated argument.

'You're not reading me, Hans,' said an American, 'You're taking a non-power-oriented standpoint. Now what I'm saying is that from the proven experimental evidence of the past there is no alternative to Realpolitik or Machtpolitik if you like . . .'

'I don't like,' said a man with a foreign accent, 'and I should know. I was there at the Battle of the Kursk. You think I liked that?'

'Sure, sure. I guess not. But what happened there was the breakdown of Machtpolitik powerwise.'

'You can say that again,' said the German. 'You know how many Tigers we lost?'

'Jesus, I'm not talking logistically. You had a pre-War situation which was unbalanced.'

'We had a man who was unbalanced too. That's what you fail to take into account. The human psyche. All you can see is the material, the non-personalistic and dehumanized product of an economically dependent species. But never psychical impulses which transcend the material.'

'That is not true. I admit the interdependency of the individual and the socio-economic environment but the basis remains the same, the person is the process.'

The German laughed. 'You know, when I hear you talk that way I am reminded of our Soviet colleague. The individual is free by virtue of the very collectivity which makes him unfree. With you the collective imposes a freedom on the individual which he does not want. In the Soviet case there is the stasis of state capitalism and in the American the chaos of the free-market economy, and in both the individual is tied with the halter of militaristic power monopolies over which he has no control. And that you rationalize as Realpolitik?'

'And without it you wouldn't be sitting here, Heinie,' said the American savagely.

'Professor Botwyk,' said the German, 'I would remind you that we neither of us would be sitting here if twenty million Russians hadn't died. I would ask you to remember that also. And so, good night.'

He left the room and for a while Peregrine could hear the other man pacing the room above. He had understood nothing of what they had been talking about except that it had had something to do with the War. Presently, the American moved out of the room. Below him in the passage Peregrine followed the sound of his footsteps. Halfway along the passage they turned away. Peregrine stopped and flashed his torch briefly. Some steps led up to a door. Very cautiously he climbed them and softly opened the door. A figure was standing on the terrace and had lit a cigar. As Peregrine watched he walked away. Peregrine slipped after him. Here was the perfect opportunity to learn what had happened to Glodstone. As the man stood staring contemplatively over the valley puffing his cigar Peregrine struck. To be precise he sprang and locked one arm round his victim's throat while with the other he twisted his arm behind his back. For a second the cigar glowed and then grew dim.

'One word out of you and you'll die,' whispered Peregrine gratuitously. With rather more smoke in his lungs than he was in the habit of inhaling and with what felt like a hangman's noose in human form round his neck, the advocate of Machtpolitik was for once speechless. For a moment he writhed but Peregrine's grip tightened.

'What have you done with him?' he demanded when the struggling stopped. The American's only answer was a spasm of

114

coughing. 'You can cut that out too,' continued Peregrine and promptly made the injunction entirely unnecessary. 'You're going to tell me where you've put him.'

'Put who, for Chrissake?' gasped the professor when he was allowed to breathe again.

'You know.'

'I swear —'

'I shouldn't if I were you.'

'But who are you talking about?'

'Glodstone,' whispered Peregrine. 'Mr Glodstone.'

'Mr Gladstone?' gurgled the professor whose ears were now buzzing from lack of oxygen. 'You want me to tell you where Mr Gladstone is?'

Peregrine nodded.

'But he's been dead since —'

He got no further. The confirmation that Glodstone had been murdered was all Peregrine needed. With his arm clamped across Professor Botwyk's windpipe he shoved him against the balustrade. For a moment the professor fought to break loose but it was no use. As he lost consciousness he was vaguely aware that he was falling. It was preferable to being strangled.

Peregrine watched him drop without interest. Glodstone was dead. One of the swine had paid for it but there was still the Countess to consider. With his mind filled with terrible clichés, Peregrine turned back towards the Château.

Chapter 14

For the next hour the occupants of the Château Carmagnac were subjected to some of the horrors of Peregrine's literary education. The fact that they were a strange mixture, of British holidaymakers who had answered advertisements in the *Lady* offering a quiet holiday *au château* and a small group of self-styled International Thinkers sponsored by intensely nationalistic governments to attend a symposium on 'Détente or Destruction', added to the consequent misunderstanding. The Countess's absence didn't help either.

'Haven't the foggiest, old chap,' said Mr Hodgson, a scrap-iron merchant from Huddersfield whom Peregrine had caught in the corridor trying to find the lightswitch. 'You wouldn't happen to know where the loo is, would you?'

Peregrine jabbed him in the paunch with his revolver. 'I'm not asking again. Where's the Countess?'

'Look, old chap. If I knew I'd tell you. As I don't, I can't. All I'm interested in now is having a slash.'

Peregrine gave him one and stepping over his body went in search of someone more informative. He found Dimitri Abnekov.

'No capitalist. No roubles. No nothing,' he said taking hurriedly to broken English instead of his normally fluent American in the hope that this would identify him more readily on the side of whatever oppressed masses Peregrine's anti-social action might be said to express. In his pyjamas he felt particularly vulnerable.

'I want the Countess,' said Peregrine.

'Countess? Countess? I know nothing. Countess aristocratic scum. Should be abolished like in my country. Yes?'

'No,' said Peregrine. 'You're going to tell me where . . .'

Dr Abnekov wasn't. He broke into a spate of Russian and was rewarded by one of Major Fetherington's Specials which left him unable to say anything. Peregrine switched out the light and hurried from the room. Outside he encountered Signor Badiglioni, a Catholic Euro-Communist, who knew enough about terrorism to have the good sense to hurl himself through the nearest door and lock it behind him. That it happened to be the door to the room of Dr Hildegard Keister, a Danish expert on surgical therapy for sexual offenders, and that she was cutting her toenails with a pair of scissors and exposing a good deal of thigh in the process, rendered Signor Badiglioni totally incoherent.

'You want me? Yes?' asked the doctor in Danish, advancing on him with a Scandinavian broadmindedness Signor Badiglioni entirely misinterpreted. Babbling frantic apologies, he tried to unlock the door but the good doctor was already upon him.

'Terrorist outside,' he squealed.

'The reciprocated sensuality is natural,' said the doctor and dragged him back to the bed.

Further down the corridor, Peregrine was engaged in an attempted dialogue with Pastor Laudenbach, the German who had been through the Battle of the Kursk Salient and whose pacifism was consequently sufficiently earnest for him to refuse to give in to Peregrine's threat to blow his head off if he didn't stop saying his prayers and tell him where the Countess was. In the end, the Pastor's convictions prevailed and Peregrine left him unscathed.

He was even less successful with his next victim. Professor Zukacs, an economist of such austere Marxist-Leninist theoretical principles that he'd spent a great many years in Hungarian prisons to save the country's industrial progress and who had been sent to the conference in the vain hope that he would defect, was too used to young men with guns patrolling corridors to be in the least disconcerted.

'I help you find her,' he told Peregrine. 'My father was with Bela Kun in the First Revolution and he shot countesses. But not enough, you understand. The same now. The bourgeoisification of the masses is detrimental to the proletarian consciousness. It is only by –'

They were interrupted by the Mexican delegate who poked his head round the door of his bedroom and expressed the wish that they would shoot countesses somewhere else and said that he had enough trouble with insomnia without having proletarian consciousness added to it.

'Trotskyite,' snapped Professor Zukacs, 'imperialist lackey . . .' In the ensuing row Peregrine made his escape. Even to his limited intellect it was obvious the Countess wasn't in this wing of the Château. He hurried along the corridor and found a passage to the right. He was just wondering which room to enter when the matter was decided for him. Someone was moaning nearby. Peregrine moved towards the sound and stopped outside a door. The moaning was quite distinct now. So was the creak of bedsprings.

Peregrine had no difficulty interpreting them. Someone who had been gagged and tied to a bed was struggling to escape. He knew who that someone was. Very gently he tried the handle of the door and was surprised to find it opened. The room was as dark as the passage and the sounds were even more heartrending. The Countess was obviously in agony. She was panting and moaning and the depth of her despair was rendered more poignant by the occasional grunt. Peregrine edged silently towards the bed and reached out a hand. An instant later he had withdrawn it. Whatever other physical peculiarities the Countess might have, one thing was certain, she had a remarkably hairy and muscular behind. She was also stark naked.

Anyway she had got the message that help was on the way. She'd stopped bouncing on the bed and Peregrine was about to explain that he'd have her out of there in a jiffy when she moaned again and spoke.

'More, more. Why've you stopped? I was just coming.' It was on the tip of Peregrine's tongue to say that she didn't have to because he was there and would untie her when a man's voice answered.

'How many hands have you got?' he asked.

'Hands? Hands? How many hands? Is that what you said?'

'That's exactly it.'

'That's what I thought,' muttered the woman, 'at a time like this you've got to ask fool questions? How the hell many hands do you think I've got, three?'

'Yes,' said the man, 'And one of them is cold and horny.'

'Jeepers, horny! Only thing round here that's horny has got to be you. I should know. So come on, honey, lay off the gags and give it to me.'

'All right,' said the man doubtfully, 'All the same I could have sworn . . .'

'Don't be crazy, lover. Get with it.'

The bouncing began again though this time it was accompanied by rather less enthusiastic grunts from the man and by frantic requests for more from the woman. Crouching in the darkness by the bed Peregrine dimly understood that for the first time in his life he was in the presence of a sexual act. He wondered what to do. The only thing he was sure of was that this couldn't be the Countess. Countesses didn't writhe and moan on beds with hairy men bouncing on top of them. All the same, he was interested to see what they were doing but he couldn't stay there when the Countess's life was at stake. He was just getting up when the mat on the floor slid away from him. To stop himself from falling Peregrine reached out and this time grasped the woman's raised knee. A strangled yell came from the bed and the bouncing stopped. Peregrine let go hurriedly and tiptoed to the door.

'What's the matter?' asked the man.

'Hands,' gasped the woman. 'You did say hands?'

'I said one hand.'

'I believe you. It just grabbed my knee.'

'Well, it wasn't mine.'

'I know that. Where's the lightswitch? Get the lightswitch.'

As her voice rose hysterically, Peregrine groped for the door-handle and knocked over a vase. The sound of breaking china added to the din.

'Let me go,' shrieked the woman, 'I've got to get out of here. There's something awful in the room. Oh, my God. Someone do something!'

Peregrine did. He wasn't waiting around while she screamed blue murder. He found the door and shot into the corridor. Behind him the woman's screams had been joined by those of her lover.

'How the hell can I do anything if you won't let me go?' he bawled.

'Help,' yelled the woman.

As doors along the passage opened and lights came on, Peregrine disappeared round the corner and was hurtling down a large marble staircase towards the faint light illuminating the open doorway when he collided with the British delegate, Sir Arnold Brymay, who had been trying to think of some rational argument to the assertions of all the other delegates that Britain's colonial role in Ulster was as detrimental to world peace as the Middle East question, U.S. involvement in South America and Russia's in Afghanistan and Poland, about which topics there was no such agreement. Since his expertise was in tropical medicine, he hadn't come up with an answer.

'What on earth . . .' he began as Peregrine ran into him but this time Peregrine was determined to get a straight answer.

'See this?' he said jamming the revolver under Sir Arnold's nose with a ferocity that left no doubt what it was. 'Well, one sound out of you and I'm going to pull the trigger. Now, where's the Countess?'

'You tell me not to utter a sound and then you ask me a question? How do you expect me to answer?' asked Sir Arnold, who hadn't been debating the Irish question for nothing.

'Shut up,' said Peregrine and forced him through the nearest doorway and shut the door. 'Any funny tricks and your brains will be all over the ceiling.'

'Now look here, if you'd kindly remove that firearm from my left nostril we might be able to get down to the agenda,' said Sir Arnold, jumping to the natural conclusion that he was either dealing with one of the other delegates who'd gone clean off his head or, more probably, with the I.R.A.

'I said where's the Countess,' growled Peregrine.

'What Countess?'

'You know. If you don't answer it's curtains.'

'It rather sounds like it,' said Sir Arnold, buying time.

Upstairs a fresh problem had obviously arisen. 'Let me out,' bawled the erstwhile lover.

'I can't,' screamed the woman, 'I'm all tensed up.'

'As if I didn't know. And stop pulling my legs, you bastards. You want me to be disembowelled or something? Can't you see I'm dog-knotted?'

'Dear God,' said Sir Arnold, 'This is terrible.'

'Answer the question.'

'It rather depends on which countess you mean.'

'The Countess of Montcon.'

'Really? An unusually revealing name, and one that by the sound of things upstairs that young man would have found infinitely more inviting, don't you think?'

'Right,' said Peregrine. 'You've asked for it and you're going to get it.' And shoving Sir Arnold against the wall he aimed the revolver at him with both hands.

'All right, all right. As a matter of fact she's not here,' said the expert on bilharzia, deciding that, while he hadn't asked for anything, the time had come to invent something in preference to being shot. 'She's at Antibes.'

'And where's she live, this aunt?' asked Peregrine.

'Live?' said Sir Arnold, his sangfroid crumbling under this line of questioning and the discussion going on above. Some voluble woman who claimed to know all about dog-knotting from personal experience with her bull terriers had just tried throwing a bucket of cold water over the loving couple with predictably aggravating results.

'Shit,' yelled the young man. 'Get it into your stupid head I'm not a fucking bull terrier. Do that again I'll be clamped in a corpse.'

Sir Arnold dragged his attention away from this academic question and faced up to his imminent death. Peregrine had begun the coundown.

'Antibes is a place, for God's sake,' he said, beginning to gibber.

'I know that, but where?' demanded Peregrine.

'Near St Tropez.'

'And what's the address?'

'What address?'

'Aunt Heeb's.'

But the strain of being held at gunpoint by a maniac who thought that Antibes was a person while a couple who claimed they weren't bull terriers were being drowned upstairs was proving too much for Sir Arnold.

'I can't stand it. I can't stand it,' he gibbered, and proved his point by slumping down the wall. For a moment Peregrine hesitated. He was tempted to kick some life into the swine but the sound of footsteps and someone talking excitedly in the hall deterred him. Besides he fairly sure now that the Countess wasn't in the Château, and there was no point in risking capture. Opening a window, he checked that the courtyard was clear and then jumped lightly across the flowerbed. Five minutes later he had reached the roof and was scrambling down the lightning conductor with a lack of vertigo that would have appalled Glodstone.

Not that Glodstone needed appalling. Ever since he had scrambled onto the ledge at the bottom of the cliff he had come to feel differently about adventures. They were not the splendid affairs he had read about. Quite the contrary, they were bloody nightmares in which one stumbled across miles of foul countryside carrying an overweight rucksack, spent sleepless nights shivering with cold in the rain, ate burnt corned beef out of tins, learned what it felt like to be drowned and ended up soaked to the skin on rock ledges from which the only escape had to be by drowning. Having experienced the Boose's horrid habit of sucking things down like some torrential lavatory pan, he knew he'd never be able to swim across.

On the other hand there was little enough to be said for staying where he was. The simile of the lavatory didn't apply there; it was literal. The Château's sewage system was extremely primitive and, in Glodstone's opinion, typically French. Everything it carried issued from some encrusted pipe in the cliff above and was discharged into the river. In practice, a good deal of it landed on Glodstone and he was just wondering if it wouldn't be preferable to risk drowning than be treated as a human cesspit when he became aware that something more substantial was bouncing down the cliff. For a moment it seemed to hang on the pipe and then slid forward out into the river. With the demented thought that this would teach Peregrine not to be such a stupid idiot as to climb cliffs in the middle of the night, Glodstone reached for the body and dragged it onto the ledge. Then he groped for its mouth and had already given it the kiss of life for half a minute before it occurred to him that there were one or two discrepancies between whatever he was trying to resuscitate and Peregrine. Certainly Peregrine didn't have a moustache and wasn't entirely bald, added to which it seemed unlikely that he had suddenly developed a taste for brandy and cigars.

For a moment or two Glodstone stopped before his sense of duty forced him to carry on. He couldn't let the bastard die without doing anything. Besides, he'd begun to have a horrid suspicion what had happened. Peregrine must have assumed he'd been drowned while trying to cross the river and instead of coming to his rescue had somehow got into the Château and was evidently bent on murdering everyone he could lay his hands on. Glodstone wanted to dissociate himself from the process. Rescuing Countesses was one thing, but bunging bald-headed men off the top of cliffs was quite another. In any case the blithering idiot would never make it. He'd get himself killed and then . . . For the first time in his life Glodstone had a glimmering sense of reality.

That was more than could be said for Professor Botwyk. Thanks to Peregrine's gruesome handling he had been unconscious during his fall and his limpness had saved him. Now he began to come round. It was a doubtful relief. For all his convictions that the future of the world depended on stock-piling weapons of mass, not to say universal, destruction, the Professor was an otherwise conventional family man and to find himself lying soaked to the skin being inflated by someone who hadn't shaved for three days and stank like a public urinal was almost as traumatic as being strangled with a lungful of cigar smoke still inside him. With a desperate effort he tore his mouth away from Glodstone's.

'What the fucking hell do you think you're doing?' he snarled feebly. Glodstone recoiled. He knew exactly what he'd been doing, reviving one of the most dangerous gangsters in the world. It didn't seem the time to say so.

'Now just take it easy,' he muttered and hoped to hell the swine wasn't carrying a gun. He should have thought of that before. 'You've had a nasty fall and you may have broken something.'

'Like what?' said Botwyk, peering at his shape.

'Well, I don't really know. I'm not an expert in these things but you don't want to move in your condition.'

'That's what you fucking think,' said Botwyk, whose memory of some of the horrors he had been through was slowly returning.

'Just wait till I lay my hands on the bastard who strangled me.'

'That's not what I mean,' said Glodstone, who shared his feelings about Peregrine. 'I'm just advising you not to move. You could do yourself an injury.'

'When I get out of here I'm going to do more than an injury to that son of a bitch. You'd better believe me. I'm going to –'

'Quite,' said Glodstone to prevent hearing the gory details. He didn't want any part of that retribution. 'Anyway, it was a good thing I happened to be passing and saw you fall. You'd have been dead by now if I hadn't rescued you.'

'I guess that's so,' said Professor Botwyk grudgingly. 'And you say you saw me fall?'

'Yes. I dived in and swam across and managed to pull you out,' said Glodstone, and felt a little better. At least he'd established an alibi. Professor Botwyk's next remark questioned it.

'Let me tell you something, brother. I didn't fall. I was pushed.'

'Really?' said Glodstone, trying to mix belief with a reasonable scepticism. 'I mean, you're sure you're not suffering from shock and concussion?'

'Sure I'm not sure,' said Botwyk, whose latent hypochondria had been understandably aroused, 'the way I feel I could have anything. But one thing's certain. Some goon jumped me and the next thing I'm down here. In between being strangled, of course.'

'Good Lord,' said Glodstone, 'and did you . . . er . . . see who . . . er . . . jumped you?'

'No,' said Botwyk grimly, 'but I sure as shit mean to find out and when I do . . .'

He tried to raise himself onto an elbow but Glodstone intervened. It was awful enough to be stranded on a ledge with a murderous gangster without the swine learning there was nothing much the matter with him.

'Don't move,' he squawked, 'it's vital you don't move. Especially your head.'

'My head? What's so special about my head?' asked Botwyk, 'It's not bleeding or something?'

'Not as far as I can tell,' said Glodstone, edging round towards the Professor's feet. 'Of course, it's too dark to see exactly but I'd –'

124

'So why the spiel about not moving it?' said Botwyk eyeing him nervously.

'I'd rather not say,' said Glodstone, 'I'm just going to . . .'

'Hold it there,' said Botwyk, now in a state of panic, 'I don't give a dimestore damn what you'd rather not say. I want to hear it.'

'I'm not sure you do.'

'Well, I fucking am. And what the hell are you taking my shoes off for?'

'Just making a few tests,' said Glodstone.

'On my feet? So what's with my head? You start yapping about my fucking head and not moving it and all and now you're doing some tests down there. Where's the goddam connection?'

'Your spine,' said Glodstone sombrely. The next moment he was having to hold the Professor down. 'For Heaven's sake, don't move. I mean . . .'

'I know what you mean,' squealed Botwyk. 'Don't I just. Sweet Jesus, I've got to. You're telling me . . . oh my God!' He fell back on the rock and lay still.

'Right,' said Glodstone, delighted that as last he'd gained the upper hand. 'Now I'm going to ask you to tell me if you feel anything when . . .'

'Yes, I do,' screamed Botwyk, 'Definitely.'

'But I haven't done anything yet.'

'Guy tells me he hasn't done anything yet! Just tells me my spine's broken. And that's nothing? How would you feel if you'd been strangled and dropped over a cliff and some limey at the bottom gives you mouth-to-mouth and then says you've got a broken spine and not to move your fucking head? You think I don't feel nothing? And what about my fucking wife? She's going to love having me around the house all day and not being able to get it up at night. You don't know her. She's going to be hot-tailing it with every . . .' The prospect was evidently too much for him. He stopped and glared up at the sky.

'Now then,' said Glodstone, getting his own back for being called a limey, 'if you feel . . .'

'Don't say it,' said Botwyk, 'no way. I'm going to lie here and not move until it's light enough for you to swim back over there

125

and get an ambulance and the best medical rescue team money can buy and . . .'

It was Glodstone's turn to panic. 'Now wait a minute,' he said, wishing to hell he hadn't boasted about swimming across so readily, 'I've sprained my ankle rescuing you. I can't go back into . . .'

'Ankle yankle,' shouted Botwyk, 'you think I care about ankles in my fucking condition, you've got to be crazy. Somebody is for sure.'

'Oh well, if you feel like that about it,' said Glodstone rather huffily only to be stopped by Botwyk.

'Feel?' he yelled. 'You use that fucking word again and someone's going to be sorry.'

'Sorry,' said Glodstone, 'All the same . . .'

'Listen, bud,' said Botwyk, 'It's not all the same. Not to me it isn't. Your ankle and my spine are in two different categories, right?'

'I suppose they'd have to be,' said Glodstone.

'You don't need a fucking ankle to get it up and feel and all. Well, it's not that way with spines. Not the way I read it. So lay off the feeling part.'

'Yes,' said Glodstone, not too sure now if he'd been wise to raise the issue in the first place. 'All the same . . .'

'Don't,' said Botwyk menacingly.

'I was going to say . . .'

'I know what you were going to say. And I've answered that one already. It's not the fucking same. Same is out, same as feel is.'

'Even so,' said Glodstone after a pause in which he had searched for a phrase which wouldn't infuriate the blighter, 'for all we know there may be nothing the matter with your spine. The way to find out is to . . .'

'Take my fucking shoes off like you did just now,' said Botwyk, 'I've got news for you . . .'

But whatever he was about to impart was drowned by the sound of sirens. A car followed by an ambulance hurtled along the road opposite and turned over the bridge to the Château.

'For hell's sake do something,' yelled Botwyk, 'We've got to get their attention.'

But Glodstone was too preoccupied to answer. Whatever

Peregrine had done had included more than dumping this foul-mouthed swine over the cliff and if he was caught . . . The notion horrified him. In the meantime, he had better keep on good terms, or as near good as he could get, with the sod.

'Did you notice that?' he enquired, jabbing his finger into the sole of Botwyk's foot when the professor had stopped shouting.

Botwyk sat bolt upright. 'Of course I fucking did,' he snarled, 'What do you expect me to fucking notice if you do a thing like that? I've got sensitive feet for Chrissake.'

'That's a relief,' said Glodstone, 'for a while there I thought you'd really broken your back.'

'Jesus,' said Botwyk, and sank back speechless on the rock.

Chapter 15

He was not alone in this. Mr Hodgson, the scrap-iron merchant who had been dying for a slash and had been the recipient of one of Major Fetherington's Specials, was still incapable of doing more than scribble that he'd been the victim of an attack by one of those damned foreigners and the sooner he got home to Huddersfield the safer he'd feel. Dimitri Abnekov's opinion, also given in writing, was that a deliberate attempt had been made by a CIA hit-team to silence the Soviet delegate and was a violation of the UN Charter and the Helsinki Agreement as regards the freedom of speech. Signor Badiglioni, having been subjected to Dr Keister's clinical approach to what she called 'reciprocated sensuality' and he didn't, wasn't prepared to say anything. And Sir Arnold Brymay preferred not to. Professor Zukas had been too engaged in a polemic with the Mexican delegate on the question of Trotsky's murder and the failure of the Mexican government to collectivize farms it had already distributed to the peasants to remember anything so contemporary as his encounter with Peregrine. Finally, Mrs Rutherby and Mr Coombe, once they have been extricated from one another by Dr Voisin, were blaming their agonizing ordeal on Mrs Branscombe, the bull terrier judge, who denied that she made a habit of entering other people's bedrooms to indulge her latent lesbianism by hurling buckets of water over heterosexual couples.

Only Pastor Laudenbach approached the problem at all rationally. 'The question we must ask ourselves is why a young man should want so desperately to find a countess. It is a phenomenon not easily explicable. Particularly when he was obviously British.'

'Oh, I wouldn't say that,' said Sir Arnold, who could see an extremely awkward international incident heading his way.

'I would,' said Dr Grenoy, the French delegate. He had slept through the whole affair but the honour of France was at stake and in any case he was looking for an opportunity to divert the symposium away from his country's rôle in Central Africa. On the other hand, he was anxious to prevent the scandal reaching the media. 'I am sure there is a simple hooliganistic explanation for this regrettable occurrence,' he continued. 'The essential factor is that while we have all been put to some inconvenience, no one has actually been hurt. In the morning, you may rest assured that adequate protective measures will have been taken. I myself will guarantee it. For the moment, I suggest we return to our rooms and . . .'

The Soviet delegate was protesting. 'Where is the American Botwyk?' he whispered, 'In the name of the Union of –'

'Let's not get too excited,' pleaded Dr Grenoy, now as anxious as Sir Arnold to avoid an international incident. 'The Professor's absence is doubtless due to a comprehensible prudence on his part. If someone will go to his room . . .'

Pastor Laudenbach volunteered but returned in a few minutes to announce that Professor Botwyk's room was empty and that his bed had not been slept in.

'What did I say?' said Dr Abnekov, 'There has been a deliberate conspiracy to destabilize the conference by elements . . .'

'Oh Lord,' said Sir Arnold, appealing uncharacteristically to his French counterpart, 'can't someone bring an element of commonsense to this trivial affair? If that damned Yank had instigated anything he wouldn't have been idiotic enough to disappear. Anyway, there were no political implications. The lunatic simply wanted to know where some Countess was. I told him she was in Antibes. He's probably pushed off there by now.'

'Countess? Countess? Mere subterfuge,' said Dr Abnekov, finding his voice. 'Typical imperialistic tactics to obscure the real issue. There are no Countesses here.'

Dr Grenoy coughed uncomfortably. 'I am afraid to announce that there are,' he said, 'The proprietor of the Château . . .' He shrugged. The name Montcon was not one he wished to announce to the world.

'There you are,' said Sir Arnold more cheerfully, 'The woman has some lover . . .'

He was interrupted by the arrival of one of the ambulance drivers.

'There appears to be an explanation to the disappearance of Professor Botwyk,' Dr Grenoy announced after a whispered consultation with the man. 'He has been found on a rock in the river.'

'Dead?' asked Dr Abnekov hopefully.

'No. In the company of another man. The Emergency Services have been alerted and they should be rescued at any moment.'

The delegates trooped out onto the terraces to watch. Behind them Dr Grenoy and Sir Arnold consulted one another on the need to re-establish Franco-British collaboration, at least for the time being.

'You keep the British out of this and I won't spread the word about Madame de Montcon,' said Sir Arnold.

'It's the wretched American I'm worried about,' said Dr Grenoy. 'He may demand an enormous security operation. Thank God we don't have a representative from Libya.'

They went out onto the terrace in time to see Professor Botwyk and Glodstone being ferried across the river by several frogmen with an inflatable dinghy.

'I just hope he doesn't insist on holding a press conference,' said Sir Arnold, 'Americans make such a song and dance about these things.'

Beside him Dr Grenoy made a mental note to see that the State-controlled French television refused facilities.

But Botwyk was no longer interested in anything to do with publicity. He was more concerned with the state of his own health. In addition to being strangled, dropped into the river and made the victim of Glodstone's suggestion that he might have broken his back, he had also been subjected to the attentions of the Château's sewage disposal system. Being hit in the face by an unidentified sanitary napkin had particularly affected him. With a haunted look he was hauled up the bank and helped into an ambulance. Glodstone was brought up too and together they were driven up to the Château. Only then did Botwyk open his mouth briefly.

'Just get me into a disinfectant bath and a bed,' he told Dr Voisin as he stumbled out into the dawn light. 'If you want any further information, ask him.'

But Glodstone had his own reasons for being reticent. 'I just happened to be in the right place at the right time,' he said, 'I was passing and saw him fall. Swam across and got him out.'

And conscious that he was now in the enemy's camp, he followed Botwyk and the doctor miserably up the stairs to the bathroom.

From the far side of the valley Peregrine watched these proceedings with interest. It was good to know that Glodstone was still alive but rather disappointing that the swine who had said he was dead had somehow survived. Anyway, there was nothing he could do now until darkness came again. He wriggled back to the bivouac and hung his clothes out to dry and climbed into his sleeping bag. For a moment he wondered if he shouldn't take the precaution of moving somewhere else in case they tortured Glodstone into telling them where the base was, but Gloddie would never talk no matter what they did to him. On this reassuring note he fell asleep.

Deirdre, Comtesse de Montcon, never slept in the Château during the holiday season. She would never have slept there at any other time if she could have helped but during the summer she had her anonymity to think about, and besides, by staying the night in Boosat, she was sure of getting the best vegetables in the market and the finest cuts of meat at the butcher. Nobody at the Château Carmagnac could complain that the cuisine wasn't excellent or the service poor. Nor would they know that the expert cook was a countess. More importantly, no one would suspect that the woman who drove up in the Renault van each morning and spent the day scurrying about the kitchen and shouting orders to the other servants was English or that her greatest ambition was to retire to an even greater anonymity in her bungalow in Bognor Regis. Above all, they must not know that she had a past.

Born Constance Sugg, of 421 Selsdon Avenue, Croydon, she had risen by a series of changed identities and useful adulteries to her present title. In fact it could be truthfully said that she had a great many pasts. She had been Miss Croydon at seventeen, a starlet in Hollywood at nineteen, a masseuse in an extremely dubious parlour in San Francisco at the age of twenty-two, a hostess at a dude-ranch three years later and for ten years the wife of Siskin J. Wanderby. By then Wanderby, a man who believed in putting his money where his mouth was, had made and lost several fortunes and Constance, now Anita Blanche and mother of Anthony B. Wanderby, had divorced him on the grounds that never knowing from one week to another whether she was the wife of a millionaire or something destined for Skid Row constituted a particularly sadistic form of mental cruelty. At the time, Wanderby had been on the point of making a fortune out of capped oil wells in Texas and had looked good for a gigantic alimony. Instead, the oil glut had put paid to her hopes and she had been forced to provide for her own future. Since she was in Las Vegas she had changed her name to Betty Bonford and had stayed on as sucker-bait at Caesar's Palace. It was there she met her future husband, Alphonse Giraud Barbier, Comte de Montcon.

At fifty, the count had already gained a considerable reputation as a playboy, a gambler and a piss-artist, a consequence of his having followed his widowed mother's advice to the letter. 'Don't marry for money, Alphonse,' she had told him, 'go where money is.' And Alphonse had. By the time he landed in Las Vegas he had been to almost every expensive hotel, ski-resort, exclusive club and casino in Europe and was down to his last million francs and the Château Carmagnac. He was also under orders to marry the first rich woman who would have what was left of him. Again the Count had done what he was told and had proposed to Deirdre Gosforth (she had changed her name once more for this eventuality) in the mistaken belief that a woman who could win a hundred thousand dollars three nights running in crap games had to be loaded. The fact that it was the dice that were, and that she handed back her winnings to the management, never occurred to him, even when she had steered him in an alcoholic haze through a marriage ceremony and onto a jet to Paris taking with her, for once, all her winnings.

It was only when they reached the Château that the Count realized his mistake and the new Countess knew that in hooking her last sucker she had been hooked herself. Worse still, there was no way she was going back to the States with a hundred grand of the Syndicate's money. She had reconciled herself with the knowledge that any man who breakfasted on black coffee laced with Armagnac was heading for the hereafter at a rate of knots and as his widow she'd be able to flog the Château. The illusion hadn't persisted. The Count's constitution proved stonger than his intellect and while the Château might be in his possession it couldn't be in his will. Without an heir it would revert to the family and the Count's two sisters had no intention of losing it to a Yankee gold-digger. In fact they had done their damnedest to get the marriage annulled. Deirdre had fought back by keeping the Count's alcohol level too high for him to remember where he'd been married, or to care.

In the ensuing vendetta neither side could be said to have won. Deirdre's premature announcement that she was pregnant had driven the two sisters to consult the family lawyers while her efforts to achieve the only partially desired result had killed the Count. Since the traumatic moment when she had realized his brandy droop was terminal and that for the past ten minutes she had been having coition with nothing more responsive than a corpse with a strangulated hernia, the Countess had come to an accommodation with the family.

'You want me out, you buy me out,' she told the relatives after the funeral, 'and that means a million.'

'Francs?' asked ancient Uncle René hopefully.

'Dollars.'

'Impossible. Impossible. Where would we get such a fantastic sum?'

'By selling this dump.'

'Only a madman would pay . . .'

'Not as it stands,' said Deirdre, 'We turn it into a château de luxe. Best food in France, the finest wines, get top ratings in the *Guide Bleu*. We climb on the cuisine gravy train and charge through the nose.'

The relatives had looked at one another thoughtfully. Money talked, but they had their family pride to consider.

'Are you expecting us to become restauranteurs?'

'Leave it to me,' Deirdre told them, 'I run the joint and –'

'The name Montcon means something still in France. We are not petit bourgeois,' said one of the sisters.

'So we don't muddy the name. I'll take the flak. You can keep your hands clean and inside five years we put it on the market and scoop the pool.'

After a great deal of argument, the family had agreed and the Countess, now plain Deirdre, had set to work only to discover that she had been taken for a sucker yet again. The family had no intention of ever selling. She could have her cut of the profits but that was all. Even her threat to drag the name of Montcon through the mud of the courts had backfired. The family no longer existed and the sisters and nieces were content with their husband's names and the income they drew from Deirdre's efforts. Worse still, the youngest sister of the late Count had married Dr Grenoy, the Cultural Attaché to the Embassy in Washington, who had used his position to look a little more closely into Deirdre's background. From that moment, Deirdre had become a dependant. Dr Grenoy had made that clear enough. 'There are . . . how shall I say? . . . certain gentlemen in a town renowned for gambling and violence who have long memories. It would interest them to know where their money has been invested.' Deirdre's eyes had hardened and Dr Grenoy continued. 'However that need not concern us. In France we are more civilized. Naturally we will have to readjust your percentage to prepare for any unfortunate contingencies . . .'

'Hold it there,' said Deirdre, 'I work my butt off and you tell me . . .'

'Madame,' interrupted Dr Grenoy, 'there are additional advantages I have yet to mention. I need not stress your understandable desire for anonymity but I have something to offer. Conferences funded by international corporations, UNESCO, the World Wildlife Conservation. I am in a position to influence the venue and with the service you provide . . . Need I say more?'

'And the cut off my percentage goes to you?'

Dr Grenoy nodded. Deirdre had agreed, with the private reservation that she'd keep meticulous records of Dr Grenoy's new source of income. Two could play that game. And one of these days she would skip France and resume her original identity in her bungalow at Bognor Regis. Constance Sugg was not a name she'd have chosen for herself but it had the great advantage of being on her birth certificate.

Now as she drove the little van back from Boosat her mind was concerned with a new problem. Once it had been impossible to get money out of Britain and easy to shift it from France. The situation had changed and the little gold bars she had slowly accumulated over the years, while they had appreciated enormously in value, made the matter even more difficult. Perhaps if she bribed a fisherman to take her across to Falmouth . . . At least there would be no trouble with Immigration Officials. She was a British subject born and bred . . . But the problem was never to be resolved.

As she drove into the courtyard and saw the ambulance, her mind switched to the terrible possibility that one of the visitors had gone down with food poisoning. Those mushrooms she had used in the *coq au vin* . . . She got out and hurried into the hall and was stopped by Dr Grenoy.

'What has happened?' she asked.

'I can't explain here,' said Grenoy, hustling her into the dining room and shutting the door. 'They've found you. A man with a gun was here during the night looking for you.'

The Countess sat down. She felt sick. 'For me?'

'He demanded of the guests where you were. He asked specifically for the Countess.'

'But no one knows. Except you and Marie-Louise and some of the servants,' she said. 'This is all your fault. They must have traced me through you and your stupid enquiries in the States.'

'I didn't make enquiries myself. I hired a detective. He didn't know who I was.'

'He knew you were French. And doubtless you paid him by cheque.'

'I paid in cash. I am not indiscreet. You think I wanted my wife's family to be known to be involved with such people? I have my reputation to consider.'

'And I've got my life.'

'Exactly,' said Dr Grenoy, 'You must leave here at once. Go to Paris. Go anywhere. This affair could become a national scandal. Professor Botwyk has already had to be rescued from the river and the Russian delegate and the dreadful Englishman, Hodgson, were both assaulted. Not to mention other most unpleasant events concerning the wife of Mr Rutherby and Mr Coombe. The situation is extremely awkward.'

Deirdre smiled. It had occurred to her that there was another explanation. They wanted her out of the Château and she had no intention of leaving except in her own good time. 'Dr Grenoy,' she said, 'with your influence I am sure I shall be well protected. In the meantime, no one knows who I am and, if what you say is correct, no one need know. I shall speak to the servants. You need have no worry. I can take care of myself.'

She went down to the kitchen and found Dr Voisin gleefully helping himself to coffee from the pot on the stove. 'Ah, madame la Comtesse,' he said, 'my illusions of a lifetime have been destroyed. I had always believed that French women, my dear wife in particular, were the most possessive in the world. But now I know better. Madame Voisin, and I thank the good God for it, is only interested in possessing material things. True, one may count the male organ as material, though for myself I prefer a more personalistic approach. Monsieur Coombe shares my prejudice. But Madame Rutherby . . . what a woman! Passion and possessiveness to that degree are fortunately beyond my experience. And one speaks of women's liberation . . .'

'What on earth are you talking about?' asked the Countess, when she could get a word in. 'I understood a gunman was here . . .' She stopped. The less said about the purpose of his visit the better.

'The English,' continued Dr Voisin. 'An amazing species. One cannot designate them as a race. And one would not describe Madame Rutherby as a particularly desirable woman. It is all a mystery. And finally to find that the American has been rescued by an English eccentric with one eye who claims to be on a walking tour in the middle of the night, no, that is not explicable either. And when I offered him a sedative it was as though I was trying to poison him.'

'An Englishman with one eye rescued Mr Botwyk? Did he give his name?'

'I think he said Pringle. It was difficult to tell, he was in such an agitated state. And how the American came to be at the foot of the cliff is another mystery. But I must be off. I have my other patients to think of if I can bring my thoughts to bear on anything except the English.'

And muttering to himself about barbarians he went out to his car and drove off. In the kitchen, the Countess busied herself with the preparations for breakfast but her thoughts were still on the bizarre events of the night. A one-eyed Englishman? Where had she heard of such a person before? It was only when Marie-Louise brought the two men's clothes down to be laundered and dry-cleaned that the puzzle was resolved. And made more mysterious. Inside Glodstone's shirt and underpants were sewn little labels on which were written his name. It was something the school laundry demanded and he had entirely forgotten.

Chapter 16

In the case of Mr and Mrs Clyde-Browne there would never be any forgetting their holiday in Italy. From the first it had been an unmitigated disaster. The weather had been lousy; their hotel accommodation had included cockroaches; the Adriatic had been awash with untreated sewage and the whole damned place, in Mr Clyde-Browne's opinion, polluted by ubiquitous Italians.

'You'd think they'd have the gumption to go to Greece or Turkey for their own blasted holidays instead of cluttering up the beaches here,' he complained, 'their economy's on the brink of collapse and without the money they get from tourism the lira would be worth even less than it is now.'

'Yes, dear,' said Mrs Clyde-Browne with her usual apathy when politics came up in their conversation.

'I mean, no sane Englishman would dream of going to Brighton or even Torquay in August. Mind you, you'd have less chance of bumping into a turd in the Channel than you do here.'

In the end a bout of Adriatic tummy had persuaded them to cut their losses and fly home a week early. Mr Clyde-Browne waddled off the plane at Gatwick wearing one of his wife's tampons and determined to institute legal action against the travel agent who had misled them. His wife, more philosophically, looked forward to being with Peregrine again. 'We've hardly had a chance to see him all year,' she said as they drove home, 'And now that he's left Groxbourne . . .'

'He'll be lounging about the house all day unless I can get him into the Army.'

'All the same, it will be nice . . .'

'It won't,' said Mr Clyde-Browne. 'It'll be pure hell.'

But his attitude changed when he found among the mail cluttering the floor in the hall a letter from the Headmaster apologizing for the cancellation of the Overactive Under-achiever's Survival Course in Wales owing to unforeseen circumstances. 'Unforeseen circumstances, my foot, every circumstance ought to be foreseen. That's what we're given brains for, to foresee circumstances and make contingency plans. Now if that infernal idiot at the travel agent's had done his homework, he'd have foreseen that our bloody holiday would be a downright catastrophe.'

'Yes, but where's Peregrine?' asked Mrs Clyde-Browne before her husband could launch too thoroughly into an impassioned rehearsal of his claim against the firm.

'Peregrine? What do you mean, where is he? He's bound to be at the school. You don't imagine they'd be mad enough to let him try and find his own way home?'

But Mrs Clyde-Browne had already gone into the study and was dialling the school's number. 'I want to speak to my son, Peregrine Clyde-Browne,' she told the School Secretary, only to be told in turn that Peregrine wasn't there.

'He's not there? Then where is he?'

'I'm afraid I've no idea. If you'll just hold the line I'll try and find out.'

Mrs Clyde-Browne held the line and beckoned to her husband who was examining a gas bill suspiciously. 'They don't know where he is.'

'Probably lurking in the school bogs.'

'He isn't at Groxbourne. He's somewhere else.'

'If he isn't there, he's bound to be somewhere else. It stands to reason . . . What?'

'The secretary's gone to see if she can find out where he went to.'

But the strain of his holiday and his fury at the travel agency had been exacerbated by the gas bill. Mr Clyde-Browne seized the phone. 'Now listen to me,' he shouted, 'I demand to know . . .'

'It's no use bawling like that, dear,' said Mrs Clyde-Browne pacifically, 'There's no one there to hear you.'

'Then who the hell were you talking to?'

'The School Secretary. I told you she's gone to see if anyone knows where Peregrine –'

'Damn,' said Mr Clyde-Browne, cursing both the school and the state of his bowels. 'Then call me back the moment . . .' He shot into the downstairs lavatory and it was left to his wife to learn that Peregrine had gone to stay with his uncle.

'His uncle?' she asked, 'You wouldn't happen to know which one?'

The secretary didn't. Mrs Clyde-Brown put the phone down, picked it up again and called her sister-in-law in Aylesbury, only to find that Peregrine wasn't there. It was the same with Uncle Martin and all the other uncles and aunts. Mrs Clyde-Browne broke down. 'They said he'd gone to stay with one of his uncles but he hasn't,' she moaned through the lavatory door. Inside, Mr Clyde-Brown was heard to mutter that he wasn't surprised and gave vent to his paternal feelings by flushing the pan.

'You don't seem to care,' she wept when he came out and headed for the medicine cupboard. 'Don't you have any normal feelings as a father?'

Mr Clyde-Brown took two tablespoonfuls of kaolin and morphine before replying. 'Considering I have just flown halfway across Europe wearing one of your sanitary napkins to contain myself, what feelings I have whether as a father or not can't by any stretch of the imagination be called normal. When I think what might have happened if the Customs officer you tried to bluff about that silk had given me a body search, my blood runs cold. As a matter of fact, it's running cold now.'

'In that case, if you're not prepared to do anything, I'm going to call the police,' said Mrs Clyde-Browne, realizing for the first time in her married life that she was in a strong position.

Mr Clyde-Browne, who had been heading for the stairs and bed, stopped in his tracks. 'Police? What on earth are you going to do that for?'

'Because Peregrine is a missing person.'

'He's certainly missing something, though I'd qualify the word "person", but if you think for one moment the police are going to be involved . . .'

140

It was an acrimonious exchange and was only ended by Mr Clyde-Browne's inability to be in the lavatory and to stop his wife reaching the phone at the same time. 'All right,' he conceded frantically, 'I promise to do everything humanly possible to find him as soon as I'm physically able provided you don't call the police.'

'I can't see why not. It seems the sensible thing to do.'

'Because,' snarled her husband, 'if there's one thing a prospective employer – and God know they're few and far between in Peregrine's case – dislikes as a reference it is a police record.'

'But Peregrine wouldn't have a police record. He'd be . . .'

'Listed on the Missing Persons Computer at New Scotland Yard, and where the Army and banks are concerned that constitutes a police record. Oh, damnation.' He stumbled back into the lavatory and sat there thinking dark thoughts about dysentery and idiot sons. He emerged to find his wife standing by the front door.

'We're leaving now,' she said.

'Leaving? Leaving for where?'

'Groxbourne. You said you'd do everything possible to find poor Peregrine and I'm holding you to it.'

Mr Clyde-Browne hung onto the door sill. 'But I can't drive all that way in my condition.'

'Possibly not,' said Mrs Clyde-Browne, 'but I can. And since we haven't unpacked, we can leave straight away.'

Mr Clyde-Browne climbed submissively into the seat beside her. 'I just hope to hell you know what you're doing,' he moaned, 'and you'd better be prepared to stop fairly frequently.'

'I do and I am,' she said with a terseness he'd never heard before.

An hour later, his experience of the three motorway toilets his wife had allowed him to use had been so revolting that he was half disposed to think more highly of Italians. 'If further proof were needed that this country's gone to the dogs . . .'

'Never mind about the country,' snapped Mrs Clyde-Browne, hurtling past a petrol tanker at ninety miles an hour, 'What I want to know is where Peregrine has gone to. You don't seem to realize our son is lost.'

Mr Clyde-Browne checked his safety belt again. 'Not the only thing we'll lose if you continue to drive . . . Mind that flaming motorbike! Dear God!'

All in all it had been a hair-raising journey and by the time the car skidded to a halt outside the school office Mr Clyde-Browne was in a state of shock and his wife wasn't to be trifled with.

'I'm not trifling with you,' said the School Secretary indignantly, 'I am simply telling you that the Headmaster is on holiday.'

'Where?'

'On the Isle of Skye. I can find the address of his cottage if you like. He's not on the phone.'

But Mr Clyde-Browne had heard enough. To ward off the terrifying possibility that his wife might insist on driving through the night to the West Coast of Scotland he interposed himself between them. 'Our son Peregrine is missing,' he said, 'He was supposed to go on the Survival Course in Wales. He has not returned home. Now since Major Fetherington was in charge of the course he's *in loco parentis*, and . . .'

'He's not,' said the secretary, 'he's in the Sanatorium. If you ask Matron nicely she may let you see him. It's across the quad and up the steps by the chapel.'

'Impudent hussy,' said Mrs Clyde-Browne when they left the office. Her husband said nothing. As they marched across the grim quad and past the looming chapel, he was praying that Peregrine hadn't been left in Wales. The notion of being driven there was almost as bad as Scotland.

'Is there anyone about?' Mrs Clyde-Browne shouted when they found the Sanatorium and had tried several empty rooms in vain. At the end of the passage a door opened and a woman peered out.

'We want to see Major Fetherington,' said Mr Clyde-Browne.

The woman looked doubtful. 'I'm just giving him a bed-bath,' she muttered, 'If you'll just wait a minute . . .'

But Mrs Clyde-Brown wasn't waiting for a second. Pushing past her husband, she bore down on the Matron. For a moment there was a confused scuffle and then the Matron managed to shut the door and lock it.

'Bed-bath indeed!' said Mrs Clyde-Browne, when she had got her breath back. 'If you'd seen what I saw . . .'

'Which, thankfully I didn't,' said her husband, 'now for goodness sake try and get a grip on yourself . . .'

'Grip on myself? I like that. If you ask me those two were . . .'

'I daresay,' snapped Mr Clyde-Browne, 'but if we're to get the Major's co-operation you're not going to help matters by intruding on his private affairs.'

'Private affairs indeed! That depraved creature was stark naked and wearing a French tickler and if you call that a bed-bath, I most certainly don't,' said Mrs Clyde-Browne, managing to combine a sexual knowledge her husband had never suspected with a grievance that he'd never bothered to use one. But before he could reply the bedroom door opened and the Matron appeared. Mr Clyde-Browne was grateful to note that this time she was wearing a skirt.

'Well I must say . . .' she began.

'Don't,' begged Mr Clyde-Browne, 'We're extremely sorry to have . . .'

'I'm not,' interrupted his wife, 'considering that that filthy man in there –'

Mr Clyde-Browne had had enough. 'Shut up,' he told her violently and, leaving her speechless, explained the situation as swiftly as he could to the Matron.

By the time he had finished she was slightly mollified. 'I'll go and see if the Major is prepared to see you,' she said, pointedly ignoring Mrs Clyde-Browne.

'Well I like that,' Mrs Clyde-Browne exploded when the door was shut. 'To think that I should be told to shut up in front of a –'

'Shut up!' roared Mr Clyde-Browne again. 'You've already done enough damage and from now on you'll leave the matter in my hands.'

'In your hands? If I'd had my way none of this would have happened. In the first place –'

'Peregrine would have been aborted. But since he wasn't you had to delude yourself that you'd given birth to a bloody genius. Well, let me tell you –'

By the time he had got his feelings about Peregrine off his chest, Mr Clyde-Browne felt better. In the next room Major Fetherington didn't. 'If he feels like that about the poor sod I'm not surprised Perry's gone missing. What I can't understand is why that maniac wants to find him. He'd be better off in the Foreign Legion.'

'Yes, but what are you going to tell them?' asked the Matron.

'Lord alone knows. As far as I can remember, he told me he was going to stay with his uncle and then pushed off. That's my story and I'm going to stick to it.'

Five minutes later, Mr Clyde-Browne's legal approach had changed his mind. 'Are you suggesting, Major, that my son was guilty of a deliberate falsehood?'

The Major shifted uncomfortably under the bedclothes. 'Well, no, not when you put it like that. All the same he did say he'd phoned his uncle and . . .'

'The inescapable fact remains that he hadn't and that no one has seen him since he was left in your care.'

Major Fetherington considered the inescapable fact and tried to elude it. 'Someone must have seen him. Stands to reason. He can't have vanished into thin air.'

'On the other hand, you were personally responsible for his welfare prior to his disappearance? Can you deny that?'

'Prior to, old boy, prior to. That's the operative word,' said the Major.

'As a matter of fact it's two words,' said Mr Clyde-Browne, getting his own back for being called an old boy.

'All right, two operative words. Doesn't make any difference. As soon as he said he was going to his uncle's and shoved off I couldn't be responsible for his welfare, could I?'

'Then you didn't accompany him to the station?'

'Accompany him to the station?' said the Major indignantly, 'I wasn't capable of accompanying anyone anywhere. I was flat on my back with a fractured coccyx. Damned painful I can –'

'And having it massaged by the Matron no doubt,' interrupted Mr Clyde-Browne, who had taken out a pocket book and was making notes.

Major Fetherington turned pale and decided to change his tactics. 'Look,' he said, 'I'll do a deal.'

'A deal?'

'No names, no packdrill. You don't mention anything to the Headmaster about you-know-what and . . .' He paused to see how Mr Clyde-Browne would respond.

The solicitor nodded. 'Do go on,' he said.

'As I was saying, no names, no packdrill. The chappie you really want to see is Glodstone . . .'

Outside, Mrs Clyde-Browne sipped a cup of tea reluctantly. It was a peace offering from the Matron but Mrs Clyde-Browne wasn't mollified. She was wondering how her husband could have condemned her Peregrine to such a terrible environment. 'I blame myself,' she whimpered internally.

In the school office her words would have found an echo in Slymne. Ever since he had wrecked the Blowthers' brand-new Jaguar he had been cursing himself for his stupidity. He had been mad to plan Glodstone's prepackaged adventure. In an attempt to give himself some sort of alibi he had returned to the school, ostensibly to collect some books, only to learn that events had taken another turn for the worse.

'I've never seen parents so livid,' the School Secretary told him. 'And rude. Not even Mr and Mrs Fairchild when their son was expelled for tying a ferret to the crotch of Mr Paignton's pyjamas.'

'Good Lord,' said Slymne, who remembered the consequences of that awful occasion and had examined his own pyjamas very carefully ever since.

'And all because that stupid Peregrine Clyde-Browne hasn't gone home and they don't know where he is.'

Slymne's heartbeat went up alarmingly. He knew now why the youth he had seen washing the Bentley in Mantes had seemed so familiar. 'What did you tell them?' he asked tremulously.

'I told them to see the Major. What I didn't tell them was that Mrs Brossy at the Post Office says she saw a boy get into Mr Glodstone's old banger down at the bus-stop the day he went away.'

'Who went away?' asked Slymne, his alarm growing by the minute.

'Mr Glodstone. He came back here all excited and –'

'Look,' said Slymne, 'does the Headmaster know about this?'

145

The secretary shook her head. 'I said he was on holiday on the Isle of Skye. Actually, he's in his caravan at Scarborough but he doesn't like that to be known. Doesn't sound so respectable, does it?'

'But he's on the phone?'

'The campsite is.'

'Right,' said Slymne, coming to a sudden decision, 'rather than have them bothering you, I'll deal with them. Now what's the number of the campsite?'

By the time the Clyde-Brownes left the Sanatorium Slymne was ready for them. 'Good afternoon,' he said briskly, 'my name is Slymne. I'm the geography master here. Miss Crabley tell me you're concerned about your son.'

Mr Clyde-Browne stopped in his tracks. Mr Slymne's reports on Peregrine's lack of any academic ability had always struck him as proving that at least one master at Groxbourne was neither a complete idiot nor a barefaced liar.

'More than concerned,' he said. 'The boy's missing and from what I've been able to gather from that man Fetherington there seems to be good reason to suppose he's been abducted by Mr Glodstone.'

Slymne's mouth dried up. Mr Clyde-Browne was evidently an expert investigator. 'Mr Glodstone's abducted your son? Are you quite sure? I mean it seems . . .'

'Of course I'm not sure. I'd have called the police if I were,' said Mr Clyde-Browne, bearing in mind the law on slander. 'I said I'd been given reason to believe it. What's your opinion of Glodstone?'

'I'd rather not comment,' said Slymne, glad to be able to tell the truth for the time being, 'my relations with him are not of the best and I might be prejudiced. I think you ought to consult the Headmaster.'

'Who happens to be in the Outer Hebrides.'

'In the circumstances I'm sure he'll return immediately. I'll wire him to say that you're here. Now would you like me to find some accommodation locally? There's an excellent hotel in Leominster.'

When they left, the Clyde-Brownes were slightly happier in their minds. 'Thank God someone round here seems to have his head screwed on the right way,' said Mr Clyde-Browne.

'And he did seem to think that Peregrine was in safe hands,' said his wife, 'I do hope he's right.'

Mr Clyde-Browne kept his thoughts on the subject to himself. His hopes were rather different. He was wondering how best to intimidate the Headmaster into paying considerable damages for the loss of a son.

In the school office Slymne picked up the phone and dialled the campsite in Scarborough. About the only bright spot he could see on the horizon was that the Clyde-Brownes were evidently reluctant to call in the police.

Chapter 17

It was mid-morning before the Headmaster arrived to be met by a haggard and desperate Slymne. His conversation with the Major the previous night, assisted by a bottle of whisky, had appalled him. Glodstone had told the Major where he was going. And since he had confided so much it seemed all too likely that he had kept those damning letters. Slymne had spent a sleepless night trying to think of some way to dissociate himself from the whole ghastly business. The best strategy seemed to be to show that he had already acted responsibly.

'I've checked the railway station and the bus people,' he told the Headmaster, 'and it's clear that Clyde-Browne didn't leave by bus or train on the 31st, which is the day he went missing.'

'That's a great help,' said the Headmaster. 'What I want to know is where he *did* go. I've got to have something to tell his bloody parents.'

'Well, Mrs Brossy at the Post Office thinks she saw Glodstone pick a young man up outside her shop around midday.'

The Headmaster slumped into a chair behind his desk. 'Oh, my God! And I don't suppose anyone has a clue where the lunatic took him?'

Slymne played his ace. 'Strictly in confidence, sir, I did manage to get Major Fetherington to tell me that Glodstone had said he was going to France by way of Ostend.'

'Going to France by way of Ostend? Ostend's in bloody Belgium. Are you seriously telling me that that one-eyed maniac has dragged the son of a prominent solicitor out of this country without asking his parents' permission?'

Slymne demurred. 'I'm not exactly saying that, sir. I'm merely repeating what the Major told me in strict confidence and I'd appreciate it if you kept my name out of the business. I mean –'

'Damn Major Fetherington. If Glodstone's gone to France with that ghastly boy we'll all have to go into business. We'll certainly be out of teaching.'

'Quite,' said Slymne. 'Anyway, acting on the Major's tip I phoned the Channel ferry services at Dover to ask if they could confirm it.'

'And did they?'

'Not in so many words. They wanted to know who I was and what my interest was and I didn't think I'd better say anything more until I'd spoken to you. Mr Clyde-Browne didn't strike me as a man who'd take kindly to the news that his son had gone abroad with Glodstone.'

The Headmaster closed his eyes and shuddered. From his previous dealings with Peregrine's father he'd gained the distinct impression that Mr Clyde-Browne didn't count kindliness as one of his strong points. 'So that's all the information we have? Is that what you're saying?'

Slymne hesitated. 'I can't speak for the Major but I have an idea he knows more than he was prepared to tell me.'

'By God, he'll tell me,' said the Headmaster savagely. 'Go and get the fellow.'

Slymne slipped out of the room and crossed the quad to the San. 'The old man wants to see you,' he told the Major, whose physical condition hadn't been improved by a dreadful hangover, 'and if I were in your shoes, I'd tell him everything you know.'

'Shoes?' said the Major. 'If I had shoes and wasn't in a wheelchair I'd have been out of here long ago. Oh well, into the firing line.'

It was an appropriate metaphor. The Headmaster was ready to do murder. 'Now then, I understand Glodstone told you he was going to France by way of Ostend,' he said, ignoring Slymne's plea for discretion. The Major nodded unhappily. 'Did he also tell you he was taking Clyde-Browne with him?'

'Of course not,' said the Major rallying, 'I wouldn't have let him.'

'Let him tell you or let him take the boy?' asked the Headmaster, glad to take his feelings out on a man he'd never much liked anyway.

'Take him, of course.'

'What else did he tell you?'

Major Fetherington looked reproachfully at Slymne. 'Well, if you must know, he said he'd been asked to undertake a secret mission, something desperately dangerous. And in case he bought it. . .'

'Bought it? Bought what, for Heaven's sake?'

'Well, if things went wrong and got himself killed or something, he wanted me to look after his interests.'

'Interests?' snapped the Headmaster, preferring not to dwell on 'killed'. 'What interests?'

'I really don't know. I suppose he meant let the police know or get him a decent funeral. He left it a bit vague.'

'He needn't have. I'll fix his funeral,' said the Headmaster. 'Go on.'

'Not much else to tell really,' said the Major hesitantly but the Headmaster wasn't deceived.

'The lot, Fetherington, the lot. You leave out one jot or tittle and you'll be hobbling down to join the ranks of the unemployed and I don't mean tomorrow.'

The Major tried to cross his legs and failed. 'All right, if you really want to know, he said he'd been asked by the Countess of Montcon–'

'The Countess of Montcon?'

'Wanderby's mother, he's a boy in Gloddie's, the one with allergies and whatnot, to go down to her château . . . You're not going to believe this.'

'Never mind that,' said the Headmaster, who appeared to be in the grip of some awful allergy himself.

'Well, she wanted him to rescue her from some gang or other.'

'Some gang or other? You mean to tell me . . . The man must be off his bloody rocker.'

'That's what I told him,' said the Major. 'I said, "Listen, old boy, someone's having you on. Get on the blower and call her up and see if I'm not right." But you know what Glodstone's like.'

'I'm beginning to get a shrewd idea,' said the Headmaster. 'Mad as a March fucking hare. Don't let me stop you.'

'That's about the lot really. I had no idea he was going to take Perry with him.'

'So you've said before, and it's not the lot.'

The Major tried to focus his thoughts. 'About the only other thing I can think of is that he asked me to let him have a couple of revolvers from the Armoury. Naturally I wasn't buying that one –'

'A couple of revolvers from the School Armoury? Jesus wept! And that didn't tell you anything?'

'Only that he was obviously dead serious about the whole business. I mean obviously –'

'A couple of revolvers, you moron,' shouted the Headmaster, 'not just one. Who the hell do you think the second one was for?'

'Now that you come to mention it –'

'Mention it? Mention it?' yelled the Headmaster. 'What I want to know is why you didn't mention it at the bloody time?'

'Well, since he didn't get them there didn't seem much point,' said the Major. 'If Glodstone wanted to go off on some wild goose chase that was his affair and –'

'Slymne,' interrupted the Headmaster before the Major could say it was no skin off his nose what Glodstone did, 'take him to the Armoury and see that there aren't two revolvers and half a dozen rifles missing. I want every weapon accounted for.'

'But I've just told you –'

'I know what you've told me and I'm not taking any chances on your opinion. Now get out.'

As Slymne bundled the Major's wheelchair through the door, the Headmaster put his head in his hands. The situation was far worse than he had imagined. It had been bad enough to suppose that Glodstone had merely taken the wretched boy on some jaunt round the country, but that he'd almost certainly gone abroad with the lout on a so-called 'secret mission' to rescue another boy's mother verged on the insane.

The Headmaster corrected himself. It *was* insane. Finally, collecting what thoughts he could, he reached for the phone.

'Get on to International Enquiries and put a call through to Wanderby's mother in France. Her name's the Countess of Montcon. You'll find the address in the files. And put her straight through to me.'

As he slammed the phone down he saw the Clyde-Brownes' car drive up. The moment he had dreaded had come. What on earth was he going tell them? Something soothing, some mild remark . . . No, that wouldn't work. With an almost manic smile he got up to

151

greet them. But Mr Clyde-Browne had come to be heard, not to listen. He was armed with a battery of arguments.

Peregrine had been in the school's care; he had last been seen on the school premises (the Headmaster decided not to mention Mrs Brossy's sighting in the village); the school, and on a more personal level, the Headmaster, had been and still were responsible for his well-being; Mr Clyde-Browne had paid the exorbitant sum of ten thousand pounds in advance fees; and if, as seemed likely, his son had been abducted by a possibly paedophilic master he was going to see that the name Groxbourne went down in legal history and was expunged from the *Public Schools Yearbook*, where, in his opinion, it should never have been in the first place. And what had the Headmaster to say to that?

The Headmaster fought for words. 'I'm sure there's a perfectly simple and straightforward . . .' he began without any conviction, but Mrs Clyde-Browne's sobs stopped him. She appeared to have gone into premature mourning. 'I can only promise . . .'

'I am not interested in promises,' said Mr Clyde-Browne, 'my son is missing and I want him found. Now, have you any idea where he is?'

The Headmaster shuddered to think, and had his agitation increased by the telephone.

'I can't get any number,' said the School Secretary when he picked it up, 'International Enquiries say there's no Countess de . . .'

'Thank you, Miss Crabley, but I'm engaged just at the moment,' he said to stifle any shrill disclosures. 'Please tell the Bishop I'll call him back as soon as I'm free.' And, hoping he had impressed the Clyde-Brownes, he replaced the receiver and leant across the desk. 'I really don't think you have anything to worry about . . .' he began and knew he was wrong. Through the window he could see Slymne crossing the quad carrying two revolvers. God alone knew what would happen if he marched in and . . . The Headmaster got to his feet. 'If you'll just excuse me for a moment,' he said hoarsely, 'I'm afraid my bowels . . . er . . . my stomach has been playing me up.'

'So have mine,' said Mr Clyde-Browne unsympathetically, but the Headmaster was already through the door and had intercepted Slymne. 'For God's sake put those beastly things away,' he whispered ferociously.

'The thing is . . .' Slymne began but the Headmaster dragged him into the lavatory and locked the door. 'They're only replicas.'

'I don't care what . . . They're what?' said the Headmaster.

'I said they're replicas,' said Slymne, edging up against the washbasin nervously.

'Replicas? You mean –'

'Two real revolvers are missing. We found these in their place.'

'Shit!' said the Headmaster, and slumped onto the seat. His bowels were genuinely playing him up now.

'The Major is checking the ammunition boxes,' continued Slymne, 'I just thought you'd want to know about these.'

The Headmaster stared bleakly at a herb chart his wife had pinned up on the wall to add a botanical air to the place. Even the basil held no charms for him now. Somewhere in Europe Glodstone and that litigious bastard's idiot son were wandering about armed with property belonging to the Ministry of Defence. And if the Clyde-Brownes found out . . . They mustn't.

Rising swiftly he wrenched the top off the cistern. 'Put the damned things in there,' he said. Slymne raised his eyebrows and did as he was told. If the Headmaster wanted replica firearms in his water closet that was his business. 'And now go back to the Armoury and tell that Fetherington not to move until I've got rid of the parents. I'll come over myself.'

He opened the door and was confronted by Mr Clyde-Browne, for whom the mention of stomachs and lavatories had precipitated another bout of Adriatic tummy. 'Er . . .' said the Headmaster, but Mr Clyde-Browne shoved past him and promptly backed out again followed by Slymne. 'The toilet's not working. Mr Slymne here has been helping me fix it.'

'Really?' said Mr Clyde-Browne with an inflection he relied on in cases involving consenting adults charged with making improper use of public urinals, and before the Headmaster could invite him to use the toilet upstairs he was back inside and had locked the door.

'You don't think . . .' said Slymne injudiciously.

'Get lost,' said the Headmaster. 'And see that . . . the Major doesn't stir.'

Slymne took the hint and hurried back to the armoury. The Major was looking disconsolately at several empty boxes in the ammunition locker. 'Bad news, Slimey old chap,' he said. 'Two hundred bloody rounds gone. The Army isn't going to like it one little bit. I've got to account for every fucking one.'

'Not your fault,' said Slymne. 'If Glodstone chooses to go mad and pinch the key . . .'

'He didn't. Peregrine had the thing. And to think I used to like that boy.'

'Well, the Head's got his hands full with the Clyde-Brownes and I don't think he's having an easy time.'

The Major almost sympathized. 'I don't see how he can avoid sacking me. I'd sack myself in the circumstances. More than flesh and blood can stand, that bloody couple.' He wheeled himself across to a rack of bayonets.

'Don't tell me they've taken some of those too,' said Slymne.

'I wish to God they had,' said the Major. 'The Army wouldn't worry so much. Mind you, I hate to think what Perry would get up to. Born bayoneteer. You should see what he can do with a rifle and bayonet to a bag of straw. And talking about guts I suppose if I were a Jap the Head would expect me to commit Mata Hari.'

Slymne ignored the mistake. He was beginning to feel distinctly sorry for the Major. After all, the man might be a fool but he'd never been as malicious as Glodstone and it had been no part of Slymne's plan to get him sacked.

'They probably won't use any of those bullets,' he said by way of consolation and wondered what he could do to save the Major's job.

It was not a consideration that had top priority with the Headmaster. Mr Clyde-Browne's eruption from the lavatory clutching the two replica revolvers he had dredged from the cistern in an attempt to make the thing flush had honed to a razor's edge the Headmaster's only gift, the capacity for extempore evasions.

'Well I never,' he said. 'Would you believe it?'

'No,' said Mr Clyde-Browne.

'Boys will be boys,' continued the Headmaster in the face of this blunt refusal to accept his rhetoric, 'always up to some practical jokes.'

Mr Clyde-Browne fingered the revolvers dangerously. He had yet to realize they were replicas. 'And maniacs will presumably be maniacs. Since when have you and that man Slymne made a habit of hiding offensive weapons in the cistern of your lavatory?'

'Are you suggesting –'

'No. I'm stating,' said Mr Clyde-Browne, 'I intend to present these firearms to the police as proof that you are wholly unfit either by virtue of insanity or criminal tendency to be in charge of anything more morally responsible than an abattoir or a brickyard.'

The Headmaster struggled with these alternatives but Mr Clyde-Browne was giving tongue again. 'Marguerite!' he yelled, 'Come here at once.'

Mrs Clyde-Browne crept from the study. 'Yes, dear,' she said meekly.

'I want you to bear witness that I have discovered these two guns in the water closet of this –'

But the sight of her husband aiming two revolvers at the Headmaster was witness enough.

'You're mad, mad, mad!' she wailed and promptly had a fit of hysterics.

The Headmaster seized his opportunity. 'Now look what you've done,' he said appealing to Mr Clyde-Browne's better feelings in vain. 'Your poor wife . . .'

'Keep your hands off that woman,' snarled her husband, 'I give you fair warning . . .' He waved the revolvers as the Headmaster tried to calm her.

'There, there,' he said, 'now come and sit down and . . .'

Mr Clyde-Browne was more forthright. Putting the guns on a side table, he whisked a bowl of faded roses from it and did what he had been longing to do for years. It was not a wise move. With water running down her face and a Wendy Cussons in her hair, Mrs Clyde-Browne's hysterics turned to fury.

'You bastard,' she yelled and seizing one of the guns, aimed it at her husband and pulled the trigger. There was a faint click and Mr Clyde-Browne cowered against the wall.

The Headmaster intervened and took the gun from her. 'Toys,' he explained, 'I told you it was simply a prank.'

Mr Clyde-Browne said nothing. He knew now where Peregrine had got his demonic gifts from and he no longer cared where the sod was.

'Come into the study,' said the Headmaster, making the most of the domestic rift. 'The School Secretary will see to Mrs Clyde-Browne's needs and I'm sure we could all do with a drink.'

The respite was only temporary. By the time the Clyde-Brownes drove off half an hour later, Mrs Clyde-Browne had threatened to divorce her husband if Peregrine wasn't found and Mr Clyde-Browne had passed the threat on in terms that included legal damages, the end of the Headmaster's career and the publicity that would result when the *News of the World* learnt that Major Fetherington, instead of being *in loco parentis*, had been *in loco matronae* and wearing a french tickler to boot. The Headmaster watched them go and then crossed the quad at a run to the Armoury.

'Off your butts,' he shouted, evidently inspired by the place to use Army language and ignoring the Major's patent inability to do more than wobble in his wheelchair. 'You're going to France and you're going to bring that bloody boy back within the week even if you have to drug the little bugger.'

'France?' said Slymne with a quaver. That country still held terrors for him. 'But why me? I've got –'

'Because this stupid sex-maniac can't drive. By this time tomorrow you'll be at the damned Château.'

'More than I will,' said the Major. 'You can sack me on the spot but I'm fucked if I'm going to be hurtled across Europe in a fucking wheelchair. I can't put it plainer than that.'

'I can,' said the Headmaster, who had learnt something from Mr Clyde-Browne when it came to blunt speaking. 'Either you'll use your despicable influence on your loathsome protégé, Master Peregrine Clyde-Bloody-Browne, and hopefully murder Glodstone in the process, or that damned man will have the police in and you'll not only lose your job but you'll be explaining to the CID and the Army why you gave those guns to a couple of lunatics.'

'But I didn't. I told you –'

'Shut up! I'll tell them,' said the Headmaster, 'because you were screwing the Matron with a french tickler and Glodstone threatened to blow your cover.'

'That's a downright lie,' said the Major without much conviction.

'Perhaps,' yelled the headmaster, 'but Mrs Clyde-Browne

evidently didn't see it that way and since her husband claims to be a personal friend of every High-Court Judge in the country, not to mention the Lord Chancellor, I don't fancy your chances in the witness box.'

'But can't we phone the Countess and explain . . .' Slymne began.

'What? That the school employs maniacs like Glodstone to come and rescue her? Anyway the secretary's tried and the woman isn't in the directory.'

'But the cost –'

'Will be funded from the school mission on the Isle of Dogs which is at least designated for the redemption of delinquents and no one can say it's not being put to its proper purpose.'

Later that afternoon, Slymne drove down the motorway towards Dover once again. Beside him the Major sat on an inflated inner tube and cursed the rôle of women in human affairs. 'It was her idea to use that beastly thingamajig,' he complained, 'I couldn't stop her. Had me at her mercy and anyway I couldn't feel a thing. Can't imagine why they call them French letters.' Slymne kept his thoughts to himself. He was wondering what the Countess had had to say about the letters she hadn't written.

Chapter 18

He needn't have worried. For the moment the Countess had other problems in mind. In fact the day had been fraught with problems. Mr Hodgson had refused to spend another night in a place where he was liable to be mugged every time he went to the loo and had left without paying his bill; Mr Rutherby had added to his wife's and Mr Coombe's little difficulties by threatening to commit a *crime passionnel* if he ever caught them together again, and Mr Coombe had told him in no uncertain terms that Mr Rutherby wouldn't know what a *crime* fucking *passionnel* was until he'd been clamped in Mrs Rutherby for three bloody hours with people pulling his legs to get him out.

But it had been the delegates who had given the most trouble. Dr Abnekov still maintained that he'd been the victim of a CIA conspiracy to silence him, while Professor Botwyk was equally adamant that a terrorist group had tried to assassinate him and demanded a bodyguard from the US Embassy in Paris. Dr Grenoy had temporized. If the American delegate wanted protection he would have him flown by helicopter to the nearest military hospital but he could rest assured there would be no recurrence of the previous night's dreadful events. The Château had been searched, the local gendarmerie alerted, all entrances were guarded and he had installed floodlights in the courtyard. If Professor Botwyk wished to leave the symposium he was perfectly welcome to, and Grenoy had hinted his absence wouldn't be noticed. Botwyk had risen to the taunt and had insisted on staying with the proviso that he be given the use of a firearm. Dr Abnekov had demanded reciprocal rights, and had so alarmed Botwyk that he'd given way on the issue. 'All the same I'm going to hold the French government fully responsible if I get bumped off,' he told Dr Grenoy with a lack of logic that confirmed the cultural attaché in his belief that

Anglo-Saxons were incapable of rational and civilized thought. Having settled the problem temporarily he had taken other measures in consultation with the Countess. 'If you refuse to leave,' he told her, 'at least see that you serve a dinner that will take their minds off this embarrassing incident. The finest wines and the very best food.'

The Countess had obliged. By the time the delegates had gorged their way through a seven-course dinner, and had adjourned to discuss the future of the world, indigestion had been added to their other concerns. On the agenda the question was down as 'Hunger in the Third World: A Multi-modular Approach', and as usual there was dissension. In this case it lay in defining the Third World.

Professor Manake of the University of Ghana objected to the term on the reasonable grounds that as far as he knew there was only one world. The Saudi delegate argued that his country's ownership of more oil and practically more capital in Europe and America than any other nation put Arabia in the First World and everyone not conversant with the Koran nowhere. Dr Zukacs countered, in spite of threats from Dr Abnekov that he was playing into the hands of Zionist–Western Imperialism, by making the Marxist–Leninist point that Saudi Arabia hadn't emerged from the feudal age, and Sir Arnold Brymay, while privately agreeing, silently thanked God that no one had brought up the question of Ulster.

But the main conflict came, as usual, in the differing interpretation by Dr Abnekov and Professor Botwyk. Dr Abnekov was particularly infuriated by Botwyk's accusation that the Soviet Union was by definition an underdeveloped country because it couldn't even feed itself and didn't begin to meet consumer demand.

'I demand a retraction of that insult to the achievements of the Socialist system,' shouted Abnekov. 'Who was the first into space? Who supports the liberationist movements against international capitalism? And what about the millions of proletarians who are suffering from malnutrition in the United States?'

'So who has to buy our grain?' yelled Botwyk. 'And what do you give the starving millions in Africa and Asia? Guns and rockets and tanks. You ever tried eating a goddam rocket?'

'When all peoples are freed –'

'Like Afghanistan and Poland? And what about Czechoslovakia and Hungary? You call killing people liberating them?'

'So Vietnam was freeing people? And how many murders are there in America every year? You don't even know, there are so many.'

'Yeah, well that's different. That's freedom of choice,' said Botwyk, who was against the uncontrolled sale of hand-guns but didn't feel like saying so.

Dr Grenoy tried to get the meeting back to the original topic. 'I think we ought to approach the problem rationally,' he pleaded, only to be asked by Professor Manake what rational rôle the French Foreign Legion were playing in Central Africa in solving anyone's problems except those of French Presidents with a taste for diamonds.

'I suppose the Foreign Legion absorbs some of the scum of Europe,' said Sir Arnold, trying to support Dr Grenoy, 'I remember once when I was in Tanganyika –'

'Tanzania,' said Professor Manake. 'You British don't own Africa any longer, in case it's escaped your attention.'

Dr Zukacs stuck his oar in. 'Untrue. Financial imperialism and neo-colonialism are the new –'

'Shut up, you damned Magyar,' shouted Dr Abnekov, who could see the insult to Ghana coming, 'not every country in Africa is a neo-colony. Some are highly progressive.'

'Like Uganda, I suppose,' said Botwyk. 'And who gave support to that cannibal Idi Amin? He kept heads in his deep-freeze for a quick snack.'

'Protein deficiency is rife in the Belgian Congo,' said Sir Arnold.

'Zaïre,' said Professor Manake.

Dr Grenoy tried again. 'Let us examine the structuralism of economic distribution,' he said firmly. 'It is a functional fact that the underdeveloped nations of the world have much to contribute on a socio-cultural and spiritual basis to modern thinking. Lévi-Strauss has shown that in some parts of . . .'

'Listen, bud,' said Botwyk, who imagined Dr Grenoy was about to bring up the question of Israel, 'I refuse to equate that bastard Khomeini with any spiritual basis. If you think holding innocent US citizens hostage is a Christian act . . .'

In the tumult that followed this insult to the Muslim world the Saudi delegate accused both Botwyk and Lévi-Strauss of being Zionist and Pastor Laudenbach advocated an ecumenical approach to the Holocaust. For once Dr Abnekov said nothing. He was mourning the loss of his son who had been captured and skinned alive in Afghanistan and anyway he loathed Germans. Even Dr Grenoy joined the fray. 'I wonder if the American delegate would tell us how many more Americans are going to prove their spiritual integrity by drinking orange juice spiked with cyanide in Guyana?' he enquired.

Only Sir Arnold looked happy. He had suddenly realized that Zaïre was not Eire and that the question of Ulster was still off the menu.

The Countess finished clearing up in the kitchen. She could still hear the raised voices, but she had long ago come to her own conclusions about the future of the world and knew that nice ideas about peace and plenty were not going to alter it. Her own future was more important to her and she had to decide what to do. The man who called himself Pringle was undoubtedly Glodstone. She had taken a good look at him when she had gone up to his room with his supper tray and had returned to her room to compare his drawn face with that in the school photograph Anthony had brought back. So why had he lied? And why had someone broken into the Château looking for her? She had already dismissed Grenoy's suggestion that the mob in Vegas had caught up with her. They didn't operate in that way. Not for a measly hundred grand. They were businessmen and would have used more subtle means of getting their money back, like blackmail. Perhaps they'd merely sent a 'frightener' first, but if that were the case they'd employed a remarkably inept one. It didn't make sense.

Now, sitting at the big deal table eating her own dinner, she felt tired. Tired of pandering to men's needs, tired of the fantasies of sex, success and greed, and of those other fantasies, the ideological ones those fools were arguing about now. All her life she had been an actress in other people's dream theatres or, worse still, an usherette. Never herself, whatever her 'self' was. It was time to find out. She finished her meal and washed up, all the while wondering

161

why human beings needed the sustenance of unreality. No other species she knew of did. Anyway she was going to learn what Glodstone's real purpose was.

She climbed the stairs to his room and found him sitting on the bed draped in a sheet and looking bewildered and frightened. It was the fear that decided her tactics. 'So what's Glass-Eye Glodstone doing in these parts?' she asked in her broadest American accent.

Glodstone gaped at her. 'Pringle,' he said. 'The name is Pringle.'

'That's not the way I read your Y-fronts. They're labelled Glodstone. So's your shirt. How come?'

Glodstone fought for an excuse and failed. 'I borrowed them from a friend,' he muttered.

'Along with the glass eye?'

Glodstone clutched the sheet to him hurriedly. This woman knew far too much about him for safety. Her next remark confirmed it. 'Look,' she said, 'there's no use trying to fool me. Just tell me what you were doing sneaking around in the middle of the night and rescuing so-called people.'

'I just happened to be passing.'

'Passing what? Water? Don't give me that crap. Some hoodlum breaks in here last night, beats up the clientèle, dumps one of them in the river, and you just happen to be passing.'

Glodstone gritted his dentures. Whoever this beastly woman was he had no intention of telling her the truth. 'You can believe what you like but the fact remains . . .'

'That you're my son's housemaster and at a guess I'd say he wasn't far out when he said you were a psycho.'

Glodstone tended to agree. He was feeling decidedly unbalanced. She couldn't be the Countess. 'I don't believe it. Your son told you . . . It's impossible. You're not the Countess.'

'OK, try me,' said the Countess.

'Try you?' said Glodstone, hoping she didn't mean what he thought. Clad only in a sheet he felt particularly vulnerable.

'Like what you want me to tell you. Like he's circumcised, got a cabbage allergy, had a boil on his neck last term and managed to get four O-levels without your help. You tell me.'

A wave of uncertain relief crept over Glodstone. Her language might not fit his idea of how countesses talked, but she seemed to know a great deal about Wanderby.

'Isn't there something else you want to tell me?' he asked finally to put her to the test about the letters.

'Tell you? What the hell more do you want to know? That he hasn't got goitre or something? Or if he's been laid? The first you can see for yourself or Miss Universe 1914 can tell you. And the second is none of your fucking business. Or is it?' She studied him with the eye of an expert in perversions. 'You wouldn't happen to be an asshole freak, would you?'

'I beg your pardon?' said Glodstone, stung by the insult.

'No need to,' said the Countess nastily. 'It's not my sphincter you're spearing and that's for sure. But if I find you've been sodomizing my son you'll be leaving here without the wherewithal.'

'Dear God,' said Glodstone crossing his legs frantically, 'I can assure you the thought never entered my head. Absolutely not. There is nothing queer about me.'

'Could have fooled me,' said the Countess, relaxing slightly. 'So what else is on your mind?'

'Letters,' said Glodstone.

'Letters?'

Glodstone shifted his eye away from her. This was the crunch-point. If she didn't know about the letters she couldn't possibly be the Countess. On the other hand, with his wherewithal at stake he wasn't going to beat about the bush. 'The ones you wrote me,' he said.

'I write you letters about Anthony's allergies and you make it all the way down here to discuss them? Come up with something better. I'm not buying that one.'

But before Glodstone could think of something else to say, there was the sound of a shot, a scream, more shots, a babble of shouting voices, and the floodlights in the courtyard went out. Peregrine had struck again.

Unlike everyone else, Peregrine had spent an untroubled day. He had slept until noon, had lunched on baked beans and corned beef and had observed the comings and goings at the Château with interest. Now that he knew Glodstone was alive, he wasn't worried. People were always getting captured in thrillers and it never made any real difference. In fact he couldn't think of a book in which the hero got bumped off, except *The Day of the Jackal* and he wasn't sure the Jackal had been a hero. But he had been really cunning and careful and had nearly got away with it. Peregrine made a mental note to be even more cunning and careful. No one was going to bump him off. Quite the reverse.

And so through the long hot afternoon he watched the floodlights being installed and the police van being stationed on the road by the bridge and made his plans. Obviously he wouldn't be able to go up the cliff as he'd wanted and he'd have to make sure the lightning conductor hadn't been spotted as his route in. But the main thing would be to create a diversion and get everyone looking the wrong way. Then he'd have to find Glodstone and escape before they realized what had happened. He'd have to move quickly too and, knowing how useless Glodstone was at running cross-country and climbing hills, that presented a problem. The best thing would be to trap the swine in the Château so they couldn't follow. But with the guards on the bridge . . . He'd have to lure them off it somehow. Peregrine put his mind to work and decided his strategy.

As dusk fell over the valley, he moved off down the hillside and crawled into the bushes by the police van. Three gendarmes were standing about smoking and talking, gazing down at the river. That suited his purpose. He squirmed through the bushes until they were hidden by the van. Then he was across the road and had crawled between the wheels and was looking for the petrol tank. In the cab above him the radio crackled and one of the men came over and spoke. Peregrine watched the man's feet and felt for his own revolver. But presently the fellow climbed down and the three gendarmes strolled up the ramp onto the bridge out of sight. Peregrine reached into the knapsack and took out a small Calor-gas stove and placed it beneath the tank. Before lighting it he checked again, but the men were too far away to hear and the noise of the water running past would cover the hiss of gas. Two seconds later the stove was burning and he was back across the road and hurrying through the bushes upstream. He had to be over the river before the van went up.

164

He had swum across and had already climbed halfway up the hill before the Calor stove made its presence felt. Having gently brought the petrol tank to the boil, it ignited the escaping vapour with a roar that exceeded Peregrine's wildest expectations. It did more. As the tank blew, the stove beneath it exploded too, oil poured onto the road and burst into flames and the three gendarmes, one of whom had been on the point of examining a rear tyre to find the cause of the hiss which he suspected to be a faulty valve, were enveloped in a sheet of flame and hurled backwards into the river. Peregrine watched a ball of flame and smoke loom up into the sunset and hurried on. If anyone in the Château was watching that would give them something to think about, and take their minds off the lightning conductor on the northern tower. It had certainly taken the gendarmes' minds off anything remotely connected with towers. Only vaguely thankful that they had not been incinerated, they were desperately trying to stay afloat in the rushing waters. But the Calor stove hadn't finished its work of destruction. As the flames spread, a tyre burst and scattered more fragments of blazing material onto the bridge. A seat burnt surrealistically in the middle of the road and the radio crackled more incomprehensibly than ever.

But these side-effects were of no interest to Peregrine. He had reached the tower and was swarming up the lightning conductor. At the top he paused, heaved himself onto the roof and headed for the skylight, revolver in hand. There was no one in sight and he dropped down into the empty corridor and crossed to the window. Below him the courtyard was empty and the smoke drifting over the river to the west seemed to have gone unnoticed. For a moment Peregrine was puzzled. It had never occurred to him that the gendarmes were really policemen. Anyone could dress up in a uniform and gangsters obviously wouldn't bring in the law to protect them, but all the same he'd expected them to have been on the lookout and he'd gone to a lot of trouble to draw their attention away from the Château. But no one seemed in the least interested. Odd. Anyway he was in the Château and if they were stupid enough not to be on their guard that was their business. His was to rescue Glodstone and this time he wasn't going to mingle with people in passages and bedrooms. He'd strike from a different direction.

He went down the turret to the cellar and searched the rooms again. Still there was no sign of Glodstone. But in the abandoned kitchen he could hear people arguing. He went to the dumb-waiter and listened but the voices were too many and too confused for him to hear what was being said and he was about to turn away when it occurred to him that he was in a perfect position to kill all the swine in one fell swoop. Swoop wasn't the word he wanted, because coming up in a diminutive lift wasn't swooping, but it would certainly take them by surprise if he appeared in the hatchway and opened fire. But that wouldn't help Glodstone escape. Peregrine suddenly realized his mistake. They were holding Glodstone hostage. That was why they'd only had three guards on the bridge and had put floodlights on the terrace. They knew he'd return but because they'd got Glodstone there would be nothing he could do except give himself up. It explained everything he found so puzzling.

In the darkness Peregrine's mind, as lethal as that of a ferret in a rabbit warren, gnawed at the problem: and found an answer.

Chapter 19

In the grand salon the members of the symposium had long since abandoned the topic of World Hunger. There were no experts on nutrition or agricultural techniques among them and even Dr Grenoy had failed to rally them around the topic by recourse to those generalities which, as a cultural attaché, and a French one, were his forte. In fact his attempt had made things worse. Only the multi-modular approach remained and, thanks to the enormous dinner and now the brandy, found increasing expression in national prejudices and personal feelings.

Curious bonds had been formed. Dr Abnekov's antipathy to American capitalism had been overcome by Professor Botwyk's observation to the Saudi delegate that any man who couldn't hold his liquor ought to stop spouting about the power of petroleum products, and Pastor Laudenbach had brought them even closer together by supporting the refusal of Muslims to touch alcohol. Even Professor Manake and Sir Arnold had found a common interest in big-game hunting. Only Dr Zukacs remained obstinately doctrinaire, explaining to no one in particular that the only way the under-developed countries could free themselves from imperialism was by developing heavy industry and collectivizing farms. Since he was sitting next to the Polish delegate, who was under orders to keep his mouth shut and who knew what collective farming had done to his own country, and who resented the imputation that Poland was under-developed anyway, only Dr Abnekov's threat to beat their collective heads together unless they shut up prevented a fight. Pastor Laudenbach's appeal for peace brought Botwyk to his feet.

'Listen, you dirty kraut,' he shouted, 'Don't you start yammering about peace. Two world wars your lousy country's started this century and don't think we've forgotten it. Six million died in the gas chambers and it wouldn't surprise me to learn you were the camp doctor at Auschwitz.'

'That's a lie,' snarled the Pastor inadvisedly, 'I spent four years on the Eastern Front in Panzers. I was at the Battle of the Kursk while you were bombing innocent civilians to death by the hundred thousand. I know about war. At Kursk I learnt and –'

It was too much for Dr Abnekov. 'You murdering Hitlerite,' he yelled, 'just let me get my hands on you and I'll show you what we did to butchers like you. At Kursk were you? By God –'

'Gentlemen,' appealed Dr Grenoy, 'let us try to forget the past and –'

'Shut up, you damned Frog,' shouted Botwyk. 'Without the boys who died on Omaha beach you'd be still doing what Heinie here told you even if you weren't a goddam collaborator which is open to question.'

'I was five at the time –' began Dr Grenoy, but neither Botwyk nor Abnekov were to be silenced. As Abnekov hurled himself drunkenly at the Pastor, Botwyk cursed Dr Grenoy for getting out of Vietnam and NATO, not to mention teaming up with a load of Huns in the Common Market. And what about Marshall Aid?'

'Amazing,' Professor Manake observed to Sir Arnold. 'You Europeans never seem to realize how extraordinarily barbaric you are.'

'I wouldn't call myself a European, you know,' said Sir Arnold. 'We're an island race with a seafaring tradition –'

But as he spoke, Peregrine, following another English tradition, acted. Firing with all the deadlines Major Fetherington had taught him he put his first bullet through Professor Botwyk's forehead, then shot the lights out and with two more bullets plunged the courtyard into darkness as well. As the screams and shouts of the delegates echoed through the Château he dashed for the cover of the gateway tower. There was a little office there and from it he could command a view of the entire terrace and the stableyard where the cars were parked at the back. In short, no one could move out of the buildings without being shot. Best of all, he had the swine trapped in the Château and until they released Glodstone he didn't intend to budge.

Three floors above, the Countess felt the same way about

budging. From the sound of the shots, the screams and the confusion below, she realized she had been wrong. Dr Grenoy had known what he was talking about. Some hit-man had come looking for her last night and she should have left while the going was good. Right now it was bad. Whipping to the door, she locked it and switched the light out. 'If anyone comes don't utter,' she told Glodstone. 'And wedge that bed against the door.'

For some time they sat on the floor in silence listening for more sounds of trouble and separately wondering how the hell they were going to get out of the mess. 'Must have shot one of the guests,' whispered the Countess finally.

'Guests?' said Glodstone.

'Either them or the think-tank merchants.'

'Think-tank merchants?'

'The futurologists. Though what they know about the future beats me. Still, they pay well. Or did. I can't see this being the world's favourite venue for conferences after tonight.'

Glodstone tended to agree, though he wasn't at all clear what futurologists were. Certainly international gangsters would be inclined to avoid the place.

'What beats me,' continued the Countess, 'is why that goon last night was looking for me and now he's shooting those poor eggheads down there. Unless it's the gendarmes doing the shooting.'

'The gendarmes?' said Glodstone. 'You mean they've had the nerve to call the police in?'

'You don't seriously imagine an international gathering of some of the world's most eminent intellectuals are going to sit on their fannies when there's a contract killer on the loose? It's a miracle we haven't got the United States Marines on call, the way that Professor Botwyk was carrying on this morning. Wanted to phone the Embassy.'

'The Embassy?'

In the darkness the Countess looked at him suspiciously. 'Do you always repeat everything anyone says to you?' she asked.

'No, but . . . Well, you wouldn't think men like that would have the nerve to ask for government protection.'

'I can't think why not.'

Glodstone could, but in the present circumstances it didn't seem advisable to say so. On the other hand he had the increasing feeling that there had been some terrible mistake and for a moment he began to wonder if they'd come to the wrong château, before remembering that this woman had claimed to be Wanderby's mother. Perhaps all this talk about international scholars and the police was subtle means of getting him to talk. 'It all seems very odd,' he muttered.

'You can say that again,' said the Countess as another shot rang out below. Peregrine had just winged Dr Abnekov who had made the mistake of urinating out of one of the windows and had learnt what it felt like to be circumcised by a revolver bullet. As his yells receded the Countess got to her feet. 'Where's your car?' she asked.

Glodstone hesitated. He still couldn't make head or tail of the woman but there was nothing to be gained from lying. 'I left it hidden in an old sawmill. I didn't want anyone to steal it.'

'Yeah, well I'd say you showed good sense,' said the Countess. 'We'll just have to chance it. This place is beginning to feel like the condemned cell and I don't fancy sitting here waiting. Help me move the bed. But quietly.'

Glodstone got to his feet and clutched the sheet to him. It was beginning to feel like a premature shroud. 'Is that wise?' he asked as another shot rang out, 'I mean it sounds like a battle out there.'

'Which is why we're moving now. So long as they're occupied we've got a chance.'

They moved the bed and the Countess unlocked the door and went out into the passage. Glodstone followed her unwillingly and stopped.

'So what's holding you?' demanded the Countess. 'Got cold feet or something?'

'It's just that I've got no clothes and . . . well . . . I wouldn't want to compromise you,' he murmured.

'Jesus, at a time like this he talks about compromising. If we don't hurry I'm going to get compromised by a bullet.'

Glodstone gave in and traipsed nervously down the steps after her. 'In here,' whispered the Countess when they reached a large open landing directly above the gateway. Opening a door she pushed him inside. 'You'll find some of my husband's clothes in

170

the bedroom. He was twice your size but you'll look better in something dark. That sheet goes with your complexion.'

Glodstone shuffled across the carpet into the next room and found some suits in a wardrobe. Whoever the woman's husband might be she hadn't been lying about his build. The brute must have stood six foot in his socks and his waistband was in the upper fifties. Still, anything was preferable to that sheet. Glodstone put on a shirt while the Countess busied herself in the other room. By the time he was dressed and could move about without tripping (he'd had to roll the bottom of the trousers up eight inches to achieve this feat) she had finished packing a suitcase.

'Right,' she said, fastening a rope ladder to a hook above the window that overlooked the drive and the avenue of walnut trees, 'exit one Countess followed by bear. You can hand the case to me when I'm out. And then we'll head for your car.'

'But I'll never make it dressed like this,' said Glodstone, 'where are my own clothes?'

'If they're back from the dry-cleaners they'll be in the the office down below but I wouldn't advise trying to get them. That way the only place you'll make is infinity. Let's hit the fire escape.'

She dropped the ladder out of the window and climbed over the sill. 'Now the case,' she said. Glodstone handed it to her. It was remarkably heavy. As she disappeared he stood irresolute. He had no doubt now that she was the Countess and to some extent he could be said to be rescuing her, but the thought of trying to walk fifteen kilometres in oversize men's wear and lugging that suitcase appalled him. And where was Peregrine? A shot from below should have told him. It certainly decided him. Glodstone climbed over the sill and slithered down the rope ladder.

In the little office Peregrine was in high spirits. This was the life, the world, the action he had read and dreamt about and had been prepared for. It was no longer imaginary. It was real and exciting, a matter of life and death and in the case of the latter he'd undoubtedly been successful. He'd certainly shot one swine stone-cold dead and had just potted another who'd appeared at a window. The only thing that puzzled him was that no one had fired back. He'd have welcomed an exchange of shots. But none had come and he was

171

trying to work out what this meant when a sound outside gave him the answer. Something had just bumped against the wall of the Château and he heard voices. So the bastards had managed to get round behind him and were preparing to attack him from the rear. Cunning. He'd soon put a stop to that.

Checking that the courtyard was still empty he crossed to the tiny window that gave onto the drive. As he watched, a figure appeared with a suitcase. They were going to blast him out with a bomb. Peregrine aimed the revolver through the window and then hesitated. It was a woman, and he hadn't been trained to shoot women. All the same, he was taking no chances. Slipping out to the gates he gently unlocked them. A man was out there too. He could hear him whisper. He'd strike now. Shoving the gate open with his foot he aimed the revolver with both hands. 'OK, freeze,' he shouted, now identifying with the heroes of every American thriller he'd read. 'Get your hands on your heads and don't move.'

But the woman had already done so. She was off down the drive running as fast as she could. For a second Peregrine was tempted but Bulldog Drummond prevailed. At least he'd got the man and he wasn't giving any trouble. He was wheezing and gasping but his hands were up.

'For God's sake don't shoot,' he whimpered. Peregrine recognized the voice.

'Gloddie,' he said, 'Is that you?'

'Of course it's me,' said Glodstone with a moan and sat down on the suitcase. 'Oh my God!'

'Are you all right?'

Glodstone felt his heart and thought not.

'So who's the frail?' asked Peregrine, reverting to Mickey Spillane.

'I am,' said Glodstone.

'I mean the woman.'

'That happened to be the Countess.'

'And we've rescued her. That's terrific.' Glodstone didn't reply. To his way of thinking the adjective was wholly inappropriate.

'Then we can go,' said Peregrine, 'or do you want me to finish the swine off?'

Glodstone tried to get up and promptly trod on the bottom of his trousers and fell over. 'I don't want you to do another thing,' he said savagely as Peregrine helped him to his feet, 'except see if my clothes are in an office in there and bring them out. And hurry. There's murder going on.'

'Oh I don't know,' said Peregrine, 'They're –'

'Well, I fucking do,' said Glodstone.

'Oh, all right,' said Peregrine sulkily. 'Just when it was getting to be fun.'

All the same he went into the office and presently returned with a brown paper parcel. 'Just one more thing to do,' he said and before Glodstone could protest that even one more thing would be too much for his heart he was gone. Glodstone flapped off down the drive with his clothes. If what he expected occurred he wanted to be behind a walnut tree when it did. For a few minutes everything was quiet and then a volley of shots rang out and Peregrine ran from the Château.

'That should keep them quite while we make our getaway,' he said. 'I've dumped that rope ladder and locked the gates.'

'And shot someone too, I suppose.'

'Nobody to shoot.'

'Well, get that bloody suitcase,' said Glodstone, hobbling along. He couldn't wait to put as much distance between himself and the Château as was humanly possible. The place had nothing romantic about it now.

In the grand salon the delegates crouched in the darkness surrounded by broken glass. Their concern for the future of mankind had assumed a personal and more interested dimension, but they were still at odds with one another. Dr Abnekov particularly objected to Sir Arnold Brymay's insistence that the only way to treat a badly wounded penis was to apply a tourniquet. 'But not around my scrotum,' shouted Abnekov.

'It stops the venom getting into the bloodstream,' said Sir Arnold, with a peculiar logic that stemmed from his experience of treating snakebite victims in the Tropics.

'Not the only thing it stops,' yelled the Russian. 'You want to castrate me or something?'

'I suppose we could try cauterizing it as well,' said Sir Arnold, getting his own back for the Soviet delegate's accusations that he was personally responsible for the atrocities committed by the British Army in Ireland.

Dr Keister intervened. 'Perhaps I may be of assistance,' she said. 'In Denmark I have had experiences with the genitals of sexual offenders and –'

'I am not a sex offender, you filthy cow. You do what you like in your rotten little country with all your pornography but if you touch me you'll learn what a sex offence is.'

'In Africa,' said Professor Manake, 'Some of the less progressive peoples still practise female circumcision. In Ghana it is naturally unknown but elsewere I have studied initiation rites among males. They are a symbolic preparation for manhood.'

'And what's that got to do with me, you bloody witch-doctor?' yelled Abnekov. 'There's nothing symbolic about my manhood. And stop twisting that piece of string, you imperialist pig.'

'Actually, it's my last pipe-cleaner,' said Sir Arnold. 'Still if you want to bleed to death I suppose you're entitled to.'

Under the table Dr Grenoy and Professor Badiglioni was arguing about the threory and origins of international terrorism. The Italian placed the blame squarely on Robespierre, Babeuf, Blanqui, Sorel and any other Frenchman he could think of, while Dr Grenoy countered with the Carbonari, the Mafia, Mussolini and Gramasci, whom he'd never read. The shooting of Botwyk had put all thought of the Countess' connection with gangsters in Las Vegas out of his mind.

Only Pastor Laudenbach and Sheikh Fahd bin Riyal, united by their faith in a spiritual future and certain unspoken prejudices, remained unmoved. 'It is the will of Allah. The Western world is decadent and the infidel Botwyk was clearly a Zionist. He refused to acknowledge that the return of Jerusalem and all Arab lands can only be achieved by force of arms. It is the same with Berlin and the occupied East Bank of your country.'

'I hadn't thought of it like that before,' said the Pastor. 'We have much to feel guilty about.'

In the darkness the Saudi delegate smiled. He was thinking wistfully of Eichmann.

*

174

Far to the north, Slymne drove down the N1 at ninety miles an hour. He wasn't wasting time on side roads and the Major's suggestions, made at frequent intervals, that they stop the night in a hotel had been ignored. 'You heard what the Head said,' he told the Major. 'This could be the ruination of us all.'

'Won't be much of me left to ruin at this rate,' said the Major and shifted his weight on the inner tube.

Chapter 20

Halfway down the drive the Countess paused in her flight. Too many days in the kitchen hadn't equipped her for long-distance running and anyway she hadn't been shot at. Nobody had chased after her either. She sat down on the wall to get her breath back and considered the situation grimly. She might have saved her life but she'd also lost her life savings. The seven little gold bars in the suitcase had been her guarantee of independence. Without them she was tied to the damned Château and the kitchen stove. Worse still, she might have to go elsewhere and struggle on satisfying the whims and lusts of men, either as someone's cook, housekeeper and general bottle-washer or, more distastefully still, as a wife. She would lose the bungalow in Bognor Regis and the chance of resuming her interrupted identity as Constance Sugg safe in the knowledge that her past was well and truly behind her. It was an appalling prospect and wasn't helped by the fact that she was fat, fair and forty-five. Not that she cared what she looked like. The three Fs had kept the fourth at bay but they wouldn't help her in a world dominated by lecherous men.

It was all the more galling that she would have escaped if it hadn't been for Glodstone's clumsiness. Another damned man had fouled things up for her, and an idiot at that. Baffled by the whole affair, she was about to move on when another thought struck her. Someone had certainly come looking for her and having found her they'd let her get away. Why? Unless they'd got what they'd wanted in her suitcase. That made much more sense. It did indeed. With a new and nasty determination the Countess climbed off the wall and turned back up the drive. She had gone twenty yards when she heard footsteps and the sound of voices. They were coming after all. She slipped into some bushes and squatted down.

'I don't care what you think,' said Glodstone, as they passed, 'if you hadn't come out with that bloody gun and yelled "Freeze" she wouldn't have run off like that.'

'But I didn't know it was the Countess,' said Peregrine, 'I thought it was one of the swine trying to get round behind me. Anyway we rescued her and that's what she wanted, isn't it?'

'Without her suitcase with all her clothes in it?'

'Feels jolly heavy for clothes. She's probably waiting for you at the bridge and we can give it back to her.'

Glodstone snorted. 'Frighten the wits out of the poor woman and you expect her to hang around waiting for me. For all she knows I'm dead.'

They passed out of earshot. In the bushes the Countess was having difficulty understanding what she had just heard. Rescue her? And that was what she wanted? What she wanted was her suitcase and the madman with the gun had said they could give it back to her? The statements resolved themselves into insane questions in her mind.

'I must be going crazy,' she muttered as she disentangled herself from the brambles and stood in the roadway trying to decide what to do. It wasn't a difficult decision. The young lout had her suitcase and whether he like it or not she wasn't letting him disappear with it. As the pair rounded the bend she took off her shoes and holding them in one hand ran down the drive after them. By the time they reached the bridge she was twenty yards behind and hidden by the stonework above the river.

'What's that over there?' asked Glodstone, peering at the wreckage of the police van and the remains of the driver's seat which had burnt itself to a wire skeleton in the middle of the bridge.

'They had some guards there,' said Peregrine, 'but I soon put paid to them.'

'Dear God,' said Glodstone, 'when you say 'put paid to' . . . No, I don't think I want to hear.' He paused and looked warily around. 'All the same, I'd like to be certain there's no one about.'

'I shouldn't think so. The last I saw of them they were all in the river.'

'Probably the last thing anyone will see of them before they reach the sea, if my experience of that bloody torrent's anything to go by.'

177

'I'll go over and check just in case,' said Peregrine. 'If it is all clear I'll whistle.'

'And if it isn't I'll hear a shot I suppose,' muttered Glodstone but Peregrine was already striding nonchalantly across the bridge carrying the suitcase. A minute later he whistled but Glodstone didn't move. He was dismally aware that someone was standing behind him.

'It's me again, honey,' said the Countess. 'You don't get rid of me quite so easily.'

'Nobody wants to get rid of you. I certainly . . .'

'Skip the explanations for later. Now you and me are going to walk across together and just in case that delinquent gunslinger starts shooting remember I'm in back of you and he's got to drill you before he gets to me.'

'But he won't shoot. I mean, why should he?'

'You tell me,' said the Countess, 'I'm no mind-reader even if you had a mind. So, let's go.'

Glodstone ambled forward. In the east the sky had begun to lighten but he had no eyes for the beauties of nature. He was in an interior landscape, one in which there was no meaning or order and everything was at variance with what he had once believed. Romance was dead and unless he was extremely careful he might join it very shortly.

'I'm going to tell him not to do anything stupid,' he said when they reached the ramp.

'It's a bit late in the day for that, baby, but you may as well try,' said the Countess.

Glodstone stopped. 'Peregrine,' he called, 'I've got the Countess with me so its all right. There's no need to be alarmed.'

Behind the wrecked police van Peregrine cocked the revolver. 'How do I know you're telling the truth?' he shouted, and promptly crawled away down the bank so that he could get a clear line of fire on the squat figure silhouetted against the sky.

'Because I say so, you gibbering idiot. What more do you want?'

'Why's she standing so close to you?' said Peregrine from a different quarter. Glodstone swung round and the Countess followed.

'Because she doesn't trust you with that gun.'

'Why did she ask us to rescue her?' asked Peregrine.

But Glodstone had reached the limits of his patience. 'Never mind that now. We can discuss that later. Just let's get off here and out of the way.'

'Oh all right,' said Peregrine who had been looking forward to bagging another victim. 'If you say so.'

He climbed up the bank and Glodstone and the Countess scurried past the shell of the police van.

'OK, so what's with this business of my wanting to be rescued?' asked the Countess, pausing to put her shoes on. 'And who's our friend with the itchy trigger finger?'

'That's Peregrine,' said Glodstone, 'Peregrine Clyde-Browne. He's a boy in my house. Actually, he's left now but –'

'I don't need his curriculum vitae. I want to know what you're doing here, is all.'

Glodstone looked uneasily up and down the road. 'Hadn't we better go somewhere more private?' he said. 'I mean the sooner we're out of the district the less chance they'll have of following us.'

It was the Countess's turn to hesitate. She wasn't at all sure she wanted to go anywhere too private with these maniacs. On the other hand there was a great deal to be said for getting the hell away from burnt-out police vehicles. She didn't fancy being questioned too closely about the little gold bars in her suitcase or what she was doing with several different passports, not to mention her son's housemaster and a schoolboy who went round shooting people. Above all she wanted to put this latest piece of her past behind her. Bognor Regis called.

'Nothing like burning your bridges,' she said. 'Lead on, Mac-Duff.' And picking up her bag she followed Glodstone across the road and up the hillside. Behind them Peregrine had taken her words to heart and by the time they reached the ridge and paused for breath, smoke had begun to gather in the valley and there came the crackle of burning woodwork.

'That should keep them quiet for a bit,' he said as he joined them. Glodstone stared back with a fresh sense of despair. He knew what he was going to see. The Château looked deserted but the wooden bridge was ablaze.

'Quiet? Quiet? every bloody fire-engine and policeman from here to Boosat is going to be down there in twenty minutes and we've still to break camp. The idea was to get back to the car before the hunt was up.'

'Yes, but she said –'

'Shut up and get moving,' snapped Glodstone and stumbled into the wood to change into his own clothes.

'I'll say this for you, boy,' said the Countess, 'when you do something you do it thoroughly. Still, he's right, you know. As the man said, the excreta is about to hit the fan.' She looked round the little camp. 'And if the snout-hounds get a whiff of this lot they be baying at our heels in no time.'

'Snout-hounds?' said Peregrine.

'Tracker dogs. The ones with noses the cops use. If you'll take my advice, you'll ditch every item back in the river.'

'Roger,' said Peregrine, and when Glodstone finally emerged from the undergrowth looking his dejected self it was to find Peregrine gone and the Countess sitting on her bag.

'He's just destroying the evidence,' she said, 'in the river. So now you can tell me what this caper is all about.'

Glodstone looked round the empty dell. 'But you must know,' he said. 'You wrote to me asking me to come down and rescue you.'

'I did? Well, for your information, I . . .' She stopped. If this madman though she'd written asking to be rescued, and it was quite obvious from his manner that he did, she wasn't going to argue the toss with him in the present fraught circumstances. 'Oh well, I guess this isn't the time for discussion. And we ought to do something with Alphonse's suit. It reeks of mothballs.'

Glodstone looked down at the clothes he was holding. 'Can't we just leave them?'

'I've just explained to young Lochinvar that if the police bring dogs they're going to track us down in no time.'

But it was Peregrine who came up with the solution when he returned from the river. 'You go on ahead and I'll lay a trail with them that'll lead in the wrong direction,' he said, 'I'll catch you up before you get to the sawmill.' And taking the suit from Glodstone he scrambled down to the road. Glodstone and the Countess trudged off and two hours later were on the plateau. They were too preoccupied with their own confused thoughts to talk. The sun was up now and they were sweating but for once Glodstone had no intention of stopping for a rest. The nightmare he had been through still haunted him, was still with him in the shape of the woman who quite evidently didn't know she had written to him for help. Even more evidently she didn't need helping and if anyone could be said to have been rescued Glodstone had to admit she'd saved him. Finally, as they reached the woods on the far side of the Causse de Boosat, he glanced back. A smudge of smoke drifted in the cloudless sky and for a moment he thought he caught the faint sounds of sirens. Then they were fighting their way through the scrub and trees and after another half an hour stumbled across the overgrown track to the sawmill.

The same atmosphere of loneliness and long disuse hung over the rusting machinery and the derelict buildings, but they no longer evoked a feeling of excitement and anticipation in Glodstone. Instead the place looked sinister and grim, infected with death and undiscovered crimes. Not that Glodstone had time to analyse his feelings. They rose within him automatically as he made his way across to the shed and thanked God the Bentley was still there. While he opened the doors the Countess dropped her suitcase and sat down on it. She had ignored the pain in her right arm and her sore feet, and she tried to ignore them now. At least they had a car, but what a car! Yeah, well, it fitted. A vintage Bentley. You couldn't beat that for easy identification. A one-eyed man in a Bentley. Even if they didn't have road-blocks up the cops would still stop them just to have a look at it. On the other hand, vintage car owners didn't usually go around knocking off Professors. And there was no going back now. She'd just have to say she'd been kidnapped and hope for the best.

In the shed, Glodstone replaced the plugs and started the car. He had just driven it out when Peregrine appeared, panting and dripping with sweat. 'Sorry I'm late,' he said, 'but I had to make sure they wouldn't come this way. Went down-river a couple of miles and found an old man who'd been fishing so I stuffed those clothes in the bag of his moped and waited until he rode off. That'll keep them busy for a couple of hours. Then I had to swim about a bit before doubling back. Didn't want to leave my own trail.'

'Go and shift those trees,' said Glodstone, getting out and shutting the shed doors. The countess climbed into the back seat and five minutes later they were on the road. On the wrong side.

'Drive on the right for Chrissake,' squawked the Countess. 'We aren't in England and at this rate we won't be. And where do you think you're going?'

'Back to Calais,' said Glodstone.

'So why are we on the road to Spain?'

'I just thought . . .' said Glodstone, who was too exhausted to.

'From now on, don't,' said the Countess. 'Leave the brainwork to me. Spain might not be such a bad idea, but the frontier's the first one they'll watch.'

'Why's that?' asked Peregrine.

'Because, dumkopf, it's the closest. So Calais makes a weird sort of sense. Only trouble is, can Old Father Time here last out that far without writing us all off?'

'Of course I can,' said Glodstone, stung into wakefulness by the insult.

'Then turn left at the next fork. And give me that map.'

For a few miles she pored over it while Glodstone concentrated on keeping to the right. 'Now then,' said the Countess, when they had swung onto a road that led through thick oak woods, 'the next question is, did anyone round here see this car when you came down?'

'I shouldn't have thought so. We did the last two hundred miles at night and we were on roads to the South.'

'Good. That's a bonus. So the car's not what they're going to be looking for. It's clean and it's too conspicuous to be likely for a getaway. But if they do stop us those guns are going to put you inside for a long, long time. So you'll ditch them, and not in any river. The *flics* have a penchant for looking under bridges.'

'What's a penchant?' asked Peregrine.

'What those gendarmes didn't have when you blew that van up. Now shut up,' said Glodstone.

'Yes, but if we get rid of the guns we won't have anything to defend ourselves with and anyway they're supposed to go back in the School Armoury.'

Glodstone's knuckles whitened on the steering wheel. 'Listen, you damned moron,' he snarled, 'hasn't it got through your thick

182

skull yet that we aren't going to get back to the school unless we use our wits? We'll be doing life plus thirty years in some foul French jail for murder.'

'Murder?' said Peregrine, clearly puzzled. 'But we only killed some swine and –'

'And however many gendarmes you blew out of that truck. That's all! So keep your murderous little trap shut and do what the Countess tells you.'

In the back seat the Countess listened to the exchange with interest. It was beginning to dawn on her that, by comparison with Peregrine, Glodstone was practically a genius. More to the point, he was frightened and prepared to follow her orders. 'Stop the car here,' she said to test her authority, 'and switch the motor off.'

Glodstone did so and looked at her questioningly.

'This is a good a spot as any,' she said after they had sat in silence for a minute listening. 'Now then, you, trot off into the wood a couple of hundred metres and bury those gats before anyone comes.'

Peregrine looked at Glodstone. 'Must I?' he asked. But the look on Glodstone's face was enough.

'Not a very advanced form of life,' said the Countess when he'd gone. Glodstone didn't reply. From the depths of his exhausted mind the question had surfaced again. How had he ever come to be in the power of this foul woman? He wasn't going to put it to her now but if they ever got back to Britain he'd want an answer.

'One dead, another mutilated and how many missing?' asked Inspector Roudhon.

'Two,' said Dr Grenoy looking unhappily out of the window at the little helicopter perched on the terrace. 'Madame la Comtesse and an Englishman called Pringle.'

'An Englishman called Pringle? Description.'

'Middle-aged. Medium height. Balding. Small moustache. A typical Englishman of a certain class.'

'And he was staying here?'

'Not exactly. He rescued the dead American from the river yesterday morning and he was exhausted so he was given a room and a bed.'

'If he rescued the man who was shot he doesn't sound like a killer,' said the Inspector.

'Of course he wasn't a killer. Ask your own men. They had to get him back across the river with Professor Botwyk. He was on a walking tour.'

'And yet he has disappeared?'

'In the circumstances very sensibly, Inspector,' said Dr Grenoy. 'If you had been here last night you'd have tried to leave.' He was getting irritated by the Inspector's failure to appreciate the international consequences of the night's events. The Glory of France was at stake, not to mention his own career.

'And the night before a man was here looking for Madame la Comtesse,' continued the Inspector.

'That's what I've been told. But it must be said that he made the first attempt on Professor Botwyk then. Last night the Professor was shot down in cold blood, capote-wise. And your men were supposed to be on guard for his protection.'

'So they were, but they weren't to know they were about to be attacked by terrorists. You said it was Madame la Comtesse who was in danger.'

'Naturally. What else does one think when an Englishman with a gun . . . or an American, demands to know where she is? It was your responsibility.'

'If we had been told they were terrorists it would have helped, monsieur. We can only act on the information we are given. And the roads were guarded. They didn't come from Boosat or Frisson.'

'And what about the river? They could have slipped past your road blocks in canoes.'

'Perhaps. It was clearly a well organized operation. The aim was to assassinate the American, Botwyk, and . . .'

'Castrate the Soviet delegate. Presumably to put the Siberian gas pipe-line agreement in jeopardy,' said Dr Grenoy. His sarcasm was wasted on the Inspector.

'But it is the Americans who oppose the deal. It is more likely the Iranians who are involved.'

In the dining-room the exhausted delegates were being interrogated. They too were convinced they had been the victims of a terrorist attack.

'The crisis of capitalism expresses itself in these barbaric acts,' Dr Zukacs explained to a bemused gendarme. 'They are symptomatic of the degenerate bourgeois mentality and the alliance between monopoly fascism and sectors of the lumpen proletariat. Until a new consciousness is born . . .'

'And how many shots were fired?' asked the policeman, trying to get back to the facts.

Dr Zukacs didn't know.

'Fifteen,' said Pastor Laudenbach with the precision of a military expert. 'Medium-calibre pistol. Rate of fire, good. Extreme accuracy.'

The cop wrote this down. He'd been told to treat these members of the intelligentsia softly. They'd be in a state of shock. Pastor Laudenbach obviously wasn't.

'Your name, monsieur?'

The Pastor clicked his heels. 'Obergruppen . . . er . . . Pastor Laudenbach. I belong to the Lutheran Church.'

The policeman made a note of the fact. 'Did anyone see the assailant?'

Dr Hildegard Keister pushed Badiglioni forward. 'You met him in the passage,' she said.

The Professor cursed her under his breath. 'That was the night before. It may not have been the same man.'

'But you said he had a gun. You know you did. And when you –'

'Yes,' said Badiglioni, to cut short the disclosure that he had taken refuge in her room, 'he was a young Englishman.'

'An Englishman? Can you describe him?'

Professor Badiglioni couldn't. 'It was dark.'

'Then how did you know he was a young Englishman?'

'By his accent. It was unmistakably English. I have made a study of the inter-relationship between phonetics and the socio-economic infrastructure in post-Imperial Britain and I would say categorically that the man you are looking for is of lower-upper-middle-class extraction with extreme right-wing Protestant inclinations.'

'Sod that for a lark,' said Sir Arnold. Ulster was going to be on the agenda again at this rate. 'You were into Dr Keister's room before he had a chance to speak to you. You told me that yourself.'

'I heard what he said to Dr Abnekov. That was enough.'

'And where did you pick up your astounding capacity for analysing the English language? As an Eyetie POW, no doubt.'

'As a matter of fact I was an interpreter for British prisoners of war in Italy,' said Professor Badiglioni stiffly.

'I'll put him down as English,' said the policeman.

Sir Arnold objected. 'Certainly not. I had a fairly lengthy discussion with the fellow and in my opinion he had a distinctly foreign accent.'

'English is a foreign language in France, monsieur.'

'Yes, well I daresay it is,' said Sir Arnold, getting flustered. 'What I meant was his accent was European-foreign if you see what I mean.'

The cop didn't. 'But he did speak in English?'

Sir Arnold admitted grudgingly that this had been the case. 'Doesn't mean he's British though. Probably a deliberate ploy to disguise his real nationality.'

Another helicopter clattered down onto the terrace and prevented any further questioning for the time being.

In Bordeaux Dr Abnekov was undergoing micro-surgery without a general anaesthetic. He wanted to make sure he kept what was left of his penis.

Chapter 21

'Shit, that's torn it,' said Major Fetherington as they ground to a halt at a road block beyond Boosat. Three gendarmes carrying sub-machine-guns circled the car while a fourth aimed a pistol at Slymne and demanded their passports. As the man flicked through the pages, Slymne stared in front of him. He had been staring at the road ahead for hundreds of miles while the Major had dozed beside him and it had all been in vain. Obviously something catastrophic had happened. Even the French police didn't man road-blocks and keep the occupants of cars covered with machine-guns without good cause, but Slymne was almost too tired to care. They'd have to send a cable back to the Headmaster and then find a hotel and he could get some sleep. That would be some consolation. What happened after that didn't matter now. He wasn't even worried about the letters. If Glodstone had kept them, nobody could prove he'd sent them. And in a sense he was relieved. It was all over.

It wasn't. He was woken from this rhapsody of exhaustion by the car doors being opened and with the guns aimed at them they were ordered out.

'Can't,' said the Major adamantly, 'Ce n'est pas possible. Ma bloody derrière est blessé et je m'assis sur une tube de pneu.' But in spite of his protests he was dragged out and made to stand against a wall

'Bloody disgraceful,' he muttered, as they were frisked, 'I'd like to see a British bobby try this sort of thing with me. Ouch!'

'Silence,' said the sergeant. They were prodded apart while the car was searched and their luggage was laid out on the road. It included the inner-tube and a bottle the Major had used to save himself the agony of getting out for a pee. After five minutes two police cars drew up on the far side of the barrier and several men in plain clothes moved towards them.

'Seem to be taking an interest in our passports,' said the Major and was promptly told to keep his trap shut. Slymne stared over the wall at a row of poplars by the river and tried to keep his eyes open. It was hot in the sun and butterflies soared and dropped about the meadow in the still air, alighting for no apparent reason on a small flower when there was a larger one only a foot away. Slymne took comfort in their random choice. Chance is all, he thought, and I am not responsible for what has happened. Say nothing and they can do nothing.

To the little group of policemen studying his passport, things looked rather different. The ferry ticket was in it. 'Entered France yesterday and they're here already?' said Commissaire Ficard, 'They must have driven all night without stopping.'

He looked significantly at the Major's bottle and its murky contents. 'Occupation, schoolmaster. Could be a cover. Anything suspicious in their luggage?'

Two plain-clothes cops emptied the suitcases onto the road and went through their contents.

'Nothing.'

'And what's the inner-tube doing there?'

'The other man was sitting on it, Monsieur le Commissaire. Claims to have a wounded backside.'

The mention of wounds decided Commissaire Ficard. 'Take them in for questioning,' he said, 'And I want that car stripped. Nobody drives here from Calais that fast without good reason. They must have exceeded the speed limit in any case. And check with the ferries. I'm interested in these two.'

As the Major was hustled into the van he made things worse. 'Keep your filthy paws off me, you oaf,' he snapped and found himself lying on the floor. Slymne went quietly. Being arrested had come as a relief to his conscience.

Outside Poitiers the Countess put the boot in. 'So we need gas. Now if you want to pull in at the next station with a description of a glass-eyed man circulating that's your problem. I don't want any part of it. You can drop me off here and I'll walk.'

'What do you suggest?' asked Glodstone. He had long since given up trying to think for himself.

'That you drive up the next quiet road and you and Al Capone Junior take a break and I drive on and have her filled up.'

'A car like this isn't easy to drive, you know. You have to have had experience of non-synchromesh gears and . . .'

'You double-declutch. I'll practise.'

'I suppose it might be a good idea,' Glodstone admitted, and turned onto a side road. For ten minutes the Countess drove while Peregrine sat in the back and Glodstone prayed she wouldn't strip the gears.

'OK?' she asked finally.

Glodstone nodded but Peregrine still had reservations. 'How do we know you'll come back? I mean you could just drive off and . . .'

'Leave a clever boy like you for the cops to pick up? I've got more sense. Besides, I wanted to be rescued and that's what you're doing. But if it'll make you any happier I'll leave my passport with you.'

She got out and, rifling in her suitcase, found the right one. 'I'll buy some food while I'm about it,' she said. 'Now you just take it easy in the field. Have a nap and if I'm not back inside two hours, call the cops.'

'What did she mean by that?' asked Peregrine as she drove away. Glodstone heaved himself over a gate into a field.

'She was joking,' he said hopefully and lay down in the grass.

'I still think –' said Peregrine.

'Shut up!'

Three miles further on the Countess pulled off the road again and spent some time stuffing the gold bars down behind the back seat. Then she changed into a summer frock and put on sunglasses. All the time her mind was busy considering possibilities. They could still be nabbed but, having come so far without being stopped, it seemed unlikely an alert was out for two men and a woman in a vintage Bentley. To be on the safe side, she took two of the little bars out and, making sure no one was in sight, hid them in the hedge behind a telephone pole.

An hour later she was back. The tank was full, she'd bought all the food they'd need, plus some very black coffee in a thermos, and a trowel. With this she dug a hole beside the hedge and buried the two gold bars. If the Customs found the others she wanted something to fall back on; if not she could always pick them up later. But best of all, as she drove on to where Glodstone was asleep and Peregrine still suspicious, two motor-cycle cops passed without more than a glance at her.

'Back on the trail, boys,' she said, 'We've nothing to worry about. The *flics* aren't looking for us. I've just seen two. No problems.' She poured Glodstone a mug of coffee laced with sugar. 'Keep a sloth awake for a week it's so strong, and you can eat as we go.'

'I'm not going to be able to make Calais all the same,' said Glodstone, 'not today.'

'We're heading for Cherbourg and you will.'

By midnight they were in the car-park outside the Ferry Terminal and Glodstone was asleep at the wheel. The Countess shook him awake. 'Galahad and I will cross as foot-passengers tonight,' she said, 'you come over the first boat in the morning. Right?' Glodstone nodded.

'We'll be waiting for you,' she went on, and got out with Peregrine and crossed to the booking-office. But it was another two hours before she passed through Customs and Immigration on an American passport in which she was named as Mrs Natalie Wallcott. Ahead of her, a youth called William Barnes settled himself in the cafeteria and ordered a Coke. He too was asleep when they sailed. The Countess bought a bottle of Scotch at the Duty-Free shop and went up on deck with the plastic bag and leant over the rail with it. When she came down again the bag and the bottle and any documents that might have suggested she had been the Countess de Montcon or Anita Blanche Wanderby were sinking with the Scotch towards the bottom of the Channel. By tomorrow she would be Constance Sugg once more. By today. She must be getting tired.

Slymne wasn't. He had passed through the exhaustion barrier into a new dimension of light-headedness in which he wasn't sure if he was asleep or awake. Certainly the questions being put to him by the two detectives who sat opposite him suggested the former. They were put quite nicely, but the questions themselves were horrible. The contrast made him feel even more unreal. 'I am not a member of any subversive organization, and anyway the British Secret Service isn't subversive,' he said.

'Then you admit you belong to a branch of it?'

'No,' said Slymne.

The two men gave him another cup of coffee, and consulted a file on the table. 'Monsieur Slymne, on 12 April you arrived in France and on the 22nd you left again. On the 27th you came once more and departed 3rd August. The night before last you returned and drove 900 kilometres without resting. It will help if you explain.'

Slymne tended to agree but a seemingly distant portion of his mind took over. 'I teach geography and I like France. Naturally I come frequently on visits.'

'Which is presumably why you speak our language so fluently,' said Inspector Roudhon with a smile.

'That's different. I'm not very good at languages.'

'But an incredible student of geography to investigate the country for 900 kilometres without stopping. And at night too. Unless . . .' He paused and lit a cigarette. The room stank of stale tobacco. 'Unless, Monsieur Slymne, and I merely hypothesize, you understand, you were already in France and someone provided you with an alibi by booking a crossing to Calais in your name.'

'An alibi? What would they do that for?' said Slymne, trying to keep his eyes in focus. The situation was getting madder every moment.

'That is for you to tell us. You know what you have been here for. What mission you and Major Fetherington are on.'

'Can't,' said Slymne, 'because we aren't on one. Ask the Major.'

'We have. And he has had the good sense to tell us.'

'Tell you? What's he told you?' Slymne was wide awake now.

'You really want to know?'

Slymne did, desperately. The detective left the room and returned with a signed statement a few minutes later.

'Major Fetherington admits to being a member of the Special Air Services. He was parachuted into the forest near Brive from a light aircraft . . .'

'From a light aircraft?' said Slymne in the grip of galloping insanity.

'Yes, monsieur, as you well know. He has even named the type and the airfield from which he flew. It was a Gloster Gladiator and left from Bagshot at 0400 hours Tuesday morning –'

'But . . . but they haven't made Gladiators since God knows

when,' said Slymne. What on earth was the Major up to? And there couldn't be an airfield near Bagshot. The man must have gone off his rocker.

'On landing he hurt his back but buried his parachute and made his way to the road above Colonges where you picked him up,' continued the detective. 'You were to give him his orders . . .'

'His orders?' squawked Slymne. 'What orders, for Lord's sake?'

The detective smiled. 'That is for you to tell us, monsieur.'

Slymne looked desperately round the room. Major Fetherington had landed him up to his eyeballs in it now. Talk about passing the buck. 'I don't know what you're on about,' he muttered. 'I haven't been anywhere near Brive and . . .' He gave up.

'If you will take my advice, Monsieur Slymne,' said the Inspector, 'you will tell us now what you know. It will save you from meeting certain gentlemen from Paris. They are not of the police, you understand, and they use different methods. I haven't met such men myself and I hope I never have dealings with them. I believe they are not very nice.'

Slymne cracked. But when, an hour later, he signed the statement and the Inspector left the room, he was still denied the sleep he so desperately wanted. Commissaire Ficard wasn't having it.

'Does the clown think we're mentally deficient?' he shouted. 'We have the assassination of one of America's top political theorists and the mutilation of a Soviet delegate and he asks us to believe that some English schoolmaster is responsible? And the other one has already admitted being SAS. Oh, no, I am not satisfied. The Minister is not satisfied. The American Ambassador is demanding immediate action and the Russian too and we have this buffoon telling us . . .' The phone rang. 'No, I will say nothing more to the Press. And I'd like to know who leaked the story yesterday. The media is crawling all over the ground in helicopters. What do you mean they can't crawl in 'copters? They land in them and then . . .' He slammed the phone down and lumbered to his feet. 'Just let me lay my hands on this English turd. I'll squeeze the truth out of him if it has to come out of his arsehole.'

'Monsieur le Commissaire, we have already told him some special agents are coming from Paris,' said the Inspector.

'They needn't bother. By the time I'm through with him there'll be nothing left for them to play with.'

Major Fetherington lay on his stomach with his head turned sideways and contemplated the wall uncertainly. Like everyone else in the Boosat gendarmerie, he hadn't the foggiest notion what had really happened at the Château Carmagnac but for the moment he'd spared himself the ordeal Slymne was quite clearly going through. To the Major it sounded like an advanced form of hell and he thanked God he'd given the sods what they'd wanted – a load of codswallop. And in another way it was satisfying. Old Gloddie must have done something pretty gruesome to have warranted road-blocks, helicopters and accusations that he and Slymne were agents of the Secret Service, and good luck to him. The Major had never had much time for the French and Gloddie had given it to them where it hurt and got away with it. And he wasn't sneaking on the old ass to a lot of Frog cops who were doing whatever they were doing (the Major preferred not to think about it) to Slymne. Reaching over the side of the bed he found his socks and tried to block his ears with them and had partially succeeded when Slymne stopped yelling and the cell door opened.

'What about my clothes?' asked the Major with a quaver as they dragged him to his feet. Commissaire Roudhon studied his stained Y-fronts with disgust.

'You're not going to need any where you're going,' he said softly. 'You may require shoes though. Give him a blanket.'

'What's happening?' said the Major, now thoroughly frightened.

'You're taking us to the spot where you buried that parachute.'

'Oh, my God,' whimpered the Major. He could see now he'd made a terrible mistake.

Chapter 22

The Countess sat in the coffee-lounge in Weymouth waiting for the Bentley to come through Customs. She had sent Peregrine along to the statue of George III and would have made herself scarce too if it hadn't been for the gold bars. She had bought the *Daily Telegraph* and had learnt that the assassination of Professor Botwyk was already causing an international furore. Like Slymne, she knew the efficiency of the French police and she was lumbered with two halfwits. Without her to think for them they'd end up in the hands of Scotland Yard and with the American government now involved the FBI would backtrack her to California and through her various aliases to her arrival in the States and Miss Surrey and finally to Selsdon Road and Constance Sugg. She could see how easily it would be done. Anthony at Groxbourne, the missing revolvers — she'd made a terrible mistake there — Glodstone's account of her 'letters' and Peregrine's pride in being such a good shot . . . Worst of all, whoever had set her up had done a spectacular job.

Once again she cursed men. All her life she had had to fight to maintain her independence and now just when she had it all made to be her quiet surburban self she was being forced to think ruthlessly. And think she did. By the time the Bentley nosed off the ferry, she had made up her mind. She got up and walked down the road where Glodstone could see her and waited for him. 'No problems with Customs?' she enquired as she climbed in behind him.

'No,' said Glodstone glumly. 'Where's Peregrine?'

'By the statue. He can wait. You and me is going to have a quiet talk.'

'What about?'

'This,' said the Countess and put the newspaper on his lap.

'What's it say?' said Glodstone, almost killing a pedestrian on a zebra crossing in his anxiety to get away.

194

'Nothing much. Just that the French government have assured the State Department that the killers of Professor Botwyk will be caught and brought to justice. The Russians appear to be taking a dim view too. Apparently your boyfriend shot their delegate as well, which must confuse the issue more than somewhat.'

'Oh my God,' said Glodstone and turned down a side street and stopped. 'What on earth possessed you to write those bloody letters?'

'Keep moving. I'll tell you when to stop.'

'Yes, but . . .'

'No buts. You do what I say or I'm cutting loose and calling the first cop I spot and you and Master C-B will be facing an extradition order inside a week. Turn right here. There's a parking lot round the corner.'

Glodstone pulled in and switched off and looked at her haggardly.

'Firstly I didn't write those letters,' said the Countess, 'and I want to see them. Where did you stash them?'

'Stash them? I didn't. You told me to burn them and that's what I did.'

The Countess breathed a sigh of relief. But she wasn't showing it. 'So you've no proof they ever existed?'

Glodstone shook his head. He was almost too tired and frightened to speak.

'Well, get this straight. You can think what you like but if you seriously imagine I needed rescuing you've got to be insane. Right now, you're the one in need of a rescue operation and with what you've got between the ears that's not going to be easy. Every cop in Europe is going to be hot on your trail before the day is out.'

Glodstone dragged his mind out of its stupor. 'But no one knows we were at the Château and . . .'

'Whoever wrote those letters does, doesn't he just. You've been set up, and a little anonymous call to the police is all it's going to take to have you in the net. You haven't a plastic bag's hope in hell of getting away. One glass eye, this old banger and a youth with an IQ of fifty. You were made for identification and if you ask me that's why you were chosen.'

Glodstone gazed at a bowling green and saw only policemen,

court rooms, lawyers and judges and the rest of his life in a French prison. 'What do you suggest we do?' he asked.

'*You* do. Count me out. I don't mind thinking for you but that's as far as it goes. First off, I'd say your best bet is to do a Lord Lucan but I don't suppose you've got the money or the friends. And anyway that still leaves that juvenile mobster on the loose. What's his background?' Glodstone told her.

'Then one eminent solicitor is in for a very nasty shock,' said the Countess when he'd finished, 'though from what I've seen of his offspring I'd say he'd been cuckolded or his wife had a craving for lumps of lead when she was pregnant. Doesn't make your situation any cosier. Mr Clyde-Browne's going to have his son plead insanity and hurl the book at you.'

'What on earth can I do then?' whimpered Glodstone.

The Countess hesitated. If she suggested going to the police he might just do it and she wasn't having that. 'Isn't there any place you can hang out for a few days and nobody ever comes?'

Glodstone tried to concentrate. 'I've got a cousin near Malvern,' he said, 'She may be away and anyway she'd put us up.'

'Until the police came. Think, for Chrissake. Think where you wouldn't go.'

'Margate,' said Glodstone suddenly, 'I wouldn't be seen dead there.'

'Then that's where you'll go,' said the Countess, with the private thought that he probably would be seen dead there. 'And buy a pair of dark glasses and shave your moustache. And if I were you I'd sell treasure here to the first dealer you can find.'

'Sell the Bentley?' said Glodstone. It was the final straw, 'I couldn't do that.'

'In that case, stew in a French hoosegow for the rest of your natural. You don't seem to know what your prospects are. Well, I'm telling you. They're zero minus forty. Permafrost all the way to the Judgement Day. Amen.'

'Oh God. Oh God! How did this ever happen? It's too horrible to be real.'

For a moment the Countess felt a twinge of pity for him. The world was full of people like Glodstone who played at life and only discovered reality when it kicked them in the face. 'Roast lamb and abattoirs,' she said inconsequentially and was surprised when he picked up the message.

'Or to the slaughter.' He paused and looked at her. 'What are you going to do?'

'Think about it. You go and fetch Butch Cassidy. On foot. If I'm not here when you get back stay at the Marine Hotel in Margate and register as Mr Cassidy. I'll call you there.'

'Is there a Marine Hotel in Margate?'

'If there isn't, choose one with two AA stars and I'll call them all.'

Glodstone trudged disconsolately from the car park and found Peregrine eating an ice-cream and studying some girls in bikinis with an almost healthy interest. When they returned to the car the Countess had vanished. She was sitting in the bus station waiting for one that would take her to Bournemouth and from there she'd catch a train to London.

'I don't trust that woman,' said Peregrine grimly.

'You'd better,' said Glodstone. 'She's all that stands between us and the reintroduction of the guillotine.'

'I tell you the whole thing was a joke,' said the Major, 'I did not drop by parachute so I don't know where it's buried.' He was standing by the roadside surrounded by armed gendarmes. Nobody else thought it was a joke.

'Monsieur chooses to play games with us,' said the Commissaire. 'Ah well, we too can play games. Back to the station.'

'Now hang on,' said the Major, 'I don't know what Glodstone's done but . . .'

'Glodstone? Who is this Glodstone?'

'Hasn't Slymne told you? I thought . . .'

'What did you think? No, I want to hear from you what this man Glodstone is.'

Major Fetherington told him. He wasn't going through Slymne's experience before he cracked and obviously Glodstone had asked for it.

'It fits the description of the one who called himself Pringle,' said the Inspector when he had finished, 'but he rescued Botwyk. Why should he then shoot him?'

'Who knows why the English do things? Only the good God

knows that. In the meantime, put out a full alert for him. All airports, frontier posts, everywhere.'

'Do we ask Scotland Yard?'

Commissaire Roudhon hesitated. 'I'll have to check with Paris first. And I want these two grilled for every bit of information they've got. They must have known more about the operation than they've admitted so far or they wouldn't be down here.'

He drove off in a hurry and the Major was shoved into the back of a van and taken back to Boosat. For the rest of the day he sat answering questions and at the end of it no one was any the wiser. Inspector Ficard made his report to an incredulous Commissaire.

'An adventure? The Countess wrote to him asking to be rescued? He came down in an ancient Bentley? And they come looking for a boy called Peregrine Clyde-Browne because his father wanted him back? What sort of madness is this?'

'It's what the other one, Slymne, told us.'

'So they had a ready-made story. We have a major political assassination to deal with and you expect me to believe it was carried out by an English schoolteacher who . . .' He was interrupted by the telephone. When he put it down Commissaire Roudhon no longer knew what to think.

'A man answering that description and driving a Bentley crossed from Cherbourg this morning. Ticket made out in the name of Glodstone. I'll inform Paris. They can decide how to play it from now on. I am a policeman, not a bloody politician.'

'What shall we do with these two?'

'Put them in a cell together and tape every single word they say. Better still, install a video camera. If they pass messages I want to know. In any case, it's the sort of thing that'll impress the Americans. They're flying ten anti-terrorist specialists in from Frankfurt, and they're going to need some convincing.'

Slymne was still gibbering when they came for him. He was too feeble to resist and what he said made even less sense than before but they carried him down the passage and put him in a larger cell.

'God Almighty,' said the Major when he was led in too. 'You poor sod. What did the buggers do to you, use electrodes on your bollocks or something?'

'Don't touch me,' squealed Slymne squinting at him.

'I don't intend to, old boy. Count me out. All I do know is that Glodstone's got something coming to him.'

In his hotel room in Margate, Glodstone looked at himself in the mirror. Without his moustache and wearing dark glasses he did look different. He also looked a great deal older. Not that that would help matters in the slightest if they caught him. He'd be over eighty by the time he was released – if they ever bothered to let people out who had been partly responsible for assassinating American political advisers. He rather doubted it. He was also extremely dubious about having followed the Countess's advice but he'd been too exhausted and numb with terror the day before to be able to think for himself. And Peregrine had been no help. He'd made matters worse by wanting to lie low in a hole in a hedge like the man in *Rogue Male*.

'Nobody would think of looking there,' he'd said, 'and when it's all blown over . . .'

'It isn't going to blow over, damn you,' said Glodstone, 'and anyway we'd come out stinking like a couple of ferrets with BO.'

'Not if we found somewhere near a stream and bought some soap. We could stock up with tins of food and dig a really deep burrow and no one would ever know.'

'Except every farmer in the district. Anyway, cub-hunting's coming up shortly and I'm not going to be chased across country by a pack of hounds or earthed up. Use your loaf.'

'I still don't think we should do what that woman said. She could have been lying.'

'And I suppose you think the *Daily Telegraph's* lying too,' said Glodstone. 'She told us it was an international gathering and she was bloody well right.'

'Then why did she write you those letters? She asked us to –'

'She didn't. Can't you see that? They were forgeries and we've been framed. And so's she.'

'I can't see why. I mean . . .'

'Because if we're caught and we say she wrote those letters she can't prove she didn't.'

'But you burnt them.'

Glodstone sighed, and wished to hell he hadn't. 'She didn't know that. That's how I knew she was telling the truth. She hadn't a clue about the damned things. And if she'd been going to do us down she'd have gone to the police when she went off to get petrol. Surely that told you something?'

'I suppose so,' said Peregrine, only to bring up the question of the revolvers. 'The Major's going to be jolly angry when he finds they're missing from the armoury,' he said.

Glodstone stifled the retort that what Major Fetherington felt was the least of their problems. If the damned man hadn't trained Peregrine to be such an efficient killer they might not have been in this terrible mess. And mess was putting it mildly. Their finger-prints were all over the Château, the French police must be looking for an Englishman with a glass eye, and even if they'd had the revolvers to put back the forensic experts could easily match them with the bullet that had killed Professor Botwyk. Finally, what made it insane to imagine they could resume their old lives or pretend they'd never been to France was what the Countess had said; whoever had set them up would undoubtedly drop the word to the police. After all, it would pay the bastard to. He hadn't killed anyone and they had, and it would get him off the hook. And only the Countess could save their necks – if she chose.

So Glodstone had driven to London, had changed his travellers' cheques and, leaving the Bentley with a reputable dealer in vintage cars with orders to sell as soon as he received the registration and licence papers, had caught the train to Margate. Peregrine had travelled in a separate carriage and he'd found himself a room in a guest-house. Glodstone spent half an hour changing and shaving in a public lavatory and had booked into the first Two-Star hotel to have a spare room. He hadn't been out since. Instead, he had hung about the bar, had watched the news on TV and had read the latest report in the papers of the terrorist attack in France. But for the most part he had stayed in his room in an abyss of self-pity and terror. Life couldn't be like this. He wasn't a criminal; he'd always detested murderers and terrorists; the police were always right and they should never have stopped hanging. All that was changed and he was particularly grateful that capital punishment had been abolished in France. He'd lost faith in the police too. It had been all very well to talk about going outside the law but now that he was there he knew no self-respecting policeman who would believe his story and if he did it would make not the slightest difference. And being inside meant just that. Whatever some damn fool poet had said about stone walls and iron bars, Glodstone knew better. They made prisons, and French ones at that. He'd never have a chance to urge his House on at rugger or knock a ball about in the nets again and the train-set in the basement . . . He'd be known as Glodstone the Murderer and go down in the school infamy as Groxbourne's equivalent of Dr Crippen. And how Slymne would gloat . . . He was just plumbing this new hell when the phone rang beside his bed.

Glodstone picked it up and listened to a now familiar voice.

'My, my, brother John, it's just taken me for ages to reach you.'

'Yes, well, the thing was . . .' Glodstone began before the Countess cut him short. She was thinking about girls on switchboards.

'I'm down by the pier so meet me there in five minutes and we'll have ourselves some lunch. Alone.'

'Yes,' said Glodstone. The phone went dead. With as much nonchalance as he could muster, he walked downstairs and out into the sunshine. The promenade was crowded with the sort of people he would normally have avoided at all costs, but today he was grateful for their presence. The Countess had known what she was doing when she had picked on Margate. All the same, he approached the pier cautiously, horribly conscious that he might be walking into a trap.

But the Countess was sitting on a bench and rose as he came up. 'Darling,' she said to his surprise, and put her arm through his. 'Gee, it's just marvellous to see you again.'

She dragged him across the road and down a side street to a car. 'Where's Peregrine?' she asked as they got in.

'In the amusement park probably, shooting things,' said Glodstone. 'It's called Dreamland.'

'Appropriately,' said the Countess. 'Right, so that's where he stays temporarily while I debrief you.'

'Debrief me?' said Glodstone, uncertain after that 'Darling' how to interpret the word.

'Like with astronauts, and guys that have been taken prisoner.

201

Somewhere along the line there's got to be a connection.'

'Between what?' said Glodstone more confused than ever.

'Between you and me. Mister Letter-Writer. Someone who wanted to screw us both and succeeded. Go back over those letters again. Was there anything peculiar about them?'

'Yes,' said Glodstone vehemently, 'there bloody well was. They . . .'

'No, sweetheart, you're not reading me. Did you see where they were posted?'

'In France. Definitely in France and in your envelopes. The ones with the crest on the back.'

'And in my handwriting. You said all that but how could you be so sure?'

'Because I've got your other letters to me about Anthony's allergies and whatnot. The handwriting was identical.'

'So that puts it back in my court. Now what did they say, and I mean exactly.'

As she drove slowly out of town Glodstone went through the details of the letters and their instructions with a total recall born of fear.

'Hotels you were booked into? Crossing via Ostend? Your whole route mapped out for you? And you did just what they said?'

'Until we got to Ivry. There was another letter there saying we had to turn back or you were going to die.'

'So you had to come on,' said the Countess, shaking her head sadly. 'And that was the only one that made sense.'

'That night they tried to stop us by putting oil on the road in the forest. We could have been killed. As it was, a man tried to hold us up –'

'Stop right there. Can you describe him?'

Glodstone visualized the figure of Mr Blowther covered in oil and leaves, and found it difficult.

'But he was English? You're sure of that?'

'I suppose he was. He certainly sounded English. And there was another one at Calais who told the ferry people my wife had died. I don't have a wife.'

'I can believe it,' said the Countess. 'Which doesn't help any.

Whoever used my notepaper and knew my hand and posted the letters in France, booked you rooms in hotels, tried to stop you . . . No way they can't be crazy. And how did they know you'd come? Come to that, why *did* you?'

Glodstone blushed. 'I couldn't leave you in the lurch,' he muttered. 'I mean I'd always thought of you as a lady and, well . . . it's difficult to explain really.'

'And what do you think now? Am I still a "lady"?'

'You're certainly very nice,' said Glodstone judiciously. 'You'd have gone to the police if you weren't.'

The Countess sighed. It still hadn't dawned on the poor dumb cluck that she'd have done just that if she hadn't had something to hide. Like seven gold bars and a past that would make his romantic hair stand on end. Talk about knight errant, operative word 'errant'. It was only in Britain they made them so innocent. 'And you're nice too,' she said and patted his knee. 'It wasn't your fault you were framed. So we can't let them take you to prison, can we?'

'Hopefully,' said Glodstone quivering with new devotion under the influence of the pat on the knee and the baby-talk. Her next remark blew his mind.

'So we go back and get the Sundance Kid and put the bite on the Clyde-Brownes.'

'We do what?'

'Put the squeeze on them. You're going to need money, and if they're what you say they are, and I think, they'll pay through the nose to keep themselves out of the media. I can't see Papa C-B wanting to be thrown out of the Reform.'

'I won't do it,' said Glodstone. 'It wasn't Peregrine's fault that . . .'

'He's wanted by the police in every country this side of the Iron Curtain? And he did the killing, not you. So Mr Clyde-Browne is going to have to work hard to pull both your irons out of the fire. And he has got influence. I've looked him up and he reeks of it. His brother's Deputy Under-Secretary at the Department of Trade and adviser to the EEC Commissioner for the Regularization, Standardization and Uniformity of Processed Food Products. Meaning fish fingers.'

'Good Lord, how did you find that out?'

'Holborn Public Library's latest copy of *Who's Who*. So we've got some muscle. And we're going to use it tonight.'

'Tonight? But we'll never drive all the way to Virginia Water . . . I mean it'll be after midnight by the time we get there.'

'I can't think of a better time to break the news,' said the Countess, and drove back to the Amusement Park.

Chapter 23

In fact it was almost 2 a.m. when they parked the car at the end of Pine Tree Lane and rang the doorbell of The Cones. A light came on upstairs and presently the door opened on the chain and Mr Clyde-Brown peered out. He'd had a hard evening listening to his wife argue that it was time they called in the police, and had only managed to get to sleep with a cup of Horlicks laced with yet more whisky and two Mogadons.

'Who is it?' he mumbled.

'Me, Dad,' said Peregrine stepping under the porchlight. For a moment Mr Clyde-Browne was prey to the ghastly thought that two Mogadons and a quarter of a bottle of Scotch didn't mix too well. Certainly he had to be hallucinating. The voice sounded horribly right but the face, and in particular the hair, didn't gel with his memory of Peregrine. The last time he'd seen the lout he'd been fair-haired and with a fresh complexion. Now he looked like something the Race Relations . . . He stopped himself in time. There was a law about saying things like that.

'Where the hell have you been?' he asked instead, and undid the chain. 'Your mother's been at her wit's end worrying about you. And who —'

The Countess and Glodstone stepped through the doorway after Peregrine. 'Let's hit the lounge,' said the Countess, 'Somewhere nice and private. We don't want the neighbours in on this.'

Mr Clyde-Browne wasn't sure. The arrival of his son with black hair in the company of a woman in dark glasses and a tall haggard man who looked vaguely familiar and definitely sinister, and this at two in the morning, seemed to˙ suggest he might need every neighbour within shouting distance. The Countess's language didn't help. With the feeling that he had stepped into a Cagney movie he went into the sitting-room and turned on the light.

'Now what's the meaning of this?' he demanded, trying to muster some authority.

'Tell him, baby,' said the Countess, checking the curtains were closed to unnerve Mr Clyde-Browne still more.

'Well, it's like this, dad,' said Peregrine, 'I've been and gone and shot a professor.'

Mr Clyde-Browne's eyes bulged in his head. 'I'm not hearing right,' he muttered, 'It's those fucking Mogadons. You've been and gone . . . Where the hell did you pick up that vulgar expression?'

'His name was Botwyk and he was an American and we thought he was a gangster and I shot him through the head,' said Peregrine. 'With a .38 from the School Armoury.'

Mr Clyde-Browne's knees buckled and he slumped into a chair. 'I don't believe it,' he moaned. 'This isn't happening.'

'No, not now,' said Peregrine. 'But it did. It's in all the papers. I shot a Russian too, but he didn't die. At least, he hasn't yet.'

Mr Clyde-Browne shut his eyes in an attempt to convince himself that he was having a nightmare. It failed. When he opened them again Peregrine and these two awful people were still there. The Countess handed him a copy of *The Times*.

'I've ringed the latest piece,' she said. 'Right now they're looking for a terrorist. Well, he's standing there in front of you.'

Mr Clyde-Brown hurled the paper aside. He'd read all about the murder on the train the day before and had expressed his sense of outrage. With another sense of outrage he got to his feet. 'If this is some sort of fucking joke,' he yelled, 'I'll –'

'Cool it, baby,' said the Countess. 'You want the cops in on this just keep bawling your head off. That's your prerogative. Or you can phone them. I guess the number's still 999.'

'I know what the fucking number is,' shouted Mr Clyde-Browne rather more quietly.

'So he's your son. You want him up on a murder rap, call them up. It's no skin off my nose. I don't go round bumping people off.'

Mr Clyde-Browne looked from her to Peregrine and back again. 'You're bluffing. He didn't shoot anyone. It's all a lie. You're trying to blackmail me. Well, let me tell you –'

'Oh sure. So go ahead and phone. Tell them you've got two

blackmailers and a son who just happens to be a murderer on your hands and you don't know what to do. We'll wait here for you. No sweat.'

Beads of it broke out on Mr Clyde-Browne's forehead. 'Tell me you didn't do it,' he said to Peregrine, 'I want you to say it and I want to hear it.'

'I shot a Professor, dad. I've told you that already.'

'I know you have . . .'

He was interrupted by the entrance of his wife. For a long moment she stood in the doorway gazing at Peregrine.

'Oh, my poor boy,' she cried, rushing forward and gathering him to her. 'What have they done to you?'

'Nothing, mum. Nothing at all.'

'But where've you been and why's your hair that colour?'

'That's part of the disguise. I've been to France . . .'

'And shot an American Professor. Through the head, didn't you say?' said Mr Clyde-Browne, helping himself to more whisky. He didn't give a damn what the stuff did with Mogadons any longer. A quiet death was preferable.

'Oh my poor darling,' said Mrs Clyde-Browne, who still hadn't got the message, 'I've been so worried about you.'

In the corner Mr Clyde-Browne was heard to mutter something about her not knowing what worry was. Yet.

The Countess got up and moved towards the door. Mr Clyde-Browne hit it first. 'Where do you think you're fucking going?' he shouted.

Mrs Clyde-Browne turned on him. 'How dare you use that filthy word in my house!' she screamed. 'And in front of Peregrine and these . . . er . . .'

The Countess smiled sweetly. 'Let me introduce myself,' she said. 'My name's Deirdre, Countess de Montcon. And please don't apologize for your husband's language. He's just a little over-wrought. And now if you'll excuse us . . .'

Mr Clyde-Browne didn't budge. 'You're not leaving this house until I've got to the bottom of this . . . this . . .'

'Murder?' asked the Countess. 'And of course there's the little matter of kidnapping too but I don't suppose that's so important.'

'I didn't kidnap you,' said Peregrine and blew his father's mind still further. If the sod was prepared to deny kidnapping while openly admitting he'd murdered, he had to be telling the truth.

'All right,' he said. 'How much do you want?'

The Countess hesitated and made up her mind not to go back to American slang. Kensington English would hit Mrs Clyde-Browne's gentility harder. 'Really,' she said, 'if it weren't for the obvious fact that you're not yourself I would find your attitude extremely sordid.'

'You would, would you? Well let me tell you I know sordidity when I see it and I know blackmailers and add that lot to your calling yourself a countess and –'

'But she is a countess,' said Peregrine as his father ran out of words, 'I saw her passport and she lives in this jolly great Château. It's called Carmagnac and it's ever so nice. And it's there I shot the professor.'

'Oh, you never did,' said Mrs Clyde-Browne reproachfully, 'you're making it up.'

'Christ!' said Mr Clyde-Browne, and downed his Scotch. 'Will you keep out of this. We've enough . . .'

'I most certainly won't,' retorted Mrs Clyde-Browne, 'I'm his mother . . .'

'And he's a fucking murderer. M – U – R – D –'

'I know how to spell, thank you very much. And he's not, are you, darling?'

'No,' said Peregrine. 'All I did was shoot him. I didn't know he was –'

'Know? Know? You wouldn't know mass murder from petty larceny,' shouted his father, and grabbed the paper, 'well, the rest of the bloody world knows . . .'

'If I might just get a word in,' said the Countess. 'The rest of the world doesn't know . . . yet. Of course, in time the French police will be in touch with Scotland Yard but if we could come to some arrangement . . .'

'I've already asked you how much you're demanding, you black-mailing bitch. Now spit it out.'

The countess looked at him nastily but kept her cool. 'For a man supposedly at the top of your profession you are really remarkably obtuse,' she said. 'The truism about the law applies. You are an ass.

208

And what's more, if you don't moderate your language I shall call the police myself.'

'Oh, you mustn't,' wailed Mrs Clyde-Browne on whose dim intelligence it had slowly dawned that Peregrine really was in danger. Mr Clyde-Browne edged onto a chair.

'All right,' he said, 'what are you suggesting?'

'Immunity,' she said simply. 'But first I would like a nice cup of tea. It's been a hard two days getting your son out of France and –'

'Get it,' Mr Clyde-Browne told his wife.

'But, Oscar –'

'I said get it and I meant get it. And stop blubbing, for God's sake. I want to hear what this blo . . . this lady has to say.'

Still sobbing, Mrs Clyde-Browne left the room. By the time she returned with the tea-tray Mr Clyde-Brown was staring at the Countess with something approaching respect. He was also drained of all emotion except terror. In a life devoted to the belief that all women were an intellectual sub-species whose sole purpose was to cook meals and have babies, he had never before come across such a powerful intelligence. 'And what about that?' he asked, glaring with horror at Glodstone.

'I have arranged his future,' said the Countess, 'I won't say where, though it may be in Brazil . . .'

'But I don't want to go to Brazil,' squawked Glodstone, and was promptly told to hold his tongue.

'Or it may be somewhere else. The point is that Mr Glodstone is going to die.'

On the couch Glodstone whimpered. Mr Clyde-Browne perked up. This woman knew her onions. 'And about time too,' he said.

'And isn't it time you phoned your brother?' asked the Countess. 'The sooner he can get the ball rolling the sooner we can wrap this up. And now if you'll excuse us . . .'

This time Mr Clyde-Browne didn't try to stop her. He knew when he was beaten. 'How will I get in touch with you if –'

'You won't, honey,' said the Countess patting his ashen cheek, 'from now on in the ball's in your court.'

'Well, really!' said Mrs Clyde-Browne, 'She didn't even touch her tea.'

'Bugger tea. Take that murderous bastard upstairs and bleach his hair back to normal.'

'But we haven't any peroxide and –'

'Use whatever you pour down the lavatory. Even if his hair falls out it'll be better than nothing.' And he hurried down the passage to the study and phoned his brother.

The Countess drove steadily towards London. She didn't want to be stopped by a patrol car and she had to get back into the sprawl of the metropolis and anonymity in case Mr Clyde-Browne's brother refused to cooperate.

'I've booked you a room at Heathrow,' she said.

'But I don't want to go to Brazil,' said Glodstone.

'So you're not going. You flew in on a Dan-Air Flight from Zimbabwe, arrival time 6 a.m., name of Harrison. And you're not to be disturbed. It's all arranged. I'll pick you up around noon for the funeral.'

'Funeral? What funeral?'

'Yours, sweetheart. Mr Glodstone's going to die. Officially. And don't take on so. You'll get used to the after-life.'

Glodstone doubted it.

Slymne didn't. Given the choice he'd have willingly died. Once again he was being interrogated. This time by three American agents from Frankfurt who were under the impression that he had spent time in Libya. In another room Major Fetherington was getting the same treatment. Unfortunately, he had.

'In the war,' he moaned, 'in the bloody war.'

'Yom Kippur or the Seven Days?'

'In the Eighth Army. A Desert Rat, for God's sake.'

'You can say that again, bud. You and Gaddafi both.'

'I'm talking about the war, the real war. The one against the Afrika Korps.'

'The who?' said one of the men who'd obviously never heard of any war before Vietnam.

'The Germans. You must know about Rommel.'

'You tell us. He train you or something?'

'Damned near killed me,' said the Major, rather wishing he had.

'So you were threatened into this, is that what you're saying?'

'No, I'm not. I'm not in this, whatever it is. I was sent down here by the Headmaster to try to find Clyde-Browne . . .'

'Tell us something new. We've been through that routine before.'

'But there's nothing else to tell. And what are you doing with that fucking hypodermic?'

In the passage outside Commissaire Roudhon and the man from the Quai d'Orsay listened with interest.

'The space shuttle and truth drugs and not an inkling of history,' said Monsieur Laponce. 'So much for the special relationship. The President will be pleased.'

'Monsieur?' said the Commissaire, who hadn't a clue what the Foreign Office man was talking about.

'Between London and Washington. We are standing at the end of an era.'

Commissaire Roudhon looked up and down the passage. 'If you say so, monsieur,' he said. Eras meant nothing to him.

'From now on Britain will be what she should always have been, a dependency of France,' continued Monsieur Laponce, indulging his taste for rhetoric. 'The idiots in Whitehall have played into our hands.'

'You really think the British government sent these men?'

'It is not what I think that matters, Commissaire. It is what those charming Americans in there report to Washington.'

'But Gaddafi –'

'– has nothing to do with this. Nor have the Red Brigade or any other terrorist group. It was a stratagem to worsen our relationship with the United States and it has failed.'

'I hadn't thought of it like that,' said the Commissaire.

'You will, Monsieur Roudhon. From now on you will. Bear that in mind. And no press releases. You will simply tell the press that the affair is of too delicate a nature diplomatically to speak about since British Intelligence Officers . . . You will stop yourself there in some confusion and demand that what you have just said is not to be reported. Is that clear?'

'Absolutely.'

'If you fail in the duty, you will have failed France,' said

Monsieur Laponce. 'Remember that. And now, to avoid listening to that terrible noise, I will report to the Minister.'

Inside the interrogation room Major Fetherington under the influence of the drugs he had been given was living up to Henry Ford's dictum that history was bunk.

'I'll tell you something,' said the chief American investigator after the Major had babbled on for the tenth time about dog-turds in Shrewsbury, 'you can say what you like about the limeys but when they make 'em they make 'em tough.'

'Not the other one,' said the medical expert, 'he's plain loco. Give him a shot of this stuff and he'll be psychotic for life.'

'What's all this shit about letters mean?'

'Zero. He's scrambled eggs cerebralwise.'

'So what've we got? Two names, Glodstone and Clyde-Browne. They're not going to like this in Washington.'

In Whitehall, Deputy Under-Secretary Cecil Clyde-Browne, CBE, sat staring dismally at a pigeon on the roof opposite and wondered what was being decided. Somewhere nearby, the Home Secretary, the Secretary of State for Foreign Affairs, the Police Commissioner and the Head of MI5 held his future in their hands. More accurately, they held a telex from the British Ambassador in Paris.

'Well?' asked the Foreign Secretary, when they'd all had their fill of the ghastly news. 'Do we hand the little bugger over or do we not?'

The Chief Commissioner of Police and the Head of MI5 shook their heads.

'Out of the question,' said MI5, 'I've had a look at the imbecile and if the French get their hands on him I've no doubt they can programme him to say anything. Not that they'd need much for him to say. Nobody'd believe his story anyway.'

'I'm not sure I do,' muttered the Foreign Secretary. 'This couldn't be some frightful CIA plot, could it? I've never been entirely happy about your American counterparts since they tried those damned explosive clams on Castro.'

'I can't see what they could possibly gain from it. It's more likely to be KGB-inspired.'

The Foreign Secretary looked nostalgically at a globe of the World which still showed India as part of the Empire. 'Where have you got the brute?' he asked presently.

'In a safe house in Aldershot.'

The name inspired the Foreign Secretary. 'I don't suppose you could arrange for him to have an accident, or Lassa fever, or something?'

'It's feasible, but with the man Glodstone on the loose . . .'

The Home Secretary intervened. 'I'm not prepared to be party to an unofficial execution,' he said hurriedly, 'I mean if this got out . . .'

'It is out, damn it. Whatever it is. And we've got to decide something now. The American Ambassador is due at two and with the confounded French putting it about that there's an SAS hit-squad conducting an assassination campaign to worsen Franco-US relations, I've got to tell the fellow something credible. I know he's from Arkansas but . . .'

'The truth perhaps?' murmured the Home Secretary. 'They say it always comes out in the end.'

'They can say what they bloody well please, but I haven't spent forty years in the foreign service to believe that one, and from what I can tell no one knows what the truth is.'

'I suppose we could always put the blame on the IRA,' said MI5. 'It's as good a ruse as any and it won't do the Irish lobby in Washington any harm to get a kick in the teeth!'

'And what the hell do we do with Clyde-Browne? Call the little bastard O'Brien? I know this fellow from Arkansas thinks Bombay is part of a B52, but he's not going to fall for anything as dumb as an Irish dimension.'

It was the Police Commissioner who came up with the answer. 'I should have thought the obvious thing to do was put the lad in the SAS. He's obviously a born killer and it's the last place they're going to look.'

'The first, you mean,' said the Foreign Secretary, but the Police Commissioner held his ground.

'The last. If we had organized a hit-squad along these lunatic lines with vintage Bentleys and men with glass eyes nobody would think the SAS were involved. They're experts and professionals.'

'But this raving Major Fetherington's already admitted . . .'

'Which makes it certain no one seriously believes he is. The man's in his mid-fifties. In any case he has nothing to do with it. He was in the UK at the time of the murder.'

The Home Secretary backed him up. 'It's the same with Slymne. The Headmaster sent them both off.'

'Splendid,' said the Foreign Secretary, 'so how do I explain to this Arkansas beef baron that the bloody boy isn't in the SAS when he is?'

MI5 smiled. 'I think you can safely leave that to me,' he said.

The Foreign Secretary had his doubts. He was thinking about Blake, Philby and Blunt. 'Safely?' he asked.

MI5 nodded.

By the time the American Ambassador arrived a hooded figure was standing in the ante-room.

'Of course, we wouldn't disclose the identity of any of our men in the Special Air Services,' said the Foreign Secretary after asking politely about the health of the Ambassador's cattle and learning that he was actually into natural gas and came from Texas, 'in ordinary circumstances, that is. But we're prepared to make an exception in this case.'

He pressed a bell on his desk and the hooded figure entered. 'Sergeant Clyde-Browne, remove your balaclava,' he said.

'We're going to want more identification than than,' said the Ambassador, staring at the large individual with the walrus moustache.

'Fingerprints? I mean the French have got those of the assassin, haven't they?'

'I guess so.' He was still guessing when the man, having given his fingerprints, weight, size of shoes and height in centimetres (to confuse the issue still further) donned his balaclava helmet and left the room. 'Haven't I seen him some place else?' enquired the Ambassador.

'Possibly,' said the Foreign Secretary loftily. 'Between ourselves I understand him to be in charge of certain . . . er . . . unmentionable security operations at Buckingham Palace.'

'I guess that explains it then. Those goddam Frenchies seem to have screwed things up again. I'll have our security chief check the details but they don't fit the description I'd been given. The killer was shorter and twenty years younger.'

'And doubtless French,' said the Foreign Secretary, and saw him to the door.

'Who on earth was that grisly-looking blighter?' he asked MI5 when the Ambassador's armour-plated limousine was safely out of the way. 'And what are those unmentionable duties at Buck House?'

'Actually he's Captain of the Queen's Heads,' said MI5. 'I thought that was rather a nice touch.'

'Captain of . . . you mean he's a lavatory attendant? Good God, man, no wonder that blasted Yank guessed he'd seen him before.' He stopped and looked at MI5 suspiciously. 'He's not another swine like Blunt, is he? Has he had positive vetting?'

'Oh absolutely. Comes from an eminently respectable Catholic family in the Falls Road area of Belfast. Anyway he's only in charge of the visitor's loos. Don't suppose he's set eyes on Her Majesty.'

'I should bloody well hope not. And if I were in your shoes I'd see to it she doesn't set eyes on the wallah. Wouldn't blame her for setting those damned Corgis on the brute. Anyway, thank the Lord that's settled. Even the present American administration wouldn't have the gall to start checking the Palace.'

Chapter 24

At the Cortège drove slowly out of the Crematorium, Glodstone stared miserably at the back of the chauffeur's head. It was one of the ironies of having attended his own funeral that he should now recall that 'chauffeur' came from the French for stoker; presumably even modern furnaces had to be attended by somebody to take out the ashes. Whoever had just been incinerated (probably an unidentified tramp or something they'd finished with in the dissecting-rooms at one of the teaching hospitals) had gone to his Maker bearing Glodstone's name. It was there on the death certificate and a little obituary would shortly appear in the *Old Groxbournian*. The Great Adventure had gone up in smoke.

'I know just how you feel,' said the Countess, patting his hand. '*Mourir c'est partir un peu.*'

'What?' said Glodstone.

'To die is to part a little. But it won't be for long. By the time the surgeon's finished with you you'll be a new man.'

'Surgeon?' said Glodstone. 'What bloody surgeon?'

'The plastic one. He's said to be terribly good with burns.'

'Burns? Considering where I'm supposed to be he'd have to be fucking miraculous.'

'There's no need to use that sort of language,' said the Countess sharply, 'I haven't gone to all this trouble and expense to have you swearing like a trooper.'

Glodstone considered the change in her own language and said nothing. There was something about this extraordinary woman that frightened him and it was only when she stopped the car at the top of Hampstead Heath and they were walking down to the tube station that he brought up the matter of burns and plastic surgery.

'What the hell do I need plastic surgery for? Apart from whoever went up in that coffin. . .'

'Well, we won't go into that now,' said the Countess, 'that's all past and done with. You've got to look to the future and since you refuse to go to Brazil you'll just have to do what I tell you. The main thing will be to alter the shape of your ears. They're the give-away and the police always look at them first. Then –'

'But with this wig on no one can see my blasted ears,' said Glodstone.

'I'm not going to be married to a man with a toupee. It's unbecoming and anyway it won't fit your image. As far as the rest of you . . .'

But Glodstone wasn't listening. 'Did you say "married"?' he asked.

'Of course I did. You don't imagine for one moment that I'm going to live in sin with you, do you?'

Half an hour later Glodstone entered a clinic near Portland Place. On the door a brass plaque seemed to suggest its main business lay in abortions, but Glodstone no longer cared. It was enough to know he was going to be married. It was infinitely preferable to spending the rest of his life in Brazil.

'My hero,' said the Countess, kissing him lightly on the cheek, 'Now don't forget to sign your name as Mr Smith.'

'Slymne's *where*?' said the Headmaster when Major Fetherington returned a week later, in the company of two Special Branch officers.

'Rampton,' said the Major.

'Rampton? But that's that ghastly hospital for the criminally insane, isn't it? And what on earth have you been doing to your face?'

'Dog-turd in Shrewsbury,' said the Major, who hadn't fully recovered from the effects of the truth drug and his hours of interrogation.

'But that was your backside. Now you come back here with a face looking like a . . .'

'Dog-turd in Shrewsbury,' said the Major.

'Christ,' said the Headmaster. If Slymne was sufficiently off his rocker to be in Rampton, the Major could do with some treatment himself. 'And what about Glodstone?'

'That's what we've come to see you about,' said one of the men and produced his identification. The Headmaster examined it cautiously.

'Special Branch?' he asked weakly.

The man nodded. 'Now about Mr Glodstone, sir,' he said, 'we're going to require access to his rooms and we'd be glad if you answered a few questions. For instance, were you aware that he had any Communist inclinations?'

'Communist inc . . . I thought the sod belonged to the Monday Club. He certainly read the *Daily Telegraph*.'

'That could have been cover. Homosexual tendencies? Excessive drinking? Chip on his social shoulder? Anything of that sort?'

'All of it,' said the Headmaster fervently and glanced out of the window. A number of soldiers had driven up in a lorry and were debussing on the drive. 'What the hell are they doing here?'

'If you'll just sign this,' said the Special Branch man and placed a document on his desk.

The Headmaster read it through with increasing alarm. 'The Official Secrets Act? You want me to sign –'

'Just a simple precaution, sir. Nothing more. Of course if you'd prefer to face criminal proceedings in connection with certain offences again the person committed in Belfast . . .'

'Belfast? I've never been anywhere near Belfast,' said the Headmaster, beginning to think he'd shortly be joining Slymne in a padded cell. 'You come here and tell me to sign the Official Secrets Act or be charged . . . Dear God, where's that pen?' He scrawled his signature at the bottom of the form.

'And now the key to the School Armoury, if you don't mind.'

The Headmaster handed it over and while one of the men took it out to the officer in charge of the squad the other settled himself in a chair. 'I think I must warn you that should anyone make enquiries about Mr Glodstone or a certain ex-pupil it will be in your interest not to say anything,' he said. 'The Belfast charges are still outstanding and having signed the Official Secrets Act the consequences could be slightly unfortunate. Need I say more?'

'No,' said the Headmaster indistinctly, 'but what am I going to tell Mr Clyde-Browne?'

'Who, sir?'

'Christ,' said the Headmaster. Outside the soldiers had begun to load the lorry with all the weapons from the Armoury. That was a relief anyway. He'd never liked the bloody things.

'And now if you'll just take me up to Glodstone's rooms.' They crossed the quad and climbed the staircase. 'Not that I suppose we'll find anything of interest,' said the Special Branch man. 'When the Russians employ a sleeper they do things thoroughly. Probably recruited the traitor when he was at Cambridge.'

'Cambridge? I never dreamt that Glodstone had been anywhere near a University. He certainly never mentioned it.'

'Obviously not. The man's clearly an expert. One only has to look at the sort of books he surrounded himself with to see that.'

The Headmaster gazed at the collected works of Sapper and felt peculiar. 'I really can't believe it even now,' he said. 'Glodstone was a ghastly man but he didn't have the brains to be a . . . what did you call it?'

'A sleeper,' said the Special Branch man, putting the cigar box containing the Countess's letters in a plastic bag. 'Probably in code.'

The Headmaster tried to look on the bright side. 'Well, at least I won't have the damned man around me any more,' he said. 'That's some relief. Have you any idea where he is?'

The Special Branch man hesitated. 'No harm in telling you now. We found his Bentley parked near Tilbury yesterday. An East German tramp steamer sailed on Wednesday night.'

They went back to the Headmaster's study.

'I think that'll be all we'll require for the moment, sir. If anything should occur to you that might be of use to us, we'd be grateful if you'd call this number. It's a phone drop, so just leave your name.'

'And what about him?' asked the Headmaster glancing anxiously at Major Fetherington.

'What about him?'

'I can't have a master going about muttering "Dog-turd in Shrewsbury" in front of the boys all the time. He's as mad as a hatter.'

'You should see Mr Slymne,' said the Special Branch man

grimly. 'The Major's all right. He's a hero by comparison. And you can always use him as a groundsman.'

But it was in Pine Tree Lane that feelings were most mixed.

'I'll never forgive you. Never,' wailed Mrs Clyde-Browne, ignoring the presence of ten undercover agents dressed in overalls who had already installed double glazing and were now redecorating the entire house. 'To think that I'll never see poor Peregrine again!'

'Oh, I don't know,' said Mr Clyde-Browne cheerfully, 'he'll probably get leave once in a while. They can't keep a garrison in Antarctica for ever.'

'But he isn't used to the cold and he's got such a delicate chest.'

'There is that,' said Mr Clyde-Browne almost gaily. 'You can always go out and put flowers on his grave. And he certainly won't need embalming. Things keep for ever on ice.'

'You murdering . . . No, I don't want flock fleur-de-lys in the kitchen,' she yelled, as one of the agents tactfully interposed a wallpaper pattern book between them, 'and you can stop painting the hall pink. That's a William Morris design.'

Mr Clyde-Browne made himself scarce. He had an interesting divorce case to consider involving custody of a domestic cat and now that Peregrine was out of the way it might be advantageous to goad his own wife a little further.

In Bognor Regis Glodstone looked at his face in the bathroom mirror, and failed to recognize himself. It wasn't the first time, but it still shook him to see someone he didn't know staring with such horrid amazement back at him. And horrid was the word. The Countess had been right in claiming the plastic surgeon was good with burns, though, in Glodstone's livid opinion, she ought have said 'at' them.

'Just let me get my hands on the sod,' he had shouted when the bandages had been removed and he had finally been allowed the use of a mirror. 'He must have used a bloody flamethrower. Where are my blasted eyebrows?'

'In the disposal bin,' said the Sister in charge. 'Anyway, you specifically asked for total non-recognitive surgery.'

'Non-recog . . . bugger it, I did nothing of the sort. I came in here expecting to have my ears adjusted, not to be turned into something that'd frighten a fucking punk dalek into a fit. And why am I as bald as a coot?'

'We did a scalp transplant with another patient. He had alopecia totalis. It's taken very well.'

'And what have I got then, galloping fucking ringworm?'

'It'll save you having to brush your hair again.'

'And shave,' said Glodstone, 'Who did you swop my face with, some terminal leper?'

'That's called the Spitfire effect,' said the Sister. 'Lots of pilots who crashed in the Battle of Britain looked like that.'

'In that case I'd have thought the Messerschmidt effect would have been more appropriate,' said Glodstone. 'Am I going to have to spend the rest of my life with these pustules? There's one actually swelling on what's left of my nose.'

'They're just leeches. We use them for scavenging –'

'Shit,' said Glodstone and had to be held down to prevent him from trying to dislodge the things.

'We'll have to give you a sedative if you don't behave like a good boy.'

'Madam,' said Glodstone, managing to rally some dignity under threat of the needle, 'I have had some considerable experience of boys and no sane one would allow his face to be used as a watering hole for scavenging leeches. I could get tetanus, or die from loss of blood.'

'Nonsense. We ensure they're all perfectly healthy and they're only cleaning up the scar tissue.'

'In that case they'll get bloody awful indigestion,' said Glodstone, 'they've got enough grub there for the Lord Mayor's banquet. And get that sod out of my left nostril. I can't with my hands in bandages. And what's that for?'

'Fingerprint removal,' said the Sister, and left Glodstone to contemplate a life without any physical means of identification. Even his closest friends wouldn't know him now. Or want to.

But at least the Countess had been delighted. 'Darling,' she said when she came to collect him, 'you look wonderful.'

'You've got fucking peculiar tastes is all I can say,' said Glodstone bitterly and was promptly rebuked for using filthy language.

'You were something hush-hush in the War and you'd rather not talk about it. That's the line you'll have to take,' she said, 'and from now on you're to call me Bobby.'

'But that's a boy's name,' said Glodstone, wondering if he was about to marry some sort of lesbian with a truly horrific lust for disfigured men. It was a wonder he hadn't had a sex-change operation.

'It's nice and thirtyish. Lots of girls were called Bobby then and it'll blend with the Peke.'

Glodstone shuddered. He loathed Pekes and it was clear he was no longer going to be allowed to call his life his own, let alone his face.

It had proved only too true. After a swift registry marriage at which he had had to declare himself to be Clarence Sopwith Hillary, a combination of names Glodstone found personally humiliating, unnecessarily provocative and, in the case of the last, in exceedingly bad taste, they had driven on in Bobby's dinky Mini ('We mustn't be thought to consider ourselves a cut above the neighbours, Clarence,' she told Glodstone, who knew damned well he was a hell of a lot of cuts just about everywhere else) to the bungalow in Bognor Regis. It had fulfilled his direst expectations. From its green-tiled roof to the petunias bordering the weedless lawn and the cubistic carpet in the drawing room, it represented everything he had most despised.

'But it's pure art-deco, Clarence. I mean it's us.'

'It may be you,' said Glodstone, 'but I'm damned if it's me. And can't you call me something other than Clarence? It's almost as foul as Cecil.'

'I shall call you Soppy, darling. And this is Beatrice.'

'Hell,' said Glodstone, who had just been bitten on the ankle by the Peke.

Now as he stood gazing at his own nonentity in the bathroom he knew he was beaten. They would play bridge all evening with the Shearers and he'd get told off for bidding badly and have to make the coffee and have to take that bloody Beatrice for a pee before going to bed. And he knew what they'd drink. Crême de menthe. Constance Sugg had returned to her roots.

In a hedge in South Armagh, Peregrine, now Number 960401, stared through the night-sight of his rifle at the figure moving in the field below. It could be a Garda but he didn't care. He'd already notched up five IRA men, two poachers and an off-duty RUC constable, not to mention an Army Landrover, to such awful effect that even the local Protestants had joined with the IRA in declaring his sixteen square miles a No-Go Area, and the Army avoided the place. Peregrine didn't care. He was in his element, doing what he had been trained to do. And every few weeks an unmanned balloon (there'd been an unfortunate incident with a helicopter) would drift over for him to shoot down and collect his ammunition and supplies.

Not that he needed the latter. He'd already bagged a sheep for his supper in the burrow he'd dug halfway down an old well and was rather looking forward to it. The Major had said one should live off the land, and he did. He squeezed the trigger and watched the man drop. Then he obeyed another of the Major's dicta, that an army marched on its stomach, and crawled the two miles back to his hide-out. Presently, in the happy knowledge he was doing exactly what he'd been told, he pulled his rifle through and oiled it, and settled down to leg of lamb.

About the Author

Tom Sharpe was born in 1928 and educated at Lancing College and at Pembroke College, Cambridge. He did his National Service in the Marines before going to South Africa in 1951, where he did social work for the Non-European Affairs Department and taught. He had a photographic studio in Pietermaritzburg from 1957 until 1961, when he was deported. From 1963 to 1972, he was a lecturer in History at the Cambridge College of Arts and Technology. He is married and lives in Dorset. Tom Sharpe's other books include *Riotous Assembly, Indecent Exposure, Porterhouse Blue, Blott on the Landscape, Wilt, The Great Pursuit, The Throwback, The Wilt Alternative* and *Ancestral Vices.*